RELENTLESS

BENSON SECURITY 2

JANET ELIZABETH HENDERSON

Copyright © 2019 by Janet Elizabeth Henderson

All rights reserved.

No part of this book may be reproduced in any form or by any electronic or mechanical means, including information storage and retrieval systems, without written permission from the author, except for the use of brief quotations in a book review.

ISBN: 9780473461379

Cover design by Janet Elizabeth Henderson

Editing by Liz Dempsey

❀ Created with Vellum

ALSO BY JANET ELIZABETH HENDERSON

Lingerie Wars

Goody Two Shoes

Magenta Mine

Calamity Jena

Bad Boy

Here Comes The Rainne Again

Caught

Reckless

Relentless

Rage

Ransom

Can't Tie Me Down

Can't Stop The Feeling

Can't Buy Me Love

CHAPTER 1

Julia Collins had issues. She'd even made a list of them—in order of priority, of course. Her OCD tendencies sat in joint first place with her pathological shyness. This was closely followed by the paralysis she felt when dealing with the opposite sex, then came the way she crumpled in the face of authority and, finally, the raging panic that overcame her anytime she was out of her comfort zone. In other words, she was *absolutely* the best person to ask for help when you were languishing in a foreign jail.

"Have you found me a decent lawyer yet?" her grandmother said from the other side of the bars.

Yes.

Bars.

"Not yet. I only had time to check into the hotel, leave my bags and clean up before I came straight here." All of which had taken longer than she'd anticipated, because she couldn't speak Spanish and hadn't realised the hotel she'd booked was about a two-hour taxi trip from the prison—although she suspected her driver had taken the circuitous route.

Of course, if she'd brought Joe along with her, as her boss

had insisted she do, then she would have known where to book a hotel. The ex-marine had spent time in Peru and, unlike Julia, could speak the language.

A flash of guilt speared through Julia at the thought of Joe Barone. She'd deliberately emailed Joe flight details that were false. In fact, she hadn't even booked him on a flight at all. Mainly because the thought of spending fourteen hours sitting on a plane next to a man who attracted and terrified her in equal parts was just too much to handle. She very much feared he was still sitting in Heathrow waiting for her to turn up.

"Julia? Are you awake?" Her gran's ludicrous question brought her back to her present situation.

"Of course I'm awake. I'm standing here, talking to you."

"Mmm, for a minute there, I wasn't sure. You do realise that this is a time-sensitive issue you're dealing with? I'd like to get out of prison before some woman called Bertha makes me her bitch."

"Gran!" Julia gave her a disapproving glare. "You are joking, right? I mean, you aren't being threatened or anything, are you?"

"Only by poor hygiene and terrible food. There's a good chance I'll die of the bubonic plague before I'm released." She raised her stubborn chin. "To hell with a lawyer. Just break me out of here. I mean, look at the place." She waved a hand. "How hard could it be?"

"You can't talk like that," Julia hissed as she looked around to see if anyone had overheard. All she saw was the industrial grey concrete that made up the short-term holding area of Lima's notorious female prison. It wasn't much, but after the chaos Julia had witnessed in the general area of the prison, she was glad her gran was being held separately.

She looked down at the stamps running up her forearms and shuddered. Once she'd queued outside the prison, with all the other visitors, she'd had her personal space invaded by a leering man who'd patted her body looking for weapons. Julia suspected she'd have nightmares about that for years to come. After that, her paperwork had been scrutinised and she'd been questioned in rapid-fire Spanish that she didn't understand. A lifetime later, her arms had been stamped—to prove she wasn't an inmate—and she'd been allowed inside. Julia didn't go clubbing, so she'd never had a club stamp on her arm, but she imagined it was a very similar experience to the one she'd just endured.

"Oh, darling." Patricia Matthews sighed heavily. "This is too much for you. I should have bitten the bullet and called your mother instead."

"No. I'm fine. I can do this. It's just jetlag and culture shock rolled into one. Don't worry about me; you're the one who needs help. You did the right thing. Who knows what Mum would have done if she was here?" Libby Collins wasn't exactly known for her restrained reaction in a crisis. Julia well remembered the dramas she'd endured growing up, especially seeing as, in her family, almost everything constituted a crisis.

Her gran folded her arms over her pale blue peasant blouse. There were no prison uniforms for these inmates. As far as Julia could see, there was nothing at all for the inmates. The glimpses she'd had of overcrowded cells, with pallets made of rags for beds, made her cringe.

Julia suddenly thought of something horrific. "You do have a toilet in your cell, don't you?" She put a hand over her heart as it raced at her next thought. "You have to share it, don't you? Please tell me you at least have privacy when you use it?"

Her gran pinched the bridge of her nose and closed her eyes. When she looked back at Julia, she seemed more resigned than hopeful to see her there.

"I don't want to talk about the toilet. I want to talk about your plan to get me out of here. What are you doing about finding a decent lawyer? The ones that have approached me only want money. They're promising to get the charges dropped and get me out of here in seconds—if I fork over all my cash." She rolled her eyes. "Like I'd fall for that. That's why I sent Alice off to find someone honest, or at least someone with a solid reputation." She bit her lip and suddenly looked closer to her age than usual. "Then Alice didn't come back."

Gran's best friend had been missing for four days, a fact that didn't seem to bother the Peruvian authorities any. After she got her gran out of jail, Julia planned to hire an interpreter and grill the police on exactly what they were doing to find Alice. She felt nauseated at the thought. Okay, maybe not grill. Maybe ask politely and quietly...or send a firmly worded email...or maybe a text...

"Julia, are you listening to me? What are you doing about a lawyer?"

"Sorry, I was thinking. You don't have to worry about a lawyer. I have a plan all written out. I'm going to look in the yellow pages, or do a Google search, and then I'm going to get someone at the hotel to call around for me—"

"Or," came the deep American voice behind her, "you could have trusted that I knew a guy, like I told you before you dumped me at the airport."

Julia froze.

Joe Barone.

Here.

In Lima.

Every instinct within her was screaming that if she didn't move, maybe he wouldn't see her—and eat her alive. She was pretty sure she'd react exactly the same way if she was ever confronted with a hungry T-Rex.

Julia watched her gran's eyes go wide at the sight of Joe, then she smiled with appreciation. "You must be a friend of my granddaughter."

"You must be her incarcerated grandmother." Two hands landed on Julia's shoulders and Joe was standing at her back. *Right against her back.* "I'm Joe. I work with Julia."

Her grandmother's eyes sparkled. "Is that *all* you do with my granddaughter, Joe?"

Danger! Abort! Hide! Julia's inner voice, which was remarkably similar to the robot in *Lost in Space,* was no help at all.

"With all due respect"—Joe's soft American accent vibrated through Julia as he spoke to her gran—"that's between Julia and me."

He leaned into Julia, and she felt his breath whisper against her ear. "Later, we're going to talk about the stunt you pulled at the airport."

With a gentle squeeze of her shoulders, he stepped back. Julia couldn't speak or move. She just stood useless and frozen in the middle of the room—painfully aware that her attempt to blend in with her environment and disappear entirely had failed miserably.

"This is Eduardo Sanchez," Joe said to her grandmother. "He's taking your case."

Julia kept her head down, but peeked up to see a handsome middle-aged man in an expensive navy suit. He seemed to jerk backwards when he looked at her, which made Julia step closer to Joe—for some reason. The lawyer gave a little shake of his head before turning to her gran with a smile.

"Call me Ed," he said. "When Joe here said we were running to the rescue of a grandmother, you weren't what I had in mind."

Julia almost snorted. She imagined they'd envisioned a short, round elderly woman with a cap of curly grey hair, who dressed in shapeless beige clothes and sensible shoes.

Julia looked down at her clothes, dismayed to realise she'd described her own dress sense. Yep, she wasn't going to think about that. Patricia Matthews was the exact opposite of a typical granny. She might have been in her late sixties, but she was gorgeous in the same way Helen Mirren or Susan Sarandon were gorgeous. She was tall, willowy and stylish. Even behind bars, her shoulder-length blonde hair was perfectly styled and her face was tastefully made up. Dressed in figure-hugging jeans, an embroidered peasant blouse and beige leather high-heeled boots, she was stunning. The few lines on her face did nothing but enhance her beauty. The wicked look in her eyes made her seem far more vital than her age would usually suggest.

She waved a dismissive hand at Ed's comment. "Age is just a number, darling."

His eyes sparkled; he was obviously enamoured with Julia's gran. It was no surprise—all of her female relatives stopped men in their tracks. Julia was used to being the exception.

"You're charged with stealing a mummified body." Ed consulted his notes. "Is that correct?"

"That's the charge." Patricia gave him a haughty look. "Are you going to ask me if I did it?"

"I wouldn't dare." Ed grinned as though she was delightful. "I haven't had a lot of time to go over the paperwork, but it looks to me like there are some gaping holes in the case against you. I'm pretty sure we can get you out of here in no time at all."

Patricia's eyes narrowed. "What's it going to cost me?"

"Ah, I see you've dealt with some of my esteemed colleagues." Ed seemed unfazed by the implied insult. "Don't worry—I charge a horrendous hourly fee, but there's nothing on top of that, unless you want to buy me a drink sometime as a thank you for a job well done."

Patricia beamed widely. "I think I can manage that."

Julia stared at the two of them. Were they *flirting? In a jail?*

"That didn't take long," Joe muttered with a shake of his head, which reminded Julia that they were all speaking English.

And if that was the case, there was no need for Joe to stay and interpret. Suddenly giddy with the thought of getting rid of the man who unnerved her so, she tugged on Joe's sleeve. When he looked down at her, she addressed her comments to the vicinity of his chin. "He speaks English better than I do. There's no need for you to stay. You can go back to England."

"Not going to happen, babe."

Julia frowned, her eyes still on his chin. "I wouldn't want to inconvenience you, Joe, or take you away from your other obligations. Mr. Sanchez can easily translate for us."

"I'm not only here to translate. I'm here to watch your back."

"But…"

"I'm staying." His tone told her he was immovable

Julia knew there was no point in arguing. Arguing with Joe never got her anywhere. It was better just to do what she had to and deal with the consequences later. Or, hopefully, never. That was why she'd been so underhanded at London airport. It was either that or do everything the man wanted her to do.

"Can you get me out today?" Patricia asked Ed.

He shook his head. "Tomorrow at the earliest. You okay in here for another night?"

"I'll manage." She looked at Julia. "Can you give me some cash, darling? The food they provide is abominable, but there's a delightful woman from Thailand who's here on a drug charge, and she's selling the most amazing green curry."

Julia couldn't even begin to get her head around the fact

that the Peruvian prison system seemed to involve its inmates setting up businesses to survive. She dug around in her oversized messenger bag, came out with her wallet and handed over a couple of hundred dollars.

"Is that enough?"

"More than enough, especially if Ed here can get me out tomorrow." The light in Patricia's eyes faded as she turned sombre. "I need to get out of here. I need to find Alice."

Ed consulted his notes. "That's your friend who's gone missing?"

"We've been best friends since childhood. And now I don't know where she is or what's happened to her."

"Don't worry." Joe's confidence rang out through his words. "We'll find her. But first we need to get you out of here."

"And that's where I come in." Ed motioned to the laconic guard and had a tense discussion with him in Spanish. When he was finished, he turned back to them. "Patricia and I are going to have a private meeting. We'll get this sorted. You two need to leave. I'll call with updates."

Joe nodded. Julia hesitated. It felt wrong to go back to her luxury hotel when her gran was behind bars.

Patricia seemed to read her mind, and her face softened. "It's okay, darling. You go have a good night's sleep and we'll catch up properly tomorrow."

A hand pressed against the small of her back. "I'll take care of her," Joe told her gran.

"See that you do," Patricia ordered.

"Love you, Gran," Julia whispered as Joe led her from the room.

"Love you too, sweetie." The words followed them out.

Julia looked over her shoulder at her gran and actually wished she was in the cell with her, rather than going to her doom with Joe. Okay, maybe not doom, but she was sure she was better equipped to deal with prison than she was to deal with the sexy American beside her.

THE OPPRESSIVE HEAT OF LIMA, which always seemed to press down on the city like a heavy blanket, hit them as soon as they walked out of the prison gates. Joe looked down at Julia and wondered when she'd last had something to drink. The dry heat of the desert city meant that dehydration could sneak up on a person. As they looked out at the dust-covered highway, crowded with cars and trucks, Joe reached into his day pack for a bottle of water. He unscrewed the cap and handed it to Julia.

As usual, she didn't look him in the eye when she spoke. "I'm not thirsty."

"Take it." He pressed it into her hand. "This type of heat can fool you into thinking you aren't thirsty, but you need to keep your fluids up. Drink regularly, even if you don't feel like it."

She eyed the bottle with suspicion, and Joe knew exactly what the problem was; he'd seen her do this with everything she'd consumed over the past few months. "I bought it at the airport and only just opened it. It was sealed properly and I haven't drunk out of the bottle. It's safe."

Her cheeks turned the same shade of pink as those luscious lips of hers, which made Joe's chest tighten. For some reason, Julia thought her quirks were a sign she was deficient in some way—a belief he hoped to divest her of before the trip was over. There was nothing wrong with Julia Collins. Nothing at all.

A fact Ed seemed to have noticed when he'd looked at her. Ed's reaction to Julia had made him bristle. He'd warned his old friend about Julia being painfully shy and not to force her to interact. He hadn't warned him about the impact Julia could have on a man.

Joe knew exactly how Ed felt. Seeing Julia for the first time was like a sucker punch. She was one of those rare treasures, a beautiful woman who had absolutely no idea that was what she was. Ed's gaze had taken in the shapeless beige dress, flat sports sandals and the large messenger bag Julia wore across her body like a shield, before resting on her makeup-free face. Her features were perfection. Creamy, smooth skin, a tiny upturned nose, wide amber eyes with lashes so thick it was hard to believe they were real. Pronounced cheekbones made her look even more exotic, but it was her full, peach-coloured lips that made a man's thoughts turn darker. Julia Collins had the mouth of a temptress.

"What hotel are we in?" Joe dragged his mind out of the dark, sensual places it always seemed to find when he was around Julia.

"*I'm* in the Sheraton in the city centre."

He smiled at the emphasis and the subtle rebuke it was intended to be. "I'll have someone pick up your bags and bring them to our new hotel."

"What?" Her eyes snapped up to his, and for a second Joe lost his train of thought.

"You can't stay there, babe. It's at least an hour in crap traffic to get here from there. Longer sometimes. You need to be closer to your grandmother, so you can get to the prison fast if needed."

Her eyes moved back down to focus on her feet, and Joe felt bereft at the loss. "I know, but…"

She pulled her bottom lip between her teeth and nodded as though she was having a silent conversation with herself and had come to a conclusion. She rummaged around in her bag and pulled out her iPad. "I'll see what's near here." Her slim fingers flitted across the screen before they stilled. "I forgot. I need Wi-Fi access first."

"I know a hotel." Joe held her elbow as he led them along the crowded street.

"But, I-I…"

"It's okay. I know a perfect place. Trust me." He wanted her to see that he knew her and what she needed to be comfortable in her environment. He'd made a study of Julia these past few months, and wherever possible he'd move mountains to give her what she needed.

"Okay." She sounded so resigned that Joe had to remind himself trust came with time.

He had to be patient. At least now they were together. For the past couple of weeks—since he'd kissed her—she'd taken great pains to hide from him.

He slid his hand down her arm to hold her hand, feeling her tense, and led her across the busy road, where seven lanes of traffic randomly crowded into four official lanes. Cars blasted their horns at them, but Joe ignored it. When they got to the other side of the wide street, he caught sight of something out of the corner of his eye that made the hairs on the back of his neck stand to attention.

Two men.

And they seemed to be following them.

"Maybe we should go get my bags first?" Julia said softly.

He heard her, but his attention was focused on the men. They were out of place and stood out like Trump at a feminist rally. First, they were taller than most of the people rushing around them. They were also fitter, with the kind of muscles serious working out would develop. Both men were dressed in black, when most people around them were dressed in faded clothes that had seen better days. But it was the way they moved that had Joe on alert. They moved like men who were trained. Ex-military or private army, Joe guessed. Neither option reassured him.

As he hauled Julia around the corner of the concrete prison compound, she tugged at his hand. "My legs are shorter than yours."

"Sorry." He shortened his stride, at the same time noticing that she'd almost tripped over the uneven sidewalk. He needed to be more careful. He eyed the guys behind them. But more importantly, he needed to get her to safety.

"Well, what do you think?" Julia asked.

Joe cast a glance down at her. She was looking at him nervously, but hopefully.

"About what?"

She frowned, at the same time Joe spotted the guys turn into the road behind them. They hugged the shadows, keeping their distance, clearly thinking they hadn't been spotted.

"You weren't listening," Julia gently admonished. "I said, wouldn't it be best if we stayed at the Sheraton tonight and moved closer to the prison tomorrow? That way, I could use the hotel Wi-Fi to research hotels and make a booking for us. Plus"—she cast a pointed glance around at the half-finished brick buildings surrounding them—"I don't think there are many hotels in this area."

She was right. This part of Lima was a step up from a shantytown. People here could afford to build houses, but only a bit at a time—hence all the half-finished buildings with rebar sticking out, waiting for a second floor to be added.

"Joe, what do you think?"

What he thought was that they had to get off the street. And fast. Until he knew who wanted to keep tabs on them, and what they wanted, he could better protect Julia inside a hotel.

"No." It came out more firmly than he'd intended. "We need to be close to your grandmother in case Ed needs us for something. He might even get her released tonight."

Plus, he wasn't sure if Julia had been followed from the airport, or what kind of surveillance had already been set up at her hotel. It was best if they started again—in an environment he could control.

Joe stuck his hand out and waved at passing cars. One of them had to be a cab. Seeing as most taxis didn't come with signage, it wasn't always easy to tell. He tugged Julia closer to him. He needed to get her off the street before nightfall. A small Volkswagen, which had seen better days, swerved through the traffic and screeched to a halt at the curb beside them. Joe pulled open the door to the back seat and urged Julia to get in.

"Is this a cab?" Julia was clearly horrified. No doubt she was examining the interior for the driver's official registration. She wasn't going to find any.

Joe pushed in beside her, his knees around his ears, slammed the door and ordered the driver to head for Miraflores. It was the closest suburb with decent hotels. And by decent, he meant big chain hotels. To Joe, those places were seriously lacking in atmosphere, but he knew Julia would appreciate the generic feel and familiarity.

As the car zoomed into the flow of traffic, horn blasting as it did so, Joe spotted one of the men dig into his pocket and come out with his phone. Checking in. Joe tried to keep an eye on the men, but there was too much chaos on the road behind them to see if they got into a vehicle to follow them.

"It's so dusty here," Julia whispered beside him, her eyes on the hills around Lima that housed the sandy-coloured shantytowns. The thousands of small houses, made out of reed matting and plywood sheets, were barely visible against the barren hills.

"When we get things sorted out with your gran, I'll take you to Cusco and the jungle. Lots of green there for you to look at."

She stiffened beside him, and Joe wondered if he would ever break through her defences to the point where she was relaxed and comfortable around him. He had to believe he would, because Julia Collins had become as essential to him as breathing.

"Is she going to be okay?" Julia's soft question broke into Joe's musings. "Is your lawyer friend good?"

"Yeah." Joe placed a hand on Julia's arm and watched her freeze in place. When he didn't move it, she relaxed slightly. Baby steps, Joe reminded himself, baby steps. "He's more than capable. If anyone can sort out this mess and get your gran out of there, Ed can. And she's definitely going to be okay. Patricia is in the safest part of the prison."

"But if Ed can't get her out, she'll be moved to the other part, right?"

"That's not going to happen. I promise you that."

Julia seemed to relax further at his vow, and Joe prayed he would be able to keep it. To hell with that—he would *definitely* keep it. He'd move heaven and earth to make sure he did. First, he needed to get her into their new hotel room, then he was going to make some calls to find out what the police were doing about the missing Alice. Then he planned to talk to his boss, Callum. He didn't know what was going on here, but one thing was clear—things were a whole lot more complicated than Julia's grandmother had led them to believe.

CHAPTER 2

Callum McKay swung his legs over the edge of his bed as he picked up the phone ringing on his nightstand. Well, he swung what was left of his legs. The parts that hadn't been blown off when he'd been in the service. He absently rubbed his thigh as he checked the caller ID.

"It's all gone to hell, hasn't it?" Callum said by way of hello. "It didn't take long. You've been there, what? Two hours?"

"Five," Joe said.

Callum sighed. "Spit it out, then. It's the middle of the bloody night over here." Not that he'd been sleeping, but Joe didn't need to hear about his ongoing battle with insomnia.

"We picked up a tail at the prison." Joe's voice was hushed, and Callum guessed he was keeping the information to himself for the time being.

"Law enforcement?" Callum tried to ignore the pain in his legs. Pain that shouldn't have been there, because the part of his legs that ached no longer existed.

"Don't know," Joe said. "But I don't think so. There were two of them. They were coordinated and knew what they were doing. Plus"—Joe lowered his voice—"I could have sworn I saw signs of respect as they walked through the streets."

Callum cursed. Signs of respect meant locals who were too scared to look at the men. Signs of respect generally meant one thing—cartels were involved. "Have you gotten the full story out of Julia's grandmother yet?"

"She's still in jail, but my contact—Eduardo Sanchez—is working on it."

"He can be trusted?"

"Yeah, he's dual nationality and did some time in the Marines way back when. He's good people."

"What about the missing friend? She's been gone, what? Three, four days now. Any sign of her?"

"You remember that?"

"Aye." Callum sometimes wished his memory wasn't a steel trap. He stared at his stumps. There were things he would kill to forget.

"There's been no word. We checked in with the police here, and they said they've got officers hunting for her, but…"

"But the system is disorganised and corrupt. You don't know who's really looking for her and who really wants her."

"Yeah. If she left on her own, she could be anywhere. If someone has her, there's been no word, no call for ransom. I haven't said it aloud, but there's a good chance the woman is dead."

"You think someone killed her over this damn mummy?" Callum asked.

"I don't know what to think. All I know is we have a missing woman, another in jail and guys with guns on our tail. Can you get Elle to do some hacking magic and dig up everything she can find about Alice Bridges, Patricia Matthews and this damn mummy?"

"Aye, I can do that."

Callum reached for his prosthetic legs. Although there was a ramp that led straight into the office from the old carriage house at the back of the Benson Security building, Callum didn't like to use his wheelchair. If he was going to manage the London office, he was damn well going to do it standing—even if it wasn't on his own two feet.

"Thanks." He heard Joe's relief. "I don't know what's going on here, but I'm getting a real bad feeling about it. Whatever it is, it's a helluva lot worse than Julia's gran let on."

"Another bloody family crisis. This is what I'm dealing with now. I never had to deal with this crap in the special forces." Callum put the call on speaker and started to pull the compression sock over his left leg stump. "I should have known when Julia used those doe eyes on me and asked for time off to bail her poor wee gran out of a foreign jail that this would end up being far from simple. We haven't even opened the doors of this bloody office and already we're on our second renovation because of *family issues.*"

Okay, so they'd agreed to help Dimitri find his sister before they even took over the London office and, technically, it wasn't Dimitri's fault that someone had bombed the place, but still. Callum had only just bought into the company, the London office hadn't even taken on its first paying client and already they were up to their necks in yet more of his team's family drama.

"You about done whining?" The American bastard sounded amused.

"Am I entertaining you, Joe?" Callum strapped on his prosthetic leg.

"Not at all, boss. Not at all."

"Bastard," Callum muttered. "While I remember, get Julia to call her parents. Her mother has been ringing all bloody day because she can't get her daughter on the phone, and I don't know what to tell her. All Julia said before she ran out of here was that her mother was to be kept in the dark. It's like being back in high school. I do not have time for this crap."

"I'll pass on the message," Joe drawled. "Now, if you're done ranting, can we focus on the problem in Peru? I exhausted my reliable contacts pulling a lawyer. I don't know anyone here I trust enough to do some digging for me or to watch our backs. You got anyone you can recommend?"

Callum ran a hand down his face. Man, but he felt every second of his forty-two years. "I'll see who I can dig up and call you back."

"Appreciated," Joe said.

"Yeah, yeah, yeah." Callum cut the call dead and yanked his jeans up over his half-plastic legs.

Two minutes later, he'd pulled a t-shirt over his head and was striding towards his office. It was time to call his business partners and tell them they'd somehow managed to find trouble all over again.

JOE HAD INSISTED ON A SUITE, when Julia would have rather they had separate rooms—far away from each other, on opposite sides of the hotel. The suite was decorated in a style Julia had come to think of as lush, modern chic. Lots of over-filled soft furnishings and patterned fabrics, in rich colours, interspersed with white. At least she was grateful that the suite had two bedrooms and that they were in a hotel she was familiar with. She'd stayed in the InterContinental many times with her family. That didn't stop her calling down to management while Joe was making his own calls. She grilled the poor duty manager on the temperature of her dish-washing water and frying oil, as well as on their hygiene standards concerning food preparation. To her credit, the woman was very patient with Julia's weird interrogation, and now she knew she could safely order off the menu in any of the hotel's four restaurants.

Which she would do right after she unpacked. But wait, she couldn't unpack *because her bags were in a completely different hotel*. Julia eyed the bedroom where Joe had dumped his own bag and was currently pacing while he mumbled into his phone. Maybe she could sneak out while he was talking. She could head back to her original hotel, unpack her bags, barricade the door and spend a peaceful night alone.

As though reading her mind, Joe turned and stared at her while he spoke. He said something into the phone before holding it away from his ear and pointing at her.

"Don't even think about going anywhere. It isn't safe, and I will just hunt you down anyway."

Julia gaped at the man while he continued his conversation with the local police. How did he do that? How did he read her mind? It was seriously disconcerting. Instead of bolting for the door, like any sane woman would do, Julia walked to the large window and looked out at the city.

The suite Joe had insisted on, was on one of the higher floors in the hotel, with views out over Miraflores and the cliffs, to the Pacific Ocean. Not that she'd seen any of these things, except on her iPad when she'd googled the area. Joe had told her that Miraflores was an affluent area popular with tourists. Google told her the name translated into "look at the flowers," which she thought was pretty. She was also hopeful it meant the suburb had less sand and more greenery.

"Callum says you need to call your mother."

Joe's voice startled Julia, making her jerk forward and bump her forehead against the glass.

"Come here." His hand held her shoulder and turned her

to him. He scrutinised her forehead, gently tracing a finger over the area she'd hit.

"It's nothing," Julia whispered, aware of how close he was standing.

His sinfully sensual lips quirked up at the corners. "Want me to kiss it better?"

Danger! Danger! Overload, overload, system malfunction!

Joe Barone had a tendency to eat up all the space around him, making her feel like she couldn't breathe. It wasn't just the fact he towered over her, or that his shoulders were impossibly wide—it was his intensity. Something she doubted most people noticed because he hid it behind easy charm and a quick smile. But she saw it. Probably because she'd spent so much time over the past year studying the man—covertly, of course. Joe Barone was a coiled tiger. He was dangerous, smart and relentless in everything he pursued.

Which terrified her, because Julia knew he was pursuing her.

"What did you say?" she whispered, aware of just how close he was standing.

"I said"—he ran his thumb over her forehead—"do you want me to kiss it better?

Julia jerked back, away from his touch.

"Maybe later, then." He took a half step back from her, giving her some much-needed space to breathe. "Callum said your mom has been calling every hour. You'd better deal with it or he might send someone over there to sort out the problem for him."

Great. Exactly what she needed. A conversation with her mother. Not that she didn't usually love talking to her mum. It was just that her mum could see through Julia in ways no other person could, and she would know as soon as Julia opened her mouth, that something was wrong. Talking to her mother was a minefield. Maybe she could just send her a text? Or an email? She could do an email. Maybe.

"You hungry?" Joe interrupted the discussion she was having with herself.

"I think so." A nervous stomach meant she didn't always feel hunger when she should, but she was aware she hadn't eaten much on the plane. Airline food was notorious for being badly cooked, and she couldn't risk getting food poisoning, so she'd stuck to nuts and crackers for the duration of the flight.

"I'll order something from room service. Did you check out the kitchens already?"

Julia's eyes sprang up to his. She studied him for a moment, but he didn't seem to be making fun of her.

"Yes, I did," she said cautiously.

He nodded. "Good, then call your mom while I order."

For a moment, Julia couldn't believe he'd taken her foible in his stride. It was something she'd have to think about. Later. Joe turned away from her, and for some reason, him leaving her space didn't make her feel better.

"I think it would be best if I send her a vague, but upbeat, email instead."

"Babe, she's your mom. You know how to deal with her. But if I did that to mine, she'd hunt me down until she got the real story."

So would Julia's mum. On second thought, maybe she'd send a text instead.

Joe reached for the room phone. "What do you want?"

"Fries and bananas."

Joe looked at her. "Fries and bananas?"

"Yes. The bananas come with their own packaging and fries are deep fried, which will kill any bacteria."

"Babe, please tell me you don't plan to spend this whole trip eating fries and bananas."

"No." Unless she couldn't find anything else she thought was safe enough to eat. In which case, the answer would be a most definite yes. Anyway, if she added nuts—in their shells, of course—then she'd have a balanced diet. Almost. "Can you see if they have any nuts? In shells?"

Joe shook his head and ordered the food. While he was doing that, the porter arrived with her luggage from her previous hotel. Julia had to go through it to make sure nothing had been tampered with, which made her irritated with Joe for adding to her stress and messing up her perfectly organised plan.

She had her bag open on her bed—thankfully, the lock hadn't been tampered with—when Joe sauntered into the room.

"Want to play cards?" He leaned against the doorjamb, his arms folded and his ankles crossed.

Cards? "I thought I'd eat and then get some sleep." She also thought she'd spend as little time as possible with the man who made every hair on her body stand up—as though reaching for him.

"Not a good idea. It's too early. If you go to sleep now, your body clock won't adapt properly and you'll have jetlag longer."

"Is that true?" She wouldn't put it past the charming monster to use pseudo-facts just to get her to do what he wanted.

"Babe, would I lie to you?" His smile was pure devilment.

"Yes."

He placed a hand over his heart. "Come play cards with me while we eat."

His faux-innocent look was setting off all kinds of alarm bells. This was another reason she stayed away from Joe. She was woefully out of her depth with the man.

"What kind of cards, exactly?"

"Why, Julia, do you think I would try to get you to play strip poker? Shame on you."

He was grinning now. Playing with her. Teasing. All things Julia didn't know how to deal with. Her face burned and she didn't know what to say. Even if she did, it would invariably be the wrong thing anyway.

She concentrated on her luggage instead, even though she was finished checking it. A couple of seconds passed before she felt Joe come up behind her. When his hands softly cupped her shoulders, she froze in place. Now, she not only didn't know what to say, she also didn't know what to do.

"I'm teasing," he said softly. "You're safe with me. You can't say or do anything wrong."

Her body was so tense and tight that she was sure she'd snap in two if she tried to bend.

"Come play cards, Julia. It will take your mind off things. I can promise there will be no stripping." He kissed her temple before retreating.

Julia started to breathe again as he walked away. That was, until she heard him say one word— "Yet."

CHAPTER 3

"I don't think we should be playing cards," Julia said as she sat at the tiny dining table opposite Joe. "Alice is missing. Gran is in jail. We should be doing something about that instead of wasting time."

Joe started shuffling cards. "We've called the cops, the hospitals and the airlines. Elle is checking hotels, bus companies and credit card movement for Alice. Short of going door to door, I don't know what else we can do to find her right now. As for your gran, Ed's dealing with her, and they don't let visitors hang out at the prison overnight." He started dealing cards. "And it's dark outside. You can't go wandering around the streets with a photo of Alice, looking for leads, in the dark. It's a much better idea to stay in here and play with me."

"It feels wrong. I should be doing something."

"Like what?"

She moved the cards he'd dealt, to ensure they were parallel with the table's edge. Better. "I don't know." And she hated that she didn't.

"Then we play cards. We eat. We sleep. And tomorrow we start again."

Julia looked up at him. She knew he was right. She knew there wasn't anything she could do except worry—and she was fantastic at worrying—but the thought of her gran spending another night in that awful jail and Alice lost or worse… What if she was suffering? What if Gran got ill or hurt? What if?

A big hand covered hers, the heat from Joe's touch searing her skin. "Time to take your mind off things. Pick up your cards. Spending an hour playing with me isn't going to change anything. The problems will still be there when we're done. And tomorrow, after a good night's sleep, we might think of something else we can do."

"Is it always like this?"

"Every op is different. Sometimes there's waiting when you don't want to wait. It's the nature of things."

"What did you do when you were waiting, when you were in the Marines?"

"Well, I didn't play cards with a pretty girl, that's for sure."

Julia felt her cheeks burn as she looked back down at the cards. Her stomach was doing somersaults, and she regretted eating even the small amount of fries she'd managed to get down. Joe got up, headed for the bar fridge and came back with a tiny bottle of wine and a glass.

"Here, it will help with your stomach and your sleep."

Julia looked at the glass, then at Joe. "Do you realise that most glasses found in hotel rooms haven't been washed properly? I watched a documentary about it. Maid service were just rinsing them under the tap, then polishing them with a towel."

He unscrewed the bottle and handed it to her. "Then don't use the glass."

Julia took the bottle, drank a hefty swallow of cheap red wine, then looked at Joe. "Okay, let's play."

She could do this. Right? If she didn't think about being alone with Joe. In a hotel room.

"Now that's what I like to hear." His eyes sparkled with mischief, making her stomach do the flipping thing again. "Do you know how to play poker?"

"No."

"Rummy?"

"No."

"Jules, do you know how to play any card games?"

She licked her lips, feeling more than a little foolish. "Snap?"

Joe threw back his head and roared with laughter. Once he'd calmed down, he appeared delighted. Julia didn't know why.

"Guess we're playing snap, then." His grin was wide. "Now when you lose a round, there's a penalty."

Her eyes narrowed. "What kind of penalty?" She wasn't taking off any clothes. None.

"Julia Collins, you're thinking about stripping again, aren't you? You are just desperate to get naked with me. Unfortunately, I'll have to wait for that pleasure. If you lose, the winner has the right to claim a boon."

Her head snapped up. "Boon?"

"Yeah, a reward." He waggled his eyebrows. "It could be in the form of a question the loser has to answer, or a dare they have to take, or a kiss they have to give the winner."

His eyes lingered on her lips, making her flush as she remembered the brief, sweet kiss he'd given her weeks earlier. The kiss that had made her hide from him ever since.

His eyes darkened as he watched her. "You're thinking about it, aren't you?"

Julia felt her cheeks burn, but didn't answer.

"You still playing?" he challenged.

"Is hiding in the closet an option?"

His lips twitched. "No."

"Then let's start." This might just be a game of snap, but there was no way she was letting him win. Especially with this boon system in place. The dark places of her mind were already speculating about what sort of boon Joe would claim. She shut them down and sat up straight.

"You ready?"

"Play your card, Joe."

He won the first round because his reflexes were like a cat.

"This game isn't fair," Julia pointed out. "It's more about being physical than being smart. I don't have the same level of fitness as you. Nor do I have your speed."

"I think you just insulted me." He grinned as Julia went over her words.

Her eyes went wide. "I don't mean I would have a better chance if we were playing a game that needed intellect. I just mean you're bigger. You have more muscle. You're sneaky and fast."

"Tell you what, we'll put the cards closer to you so that your shorter arms can reach them faster. Does that help?"

"You're mocking me."

"Only a little. Now I want to claim my boon."

She froze. "I'm not taking off any clothes." Not that she had many on. She'd packed a suitcase full of shapeless cotton dresses because she thought they would be the most practical option. All she had on was a beige tent that went to her ankles and beige cotton underwear.

Oh. My. Goodness.

Joe could *not* see her underwear. Ever.

"You know, just once, I'd love to be inside your mind," Joe said. "I bet it would be fascinating."

"What's the boon, Joe?" She squared her shoulders. She could take it.

"Unpin your hair. Let it fall free."

"My hair." She touched the tight bun at the back of her head.

"Yeah, I've never seen it down."

Feeling entirely too self-conscious, Julia unpinned her hair. The honey-coloured waves fell to her shoulders. Her hair was hard to style. It was never neat enough for Julia, and there was too much of it. She'd inherited her mother's thick locks.

"Beautiful." Joe reached out and played with one of the waves. "You should wear it down all the time."

"It gets in the way."

"Of what?"

She frowned at him. "Life."

With a grin, Joe played another card. "Come on, time for you to win a boon. If you can."

Julia kept her eyes glued to the growing pile of cards they threw down. Her hand shot out when two aces appeared.

"Snap!" She grinned at Joe.

"Julia Collins, you've got a maniacal competitive streak. I didn't know that about you."

"You should see me when I play Monopoly." She gathered the cards.

"I'd like that. Now what are you going to claim as your boon?"

Two thoughts slammed into her mind at the same time. One of them made her blush furiously.

"Oh, I need to hear this." Joe leaned his forearms on the table. "What just went through your head?"

Nothing—except the thought of making him play shirtless. The only thing stopping her, was that he would likely make her do the same if he won a round. The sensible thing was to go for the safe option. There were days when Julia hated her need for safety.

"I'll ask a question," she said, making him arch his eyebrow at her. "Do you like living in England?"

Joe shook his head with clear disgust. "Baby, that isn't a boon, that's polite dinner conversation. Try again. Ask something you really want the answer to."

A plethora of questions ran through her mind. To her shame, most of them involved words she couldn't say out loud. Joe Barone had a very bad effect on her it seemed.

"Time's ticking. You don't choose fast, you lose your boon."

"That wasn't in the rules."

He shrugged, clearly amused. Julia, meanwhile, tried desperately to think of something he would consider a worthy boon, but didn't involve anybody stripping. There was honestly nothing else in her brain. It was pathetic. Normally she couldn't shut her overactive mind down, but around Joe, it went blank.

"I'm counting to three, and if you don't choose, you lose. One. Two…"

"Take off your shirt." As soon as the words were out of her mouth, Julia was on her feet and running for her bedroom, humiliation fast on her heels.

A huge arm wrapped around her waist and then she was being carried back to the table.

"I need to go to bed." She struggled in his arms.

"Yeah, I saw how urgent the need was." He put her in her seat and leaned over her. "There is nothing wrong with your request. This is just us. Nobody else. And nothing you say or do here is wrong. And"—his smile was wicked—"this time, I won't make you strip as payback."

Julia groaned, hung her head and pressed her hot face

into her palms. When she looked back up, Joe was shirtless, and then her brain really stopped working.

Danger! Danger! Run!

Unfortunately, her feet had stopped working too. Her eyes however, were still very much functional. And they were glued to the most perfect set of abdominal muscles she'd ever seen. Was that an eight-pack? Was that even possible? Her fingers itched to trace over his muscles and make sure her math was correct. Perfect olive skin was tight against well-defined pecs, and there was a smattering of hair between his nipples.

Oh. My. Goodness.

It was possible she might faint and die right then and there.

"Your turn to start." Joe's rumbling baritone broke the trance his chest had put her into.

Julia eyed the bedroom door again. Maybe if she ran really fast, she could hide in the closet before he even noticed she was missing.

"Pick up your cards and play," Joe said.

Without even thinking about it, she followed his order. Her eyes flickered to his. "I'm sorry I made you strip. It was wrong of me." Especially seeing as she would die if he asked her to do the same.

"Oh, I don't know. I kind of like the look you have on your face right now. I'd say it was very right of you. Now play your card."

Dragging her attention from the half-naked Joe, Julia slapped her card down, keeping her eyes glued to the growing pile. She saw the double queens a split second before Joe's big hand smacked down on them.

"Are you cheating?" She glared at him, forgetting for once that this man made her more nervous than a mouse at a cat show.

"How can you cheat at snap?" He folded his arms, bringing her attention right back to his chest. A chest topped with shoulder muscles that made her mouth water.

With great effort, she pulled her gaze away and stared at the table instead. "I'm watching you, Joe Barone. I usually do better at this game. There's something going on here."

"Do you normally play with five-year-olds?"

That didn't even merit a reply. "What's the boon this time?"

"A kiss."

Electricity sparked between them. And it suddenly became hard to breathe. Julia could still remember the last kiss they'd shared. It haunted her dreams. There were times she was certain she could still feel his lips pressed against hers. She wasn't sure she would survive another one.

"I don't think that's a good idea," she whispered.

"Why?"

"Why?"

He cocked an eyebrow. "Yeah, tell me why it's a bad idea?"

Because you terrify me. Because you're too gorgeous to be interested in me. Because you might think you want to start something with me, but it's only a matter of time until you get fed up with my weird personality. Because...

"Julia, you have to answer out loud or I can't hear you."

"I told you we aren't suited."

"And I told you that I wanted to try. You promised to think about it. You've had enough time to come to a conclusion."

No, she hadn't. It was all she'd thought about for weeks. And she kept coming up against the same dilemma—if she started something with Joe, she'd end up getting hurt, and she wasn't sure her heart could cope with it.

"Baby." He leaned towards her, mere inches away. The heat from his body drew her like a warm open fire. "Tell me you don't want to kiss me and I'll choose another boon."

Julia almost lost herself in those chocolate-coloured eyes, but she didn't say a word. She couldn't. Because she wanted nothing more than to feel Joe's lips on hers again. Even though she knew it was a very bad idea. Even though she knew there was nothing inside her that could deal with this man. Even though she knew he could destroy her. She still wanted his kiss.

"Yeah, that's what I thought," he whispered.

As though in slow motion, he closed the gap between them. Julia's eyes fluttered shut as his lips touched hers. *Joe.* His touch was teasing, and Julia found herself leaning into it. Soft, firm lips brushed over hers as his hand clasped into the hair at the back of her head. When he nibbled softly at her lower lip, she heard a small, needy moan escape. Joe made a rumbling sound in reply, as his tongue teased the seam of her lips. There was no fighting it. Julia didn't hesitate to open her mouth for him.

His head angled and he deepened the kiss. Julia felt hot, firm muscle under her fingertips and realised her hands were on him. His scent, that masculine aroma of spice and musk, was like a drug to her senses. He tasted of coffee and Joe. He tasted of pleasure she'd never imagined. Pleasure that equally terrified and tempted.

All too soon, he slowed the kiss and leaned back, his hand still in her hair, her nails digging into his shoulders. Julia fought to lift heavy eyelids, and what she saw made her heart stutter. There was pure, ferocious need in his eyes. Need and possession.

For her.

Without thinking, Julia was on her feet and running. This time, Joe didn't stop her.

CHAPTER 4

Julia had never been so relieved as when her grandmother walked through the doors of their suite the following afternoon. Not only because she wasn't in jail, but because it meant Julia wasn't alone with Joe anymore. She rushed over to embrace her, but her gran held up her hands.

"I just spent almost a week in a cell with ten other women and no shower. You might want to wait with the hug until I've cleaned up."

"I'll take my chances." Julia wrapped her in a tight embrace while they both laughed. When they eventually separated, Julia could see the dark circles under her gran's eyes. Eyes that were filled with an equal measure of worry and relief. "Have all the charges really been dropped?"

"All of them," Patricia said. "Now, we need to find Alice."

That took the bottom out of their jubilant mood.

"We will," Julia promised, knowing it wasn't a lie. One way or another, they'd find Alice. She only hoped the woman was in one piece when they did. "We got your luggage from the police. Your bags are in my room. Go get showered and I'll order food." She pointed at the room they would share.

"Bless your heart." Patricia waved over her shoulder at the two men who were watching her. "Won't be long." And then the door closed behind her.

Julia stared at the door for a moment, enjoying the fact her grandmother was free. Then she turned to the men. Taking all of her courage in both hands, she looked up at them. "Tell me what's wrong. There's no way she should have been released like that. Something is going on, and I don't want to be kept in the dark."

"Smart," the lawyer muttered.

Julia fought a blush. Just because she had issues, didn't mean she was dumb. Plus, his comment was insulting on so many levels.

"Would you say that to a man?" Julia asked him softly, her heart racing at her temerity. "With the same degree of shock you used with me?"

"My apologies," Ed said.

Joe shook his head at the man, as he held out a hand to her. "Come on, babe. Ed will fill us in while Patricia is busy. There are things she doesn't need to know right now."

Not wanting to leave him hanging in front of Ed, she took his hand. When he sat beside her, it was just close enough that their thighs were barely touching. Julia wasn't quite sure what to make of the whole thing, so she did what she did best: she pretended it wasn't happening. She grabbed her iPad from the table beside her, opened a new document for notes and faced Ed. She stared at his chest, rather than his eyes, but didn't hesitate with her questions.

"What happened? Was there new evidence that proved she didn't do it? I went over the documents she sent, on the flight here. I might have missed some of the details because I ran them through a translation programme, but I thought the case against her was sound."

Joe's arm stretched along the back of the sofa, and she felt his fingers playing with her hair. She scooted forward an inch, out of his reach, bizarrely missing his touch once it was gone.

"Well." Ed cleared his throat. "I would be interested to see what documentation you received, because the documents I got yesterday afternoon were full of errors and gaping holes. On top of that, there's been a gross mishandling of the evidence. Based on everything I saw, your grandmother should never have been charged."

Julia had been making notes as Ed spoke. She paused when he finished, her agile mind running over everything. "There was tampering. Someone wanted Gran out of jail." She couldn't quite look at Ed, but she found she could look up at Joe. "Does Gran know who's behind this?"

"We're missing some of the facts, babe. Your gran wasn't exactly forthcoming."

"She kept saying that the walls had ears," Ed added.

"She knows, then." Julia made a note. "Does the person who wants her out of jail also have the mummy?"

"We don't know," Ed said.

Again Julia addressed her question to Joe. Something he seemed inordinately pleased with. "Did Gran and Alice steal the mummy?"

"Someone filmed the break-in on their phone and sent it to the cops," Joe said. "Your gran was on it, but Alice wasn't. Patricia was seen talking to someone off camera."

"Did it record Gran actually taking the mummy?" Julia asked.

"No, only the break-in," Ed said.

Julia nodded. "Someone wanted us to know that Gran was there, but they didn't want us to know who actually took the thing. Or they don't know who took it, and this is a setup to frame Gran."

"She was filmed in the owner's house," Joe pointed out. "On the night the mummy was stolen."

"But maybe the mummy was already gone."

"That's a stretch," Ed said. "But the recording is useless now anyway—it became mysteriously corrupted this morning and can't be used in court."

"More tampering? Somebody definitely wanted Gran out of jail. Maybe the same person had something to do with Alice's disappearance." Julia had listened in while Joe spent the morning calling everyone he could think of, to stir up the investigation into the missing woman. There was no sign of her and nobody knew where to look.

"What has Elle dug up about Alice?" Julia asked Joe, because he'd been the one to talk with her. "Did she discover anything that can help us find Alice and the person behind all these weird things happening to Gran?"

Joe reached out to play with a lock of her hair, and Julia realised she'd relaxed back into the sofa beside him at some point. Against her better judgment, she'd left her hair down instead of putting it in her usual bun—all because she knew Joe liked it that way. She was a fool. She'd spent the better part of the night lying awake worrying about what was happening with them and vowing to put an end to it. And the first thing she'd done on waking was leave her hair loose for him. She was losing her mind.

"Elle hasn't been able to dig up anything," Joe said. "Alice's credit cards haven't been used and her passport hasn't been scanned at any border."

There was silence. Julia felt what Joe didn't say. It was a rock sitting in her stomach. She took a shaky breath and said what everyone was thinking: "Either she's dead or someone has her."

Ed leaned forward. "I'm curious—why don't you think she's hiding?"

"Money," Julia said. "Alice is paranoid about carrying around a lot of cash. If she hasn't used her cards, then she doesn't have money. You need money to hide."

"That's what I've been thinking," her gran said as she strode into the room. "There's no way that woman has run off, no matter what the police tell you. We've been friends since before we started school. There have been times I've wished she'd disappear and couldn't get rid of her. She'd never wander off on her own now."

"Somebody must have her," Julia said, because the alternative was just too horrible to contemplate. "The question is why? Surely if they're going to ransom her off, they would have contacted us by now."

"You always were too smart for the rest of us," Patricia said with pride. "Give her a puzzle and she'll get to the bottom of it in no time at all. She's a genius when it comes to arranging things in patterns that no one else can see. Never could get anything past her."

Julia ducked her head, wishing she would just turn invisible. "Gran, that isn't true."

"Honey." Her gran patted her head as she passed on her way to the food trolley sitting beside the dining table. "The university think tank tried to recruit you straight out of college. I still don't know why you didn't jump at the offer. Instead you took that awful job as a production assistant with that overblown moron, just to fit in with the family." She lifted the lid on a warming plate and inhaled with a look of pure delight on her face. "Like you don't already fit in perfectly. I hear that director is in a mental institute now, getting the help he so obviously needed. Small minds, dear, they all eventually crack. Trust me. I'm old and I know these things."

Patricia grabbed a plate of steak and salad and sat at the table. "Do we have any wine to go with this?"

There was silence.

She let out a heavy sigh. "Let me eat and I'll fill you in. Promise. Julia's right—someone has Alice. I just don't know why yet. Now can someone order a bottle of wine? Trust me. After the week I've had, I need it."

CHAPTER 5

Things didn't go as planned. While Patricia was eating, a porter delivered a large manila envelope. An envelope addressed to Patricia Matthews—the woman who had been out of jail for less than two hours. The woman whom no one should have known was staying in the hotel.

"The guy doesn't know who it's from," Joe told them once the door was closed. "He says it was left at reception and they were told it was urgent."

Everyone looked at Patricia. She pushed her plate away, even though it was still half full.

"Do you know anything about this?" Joe said.

"Yes." Her shoulders slumped. "I was passed a message after Alice went missing. It told me to get out of jail as fast as possible and wait to be contacted. I assumed it was about Alice." She suddenly looked closer to her age. "I thought the same as Julia, that someone was holding Alice for ransom. It's a South American thing, isn't it? Hold wealthy tourists for ransom."

"I think that's Colombia, gran." Julia leaned over to pat her gran's hand.

"Anyway"—Patricia pointed at the envelope in Joe's hand —"I think that's them contacting me. I really hope they haven't sent me Alice's ear."

"Gran, don't say things like that. That sort of thing only happens in movies."

Joe didn't bother shattering her delusions. Kidnappers cut off ears and a whole lot more besides. And all of it was stuff Julia was better off not knowing.

"Only one way to find out what's in it." Joe ripped open the envelope.

"Joe!" Julia rushed to his side. "There could have been something dangerous in there. Like a letter bomb or something. You should have been more careful."

Joe was insanely pleased that she was worried about his safety. It showed progress. And considering she'd barely looked at him since she'd gotten up that morning, he could do with some progress. He'd been too hasty pushing her the night before, but what were his options? If he let things progress at Julia's pace, they might be dead before they ever found out if this thing between them was real. Baby steps, he told himself. He still had to take baby steps.

Baby steps sucked.

He upended the envelope over the table, and a cheap prepaid cell phone dropped out.

"Guess you're about to get a call, Patricia." Joe shared a worried look with Ed. They had no time to set up a call trace, or even to check out the phone.

The phone buzzed, making everyone in the room jump. Patricia shot to her feet as though ready to run and answer it. Joe held up a hand to stop her.

"It's a text." He hit the button and read the message. "It's an IP address."

"What does that mean?" Patricia said.

"It's an internet destination. They want you to go there."

Julia pulled out her iPad, then rooted around in her messenger bag. She came out with a cable. "I'll connect the iPad to the TV. That way we can all watch what Gran sees when she goes online. We could crowd around the screen on my tablet, but it's probably not a good idea to let everyone know we're with her—just in case they want her to enable the camera. Plus, the screen is a little small."

"If this is a two-way connection," Joe said, "it's best if the other end only see Patricia."

Julia rushed over to the large TV and connected it to her iPad. Ed was shaking his head at the mystery that was Julia, while Patricia looked on proudly.

"We'll be with you every step of the way," Joe told Patricia. "If they expect you to communicate with them, don't agree to anything without consulting me first. I want to keep you safe, and I need your help to do that."

Patricia nodded as Julia sat beside her at the small dining table. The women put their heads together, studying the screen while Julia typed in the IP address. A few seconds passed before a live feed of a nondescript room appeared on the screen. There was the sound of a scuffle, and a woman was pushed into the room.

"Alice!" Patricia gasped.

Unlike Patricia, Alice looked like someone's gran. She wore beige cotton pants and a blue button-down shirt. Her feet were clad in loafers and her grey hair was cut short, in a feathered cap over her head. She looked rumpled and tired. She stared at the screen a little vaguely, and Joe wondered if she'd been drugged.

"Is it on?" she said, and Patricia made a little mewling sound.

Alice looked around, smiled vaguely at someone off camera and then waved. "Is it on? Am I live? Hello? Is anybody out there?"

"Oh no," Julia and Patricia said at the same time.

"What?" Joe snapped.

Julia looked resigned. "I'm sorry," she said. "My whole family are like this, even the honorary members."

"Watch your mouth," Patricia said. "I'm nothing like this."

"Hellooooo," Alice sang. "Hellooooo."

"I've told her not to do this," Patricia said to Julia. "Haven't I told her?"

"Do what?" Joe almost shouted.

"She's pretending to have dementia." Julia put her palm to her brow, in a gesture that screamed long-suffering. "She thinks it makes her seem like a harmless little old lady. The problem is, Alice is the world's worst actress."

"I've told her a million times that she needs to leave acting to the professionals. There's a reason the woman's career was behind the camera."

"Okey-dokey." Alice's face filled the screen, and she smiled maniacally. "The nice man told me that the green light means I'm on TV." She waved again. "Patricia, darling, I hope you're watching. Marcus, Marcus, love, are you there? I told you I'd make a great actress, and now I have my own show." She looked off camera. "I told Marcus all about my acting plans. He's such a good listener and always full of ideas to help my career. Just wait until he hears that I'm on live TV. With my own show! What's it called again?"

Julia and Patricia shared a look of bewilderment, before focusing their attention back on the screen.

There were mumbled voices, and Alice smiled back at the camera. "It's called the Alice Show. Isn't that perfect?" She clapped her hands in delight. "Although I shall have to talk to my agent about getting a better set. This one is rather basic. And don't even get me started on the food." She spoke off camera again. "We need a new food truck." She looked back into the lens. "Jorge said if I do a good job I'll get ice cream." She beamed, looking a little demented.

Patricia threw her hands up and glared at the iPad. "Can I talk to her through this thing? I need to tell her that nobody's buying her act. A two-year-old could do a better job. Hell, Liz Hurley could do a better job, and her acting is no better than a puppet show. Wooden. Totally wooden." She poked Julia's shoulder. "Where's the mic button?"

"You can't talk to her. It's a one-way feed."

"This is embarrassing," Patricia said as she watched Alice wax lyrical about her favourite ice cream. "People with dementia don't behave like that. She should be nominated for a Razzie Award."

"Patricia!" Joe barked. "Quiet!"

"The nice producer says I have to tell you about mummy." Alice frowned with exaggerated confusion. "Do you mean my mummy? I think she's dead."

Patricia groaned loudly, and Joe shot her another glare. "I will gag you."

She made a zipping motion over her lips.

"Jorge says he wants his mummy back." Alice made a sad face that reminded Joe of a mime performance. "That's heartbreaking; he misses his mummy. What did you say, Jorge? I couldn't hear you because I'm talking to Patricia."

There was silence while Alice focused on her kidnapper.

She nodded. "Jorge says you have to bring his mummy to him or I won't get to come home." She looked slightly panicked, but smiled widely. "Don't worry about that. I like it here. I'm going to be a star! Do you hear me, Marcus? This is where I told you I'd end up. I'm going to be a star!" She waved her hands above her head, and the feed cut out.

The screen went blank and there was silence. Until the cell phone rang.

Patricia shot to her feet, her eyes went straight to Joe. "What do I say?"

"Tell them the truth. Tell them you don't have the mummy and you need time to get it."

"I don't even know where it is! It was gone by the time we broke into the house." Her voice rose with the beginnings of hysteria.

"Tell them that. Ask for more time." Joe lifted the phone and walked to Patricia. "It's important that you get more time. Make them believe you can find the mummy. Got it?"

"Got it." She didn't look like she did, but Joe had no other option than to hand over the ringing phone.

"Hello?" Patricia said in a tremulous voice.

She listened while everyone in the room leaned in towards her.

"I don't have it. Someone had already taken it by the time we got there." As she listened, Patricia paled. "No! No. I can find it. I just need some time. I'm sure I can find it." She stared into space, agony on her face. "I n-need more time than that."

The caller said something else, and then Patricia's hand fell to her side, still clutching the phone. "He says we have three days. If he doesn't have the mummy by Friday, Alice will lose her usefulness."

A grim silence enveloped the room.

"I really need wine." Patricia headed for the minibar, placing the phone carefully on the table when she passed. It was her only lifeline to Alice.

Joe looked at Julia, whose face was a mask of fear and worry. "Julia, if they plan to keep using the phone, maybe Elle can get something from it that will help us?"

"I'll email the details to her now." Julia looked less terrified now that she had a task to keep her mind occupied.

"In the meantime, we need a starting place. We need to

know everything you know about this mummy, Patricia. Including why these guys are so hot to trade your friend for a corpse that wouldn't sell for as much as a cheap used car. I get the feeling there's something about this particular mummy that isn't showing up in our research on it. Something you obviously know."

Patricia ducked her head as her cheeks turned pink. Oh yeah, she knew exactly what was going on, and it was time she shared. If there was one thing Joe hated, it was being kept in the dark. Especially when there were lives on the line.

"And Gran?" Julia looked up from her tablet. "Who is Marcus and why was Alice talking about him?"

Joe's eyes snapped to Julia. "I thought that was her husband."

"No." Patricia sighed. "Her husband was called Jonathan, and he was a film director who is probably turning in his grave at his widow's terrible performance. Marcus is something else entirely. I think mentioning him might be Alice's idea of talking in code. I'm fairly certain she was trying to give me a message."

"What message?" Julia stopped emailing Elle.

"That Marcus is up to his neck in this mess. After Alice's over-the-top declarations of love for Marcus, I get the horrible feeling that the woman I call my lifelong best friend may have had sex with my ex-lover. Honestly, I told her the man was rubbish in bed. What was she thinking?"

"Gran!" Both of Julia's hands shot up to cover her open mouth.

Patricia rolled her eyes. "We're old. Not dead."

"But the same man?"

"Not at the same time! Who knows what the crazy woman meant. It could all be part of her daft act."

Julia clapped her hands over her ears. "I didn't hear that. I can't hear you talk about your boyfriends. It didn't happen."

Patricia's eye roll was much more dramatic than anything Alice had managed during her broadcast. "You and I are going to have a talk, missy." She pointed at Julia. "A woman doesn't stop having needs just because she ages. And Marcus wasn't my boyfriend. I'm in my sixties. I don't have boyfriends. I have lovers. Your feminist education is sorely lacking."

"This isn't about being a feminist." Julia's voice rose, and Joe realised she wasn't shy when it came to family. It gave him hope that, one day, she'd feel comfortable enough to shout at him too. "It's about being a granddaughter," Julia shouted.

"Enough!" Joe held up his hands for silence and hid his shock when he got it. "Your sex life isn't interesting to anybody but you," he told the pouting Patricia. "What we need to talk about is this guy Marcus and why everybody is so damned interested in a worthless mummy."

"I'll tell you everything. But first I need a drink." Patricia looked over her shoulder at them. "I suggest you get one too."

CHAPTER 6

"Do you know what a mummy hunter is?" Patricia asked them once she had a glass of wine in her hand and was settled into an armchair.

"I thought we were going to start with this Marcus guy?" Joe said.

"I'll get there, but you need some background first. Do I need to explain what a mummy hunter is or do you all know what I'm talking about?"

"Let's assume we don't have a clue." Ed pulled out a chair at the dining table. "Start from the beginning and fill us in."

Joe was sitting on the sofa beside Julia. He leaned forward, grabbed a bottle of water from the table in front of them, unscrewed the cap and handed it to Julia. When she took it and drank without looking up from the notes she was scribbling on her iPad, he smiled indulgently. Her brain was working a mile a minute. Again. Damn, but she was gorgeous when she was thinking. He mentally rolled his eyes at himself. He was losing his mind over the woman. It was only a matter of time before he started googling Shakespearean sonnets to drop into conversation.

Patricia rested her wine glass on the arm of the chair. "There are a dedicated group of people who study mummified bodies. Most of them aren't experts in the field, but enthusiasts. Well-educated enthusiasts. We're talking research biologists and professors in palaeontology or criminal pathologists." She pointed at Julia. "You would have made a fabulous criminal pathologist, darling. It isn't too late to continue your studies, if you're interested. I could put a word in at my old university for you."

"Thanks, Gran," Julia mumbled, her focus on her iPad.

"Back to the mummy," Joe said when Patricia paused. Presumably so they could spend a moment in awe of the calibre of her fellow mummy-obsessed nut jobs.

After giving him a look of pure censure, she carried on. "These people get together every couple of years for a conference in Chile. They present papers on everything to do with mummies. They swap stories of new finds and speculate about sites for undiscovered bodies. About ten years ago, just before she officially retired, Alice made a documentary for the Discovery Channel about the conference and the people who attended."

"I thought she wasn't used to being in front of the camera?" Ed said.

"She was a producer," Patricia said. "Women can do that nowadays—in their free time away from cooking and cleaning, and looking pretty for their husbands."

Ed held up his hands in an amused, but genuine, sign of apology.

"Anyway, that's when she became hooked on the subject of mummified bodies. Alice asked me to attend the next conference with her, and I was just as fascinated. Since then, we've become part of the group and have attended all of the conferences."

"What's this got to do with your missing friend?" Joe

asked.

"I'm getting to that," Patricia snapped. "Have a little patience."

Joe rubbed a hand over his jaw and motioned for her to carry on. Seemed like they were going to do things at her pace, whether they liked it or not. It didn't appear to matter that they were working against a damned tight deadline.

He got up, wandered to the food cart, selected some prewrapped cookies and took them back to Julia. Again, she accepted the snack and ate it without even realising what she was doing. It made Joe want to keep feeding her just to see how long it would take her to register she was being fed. He glanced at the iPad, which she was furiously filling with information—all in neat, bullet-pointed columns. There was definitely something spectacular going on in her gorgeous head.

"Alice and I started researching South American mummies," Patricia said, pulling Joe's attention back. "Because there's already a lot of information out there and we were novices. The more we studied, went to meetings and read other members' papers on the topic, the more we were convinced that some Peruvian mummies held secrets."

"What kind of secrets?" Joe said.

"Will you stop interrupting me?" Patricia demanded. "Honestly, young people have no patience these days. When I was your age, I would never have dreamed of being so rude."

"Gran." Julia looked up from her iPad. "We're on a deadline here."

"Yes, I'm aware of that, Julia. It's literally a *dead*line, because if we don't meet it, Alice won't be coming home. Forgive me if I'm going too slow for you. I've just spent a sleepless week in a cell with ten other women. Not to mention the stress of worrying I'd have to spend the rest of my life as the girlfriend of a serial killer called Bertha."

Joe felt his ire rise as Julia shrank back at the rebuke.

"Do not speak to Julia like that," he said.

"Joe." Julia placed her hand on his leg, a plea for his silence. But it wasn't going to happen. There was no way Joe would sit back and let *anyone* talk to her that way.

He kept his eyes on Patricia and hoped she saw his intent. He didn't give a damn that she was family. She *would* respect Julia. "Keep in mind who's responsible for getting you into this mess in the first place. Here's a clue: it wasn't Julia. All your granddaughter has done has been to drop everything and run halfway across the world to save your ass. So watch your tone."

He felt Julia wince beside him and covered her hand with his, rubbing his thumb over the back of it.

To her credit, Patricia was instantly contrite. "I'm sorry, honey," she said to Julia. "Joe's right; this is entirely my fault, and I shouldn't be taking it out on anyone else. Forgive me." She studied the contents of her wine glass for a moment. "The obvious secrets the mummies hold are found in the things they're buried with. Each grave tells a tale. They hold insight into ancient practices and cultures. Then there are biological and environmental secrets. Sometimes, because of the drier preservation conditions over here, scientists are able to unlock information on illnesses and the cures ancient Peruvians used. Then there are other secrets." Patricia looked away and sipped from her glass. She swallowed hard before she looked back at them. "I was an art history professor. Alice was a media specialist, whose job involved investigating many different cultural and historical stories. Between us, we heard a lot of rumours and tales from this region." She fidgeted in her seat, and Joe leaned towards her. They were obviously getting to the heart of the matter.

"During our studies into mummies," she said, "and the culture surrounding the sacrificial mummified children of the Andes, we came to believe that there were messages hidden with these children. Messages that the Incas didn't want the Spaniards to find. And those messages were written in code."

"You cracked the code, didn't you?" Julia's head shot up.

Joe shared an incredulous look with Ed. Patricia thought she was a combination of Indiana Jones and Robert Langdon.

"Yes." Patricia somehow managed to look both guilty and excited at the same time. "I specialise in the study of textiles. I've spent my life on it, and it's an area of expertise that isn't common amongst mummy hunters. The code was woven into the textiles the mummies were wrapped in. You see"—she leaned forward in her seat, bubbling with enthusiasm about the topic, despite the circumstances—"for decades, scholars have believed the Incas didn't have a written language, and when they wanted to communicate, they used a series of knots in a complicated pattern on a stringed object called a quipu. But Alice and I realised the drawings in the textiles were a form of hieroglyphics—like on the walls of the Egyptian pyramids. We decoded enough samples from museums around the world to build up a language."

"Is this why you wanted to steal that mummy? There was something written on the textiles it was wrapped in?" Joe asked.

Patricia shook her head. "We never intended to steal it. We only wanted to get close enough to photograph it, for later study. We'd already petitioned the owner for time with the mummy, but he refused." Her look implored them to believe her. "It drove us mad. It wasn't like we were going to damage the thing. We only wanted to look at it because we knew that particular mummy held the key to so many riddles." She slumped back in her seat. "In the end, we were desperate and stupid. We broke in to take photos, but the body was already gone."

Joe pinched the bridge of his nose. "That's a helluva coincidence, Patricia. Kind of hard to believe that on the same night you break in to take photos, somebody else breaks in to steal the body."

"If I was going to lie, Joseph Barone, I'd have come up with something far better than that." Patricia's tone took Joe straight back to elementary school and a particularly evil teacher who could reduce him to tears just by saying his name.

He squeezed Julia's hand. "Please, if you care about me, even a little, never tell her my middle name."

A tiny giggle erupted from Julia, stunning both of them. Julia's hand shot up to cover her mouth. Joe felt like the whole world had dissolved around them. He'd made her giggle. Damn, but he felt ten feet tall.

"Do you have an explanation for the coincidence?" Ed asked, bringing the world crashing back into focus.

Joe tore his eyes from Julia to look back at Patricia, who suddenly wasn't looking all that haughty anymore.

"Well," she said to her knees, "I didn't, but then Alice kept mentioning Marcus. We only know one man with that name. He's one of the other mummy hunters, and he may have been harbouring a grudge against us...well, against me...although, after Alice's performance, it could be both of us..." Her cheeks flushed. "I can't help it if some of the men become too attached. It's not like I encourage it. I'm perfectly happy as I am. I was married for thirty-five years. My husband was my first lover. I have the right to sow some wild oats now that he's popped his clogs. But foolish Marcus took my refusal for a second night, as a blow to his teeny-tiny ego." She grinned widely. "It wasn't the only thing about him that was teeny-tiny."

"Gran!" Julia leaned forward and put her elbows on her knees and her face in her hands. Joe reached over and gently rubbed her back. She initially stiffened under his touch, but then relaxed enough to tolerate it. He took that as progress.

"Can we get back on track?" he said. "Tell us what you know about this guy."

"Marcus Delaney. He's an American archaeological professor who thinks he's Indiana Jones."

"Funny," Joe said. "I was just thinking the same about you."

That earned him another glare.

"You think Delaney took the mummy?" Ed asked.

"Who else would it be? He wants to stop me from publishing before him."

"He plans to publish the same research?" Ed said.

Patricia snorted. "Of course not. He has another theory entirely. You think I would spill my research as pillow talk? Not likely. The man was an idiot. Great body, full head of hair, but dumb as dirt. And before you ask, if Alice did sleep with him, she wouldn't have shared any secrets either."

Julia groaned again, and Joe rubbed her back some more.

The issue wasn't who told this Marcus guy about the importance of the mummy—the issue was finding out what he knew so they could get the damn thing back.

"Patricia." Joe was just about out of patience. "The guy found out somehow. It didn't happen by magic. One of you must have told him."

"It's possible we might have mentioned something at the get-together last week," Patricia said. "Things got out of hand and we got a little drunk."

"By we, you mean you and Alice?" Ed asked.

"All of the mummy crowd. We were celebrating some-one's new research and it turned into a party." Her eyes stayed firmly fixed on her drink. "And, well, we might have gotten a bit carried away with the occasion and shared a little too much with the people who were with us."

"In other words, you got drunk and blabbed your plan to a room full of mummy hunters," Joe said.

"Honestly, I can't remember what we blabbed," Patricia said. "I find it difficult to remember most of that evening."

"Was this Marcus guy there?" Joe asked.

Patricia nodded.

"So basically, you're telling me you told a guy with a grudge how to get back at you." Joe seriously hoped Patricia's crazy behaviour didn't run in the family.

"Yes, that's what I'm telling you. Obviously Marcus heard everything and is behind this whole mess. Why else would Alice mention him?"

"This guy still in Peru?" Joe said.

"If he is, and he hasn't absconded with the mummy, then he'll be regaling other idiots with his tales in the English bar at the Country Club—which is exactly where we were last week. It's his haunt. I think it makes him feel like an English lord." Patricia held out her empty wine glass and, with a smile, Ed filled it for her.

"Gran." Julia sounded weary. "What's the message on the missing mummy's textiles? What did you tell everyone that night to make Marcus want the mummy so badly?"

Patricia slumped back into her chair. "It's directions. A map, if you like." She looked at each of them in turn. "We think, but we won't know for sure until we study the textiles, that it leads to a hidden cache of Incan gold."

Ed let out a low whistle. "There are a lot of people who'd like to get their hands on some Incan gold. I know I would."

"But it can't be real," Julia said.

"Yeah, it can," Ed said. "We've only discovered a fraction of the artefacts left over from the Incan Empire. Someone finds something new every year. If Patricia here thinks she has a map that leads to gold, then people would kill to get it."

"Let's make sure Alice isn't the first to die," Joe said.

CHAPTER 7

A treasure map.

Someone had kidnapped Alice and wanted to trade her for a treasure map. One that was written in the clothing of an ancient mummified body. Julia wasn't sure what was crazier: the thought people actually believed some old textiles might show the way to buried treasure, or the fact they might be right.

"You sure this is the place?" Joe asked Patricia from behind the wheel of the SUV he'd rented.

Patricia looked out the back window at the palatial building claiming to be Lima's Country Club, and nodded. "Definitely. I remember thinking it was terribly grand, in a dated, colonial sort of way."

"My mother used to love this place," Ed said.

"Your mother was Peruvian?" Patricia asked.

"Yeah and my father was from The States. I grew up there, but we would visit family in Lima often. Mom thought Peru began and ended with Miraflores. The furthest she would venture from her house was the Country Club, she said the rest of the country was backward."

"She didn't take you to see the Incan sites?" Patricia sounded outraged.

"In her whole life, she never set foot outside Lima. My mom shuddered at the thought of anything Incan. So, no, she never took us sightseeing."

"You poor, poor man," Patricia said, making Ed laugh.

Joe swerved the SUV into a space in front of the main entrance. A liveried doorman rushed to open the passenger door for Julia, and she automatically shrank back in her seat. Thankfully, Joe was there a second later, and the man turned to help her gran out of the car instead.

"Come on, trouble." Joe held out a hand to help Julia out of the car—although she clearly didn't need the help. When she hesitated, he cocked an eyebrow.

With a sniff of disdain, she took his hand. It was a mistake. Once she was out of the car, Joe didn't let go. Instead, he held her tight as they made their way into the building.

Everything about the English Pub, in the Country Club Hotel on Lima's golf course, screamed middle-aged white man with money. From the polished dark wood, to the chairs that looked like thrones, right up to the chandelier lighting, it had been designed to make the patrons feel as though they were stars in a period drama about the British Empire. Julia could well imagine the potbellied men in the room thumping each other on the back with congratulations on eradicating the locals. The whole setup was as far from the culture outside the front door as it could get, and it made Julia's skin crawl.

She felt a warm hand span the small of her back and breath against her ear. "Still glad you fought to come along?"

"Be nice," Julia said to Joe. "Did you really want to deal with my grandmother all on your own?"

"You have a point. But if the two of you had stayed in the hotel, like I asked you to, that wouldn't have been an issue."

"You'd rather we were back in the hotel, alone, helpless, vulnerable?"

"You drive me crazy, woman." And from what she could tell, he seemed to like it.

He brushed a kiss against her temple, and Julia suddenly realised that she was no longer cowering at his touch. It was disconcerting to realise she was actually becoming acclimated to him. The sneaky man was stealing under her defences with a continuous barrage of seductive touches.

"There he is!" Her gran pointed to the end of the bar, and before they could stop her, she was off stalking in the direction of the huddled men.

"Oh no." Julia hurried after her.

Patricia turned heads as she stormed through the large room, and not solely because she was clearly furious. As usual, she was also stunning. She wore figure-hugging jeans, this time topped with a red batwing top that flowed around her, and red heeled boots to match. Julia couldn't help but glance down at her own clothes. She was wearing another beige shapeless sack of a dress and low-heeled slip-on shoes. The shoes were comfortable, but definitely far from sexy. In fact, her sister Belinda often said she had the same taste in shoes as Queen Elizabeth. Yep, she was on a par with a woman in her nineties.

"Maybe I should get some jeans," she mumbled.

She felt Joe's hand flex against her back, and realised he'd heard her. "Babe, if you want jeans, get jeans. If you don't, don't."

Julia bit at her bottom lip, desperate to keep the words in her head from erupting. It didn't work. "My grandmother is sexier than I am."

"That isn't possible," Joe said without breaking his stride. "Nobody is sexier than you."

Julia tripped over her own feet at his throwaway declaration.

"You spineless bastard!"

Julia's head snapped up in time to see her gran slap a middle-aged guy. Ed was at her back, but he didn't do anything to interfere. In fact, he was just standing there, his arms folded and a grin on his face.

"You couldn't have stepped in?" Joe grumbled at Ed.

Ed shrugged. "She seems to have it under control."

Marcus Delaney was rubbing his cheek and pouting. It wasn't a good look on him. "What the hell? Patricia, have you lost your mind?"

Patricia pointed a finger in his face. "Where is my mummy? I know you have it, you snivelling excuse for a man. Where is it?"

The man's eyes went wide, and Julia tried to figure out what had attracted her gran to him in the first place. He was pretty, the same way generic catalogue models from the seventies were pretty. Julia wondered—if he had been more charismatic, would it have transformed him from generic into handsome? She wasn't sure.

"Mummy?" Marcus blustered. "What the hell are you talking about?"

"You know exactly what I'm talking about." Patricia turned to Joe as she pointed at her ex-lover. "Joe, knock his teeth out."

Ed covered his mouth to stifle a laugh.

Joe shot the two of them a look of disgust before smiling at Marcus.

"You must be Marcus. I'm Joe Barone. It's good to meet a fellow American."

Joe held out a hand to Marcus, who had a distinct rabbit-in-the-headlights look about him. Hesitantly, Marcus shook Joe's hand. Joe used the opportunity to tug the man off his stool. He patted him on the back and whispered something in Marcus' ear. Julia couldn't make out what was being said, but she did notice the effect. All colour drained from Marcus' face.

Joe stepped back, slapped a hand on Marcus' shoulder and grinned at him. "How about we take this outside, somewhere a bit more private? Good plan?" He nodded. "Good plan." He smiled at the rapt audience. "Sorry to disturb your evening, folks." He caught the bartender's eye. "Refills for everyone. On me."

That turned the worried spectators into friends. They slapped Joe on the back as he held Marcus' arm and dragged him out of the French doors onto the patio.

"I like him," Patricia told Julia as they followed. "If I were thirty years younger, I'd steal him from you. If I could." Her eyes sparkled with mischief. "Seems like he only has eyes for my Julia."

Julia didn't even bother dignifying that with a response. Instead she kept close to Joe, who was aiming for a table against a wall at the edge of the patio, far away from curious ears. He thrust Marcus into a seat. The man wobbled before tugging at his tweed suit jacket. Tweed. In the desert.

Patricia sat in a chair beside Marcus, crossing her long legs and glaring at him. Ed leaned against the wall behind Patricia, looking amused but watchful. Julia stood beside Joe. Well, slightly behind him. She wasn't taking any chances. If Marcus was going to strike out, she knew he'd go for the weakest link. And as the weakest link, she would rather Joe was between her and the idiot her grandmother had slept with.

"Where the mummy?" Patricia demanded.

"I don't know. I wasn't the one who was jailed for stealing it." The smug sneer gave him away.

Patricia pointed a finger into his face. "You were the one who filmed us while we were in that house. You sent that video to the cops. You were there."

"I don't know what you're talking about." Marcus held his hands out, palms up. Offering them nothing.

"Rubbish." Patricia leaned forward and smacked him across the face again.

Marcus' hand flew to the reddening skin. "Will you *please* stop doing that?"

Joe pinched the bridge of his nose. "What are you doing, Patricia?"

She gave Joe a look that suggested his IQ should be tested. "What does it look like I'm doing? I'm interrogating him."

Joe stared up at the dark night sky for a second before turning his equally dark look on Julia's grandmother. "Stop it. I'll ask the questions. No more hitting."

"He deserves it." She glared at Marcus, and the fool actually leered back. "He stole the mummy and framed us. He's the reason I've been in a cell all week. He's the reason Alice is in danger. Him! And for what? To appease his fragile ego." She snorted her disgust.

"Ed," Joe said, "hold her down if you have to."

"My pleasure." Ed stepped forward to put his hands on Patricia's shoulders. She glared up at him, but only got a grin for her efforts.

"I really want to hit him," she told Ed.

"I understand," he said. "I've only just met him and I feel the same."

"I don't know what you're talking about," Marcus blustered with what was clearly a lie. "Why are you here and why are you behaving like a bitch?" He leered at Patricia. "Oh, I get it. You're put out because you didn't get a repeat visit from little Marky."

Joe groaned and shook his head. "I take it back. Feel free to hit the asshole."

Julia tugged Joe's t-shirt to get his attention. "Little Marky?" she whispered.

"His penis," her grandmother practically shouted. "And it's well named, little is exactly how I would describe it." She pointed in Marcus' face again. "For your information, I don't want a repeat. I'm still trying to get over the nightmares I have from the first time."

"Yeah, right," the idiot scoffed.

"Enough!" Joe barked, making Julia jump. She stupidly took a step closer to Joe, the guy who'd startled her. With a silent groan, she put distance between them again, hoping no one noticed her dumb move.

"Did you take the mummy?" Joe's voice was a low, menacing growl.

Marcus' eyes darted around, and he licked his lips nervously. "Yeah, yeah, we took the mummy. So what? It isn't like it's worth much. Mummies like that are a dime a dozen."

"I knew it!" Patricia shot to her feet and leaned over him. "You only took it to spite me."

"We took it to stop you from embarrassing the mummy community with your pathetic excuse for research. A treasure map? Really? Do you listen to yourself? You think you've found secret directions to El Dorado. Written. On. A. Rug." He threw up his hands in disgust.

"Not a rug—textiles. And it isn't El Dorado either, you stuck-up prick. It's El Toro de Oro."

"The golden bull." Marcus barked out a mocking laugh. "The only bull you're dealing with is *bullshit*."

Joe leaned forward, placing his hands on the armrests either side of Marcus, whose laughter suddenly evaporated.

"I've about run out of patience with you. You want to see what happens when I do, keep acting like an asshole."

There was silence as Marcus visibly swallowed. He shrank back into his seat.

"Who is we? Who helped you?" Joe stood up straight to loom over the man.

Marcus had difficulty meeting Joe's eyes. "Couple of other guys from the mummy group. We were fed up listening to Lucy and Ethel boast about their theory. About how they were gonna take the world by storm. How they'd be famous. For fuck's sake, they've only been hunting mummies for a few years." He slapped a hand to his chest. "The rest of us have dedicated our lives to this study. We struggle to be taken seriously, and it's because of people like them. They waltz in with their half-baked ideas, attracting attention they don't deserve, and give the rest of us a bad name." His chin jutted out. "We were making a stand for serious research."

"By stealing a mummy?" Julia couldn't keep quiet any longer. This was absolutely too ludicrous to believe.

"Who the hell are you?" Marcus snapped.

And just like that, Joe's fist shot out and Marcus' head snapped back. When he righted it, there was blood dripping from his nose.

"Don't ever speak to her like that again. Hear me?"

"Yeah." Marcus wiped his nose with the back of his hand, smearing blood over his cheek. "Yeah, I hear you." He kept his eyes averted from Julia.

Patricia was grinning. "I take it back, Joe. You can definitely do the interrogating."

Joe ignored her. "Where is the mummy now?"

"We sold it."

Patricia was outraged. "Why sell it? If you only intended to disrupt our research, why not replace the thing once I was arrested?"

Marcus sneered at her. "We wanted it gone. We didn't want you to get to it at a later date."

"And you wanted the money." Patricia sneered back. "You're nothing more than a grave robber."

Marcus started to bluster, but Joe leaned into him, cutting him off.

"Who did you sell it to?"

"A middleman."

"Who?"

Julia didn't know it was possible to infuse so much menace into one word.

"Juan Pablo de Santos."

"The mummy is in Bolivia?" Patricia was outraged.

The look Marcus shot her was smug and nasty. "If he still has it. You know how fast he likes to sell things on, especially seeing as it was wrapped in a *priceless treasure map*." The idiot actually laughed.

"You plan to deal with this asshole?" Ed seemed to have lost all humour.

"Oh, yeah," Joe said.

"Then we'll be in the bar." Ed hooked his arm around Patricia's waist and steered her into the building as she struggled and shouted at Marcus.

Marcus shifted nervously, squirming in his seat. "Are we finished?"

Joe hung his head for a second. "Oh yeah, we're done." And in a move too fast for Julia to track, he punched Marcus on the jaw. He slumped in his seat, out cold.

From the doorway into the bar, Patricia clapped. "He is the best! I love him. You should definitely keep him."

"I could have done that," Ed grumbled.

Julia wasn't paying attention. She was staring at Joe, who had propped Marcus up against the seat to make it look like was sleeping. Then he took Marcus' wallet out of the inside pocket of his tweed jacket and pulled out his credit card. He replaced the wallet before grabbing Julia's hand. Pulling her along behind him, he headed back into the bar. Julia was still staring at the unconscious man and wondering if she should do something. What, though, she didn't know.

Joe tossed the stolen credit card onto the bar as they passed it. "I got some great news," he announced to the room. "Food and drink are on me for the rest of the evening. Enjoy."

There were cheers and a distinctly undistinguished stampede for the bar. As they pushed their way to the front door, one of the bartenders intercepted them. He was huge, muscled like a rugby player, with close-cropped hair.

"That card doesn't belong to you." He had an Australian accent.

Julia froze as Joe seemed to increase in size. "You got a problem with that?" His tone was low and mean.

A slow smile lit up the bartender's face. "Hell no. But I thought you'd like to know that your friends caught some attention during their party last week."

"What kind of attention?" Joe said.

"The kind you don't want to attract. Know what I mean?"

Joe nodded. "I still need a name."

The guy looked around before lowering his voice. "There was a dinner meeting going on. Bunch of lieutenants in Esteban's army."

Julia didn't recognise the name, but Joe clearly did. Every muscle in his body grew tense. "Carlos Esteban."

The guy nodded.

"They show any interest in the topic of conversation coming from the partiers?"

"A whole heap of interest." The bartender took a step closer. He cocked his head at Patricia. "The MILF announced to the room that she'd cracked the Incan code on some mummy wrapping. She said it'd lead to a pot of gold. She announced that she'd be famous, rich and the best mummy hunter on the planet." His lip quirked. "She planned to donate it all to a museum, but she wanted a statue in central London for her efforts. She wanted Michelangelo to carve it, which shows you how trashed she was. That dude died a *long* time ago."

"She might as well have painted a target on her forehead."

"Sorry, man, I would have stopped it if I'd known it was real. I thought she was a nutty tourist." He looked down at the stolen credit card and then back at Joe. "Does the arsehole need a doctor?"

"Not this time. You might want to advise him to head stateside when he wakes up."

"Will do. In the meantime, I'll make sure this card gets a good workout."

"Thanks, man."

"Anytime." The guy turned, then looked back over his shoulder. "You need help, call here and ask for Michael."

Joe gave him a chin lift.

By the time they'd headed back outside to their SUV, they were all in a sombre mood.

"Is the treasure real, Gran?" Julia was beginning to side with Ed and believe it to be so.

"We did a lot of discreet investigating," Patricia said from the back seat. "The map doesn't lead to El Dorado, but we're sure it leads to some sort of hidden cache of gold. We kept hearing about a golden bull. Whether that's actual or symbolic, I don't know. I do know that it was common practice for the Incas to hide their treasure, especially after they cottoned on to the Spaniards' lust for their gold. Every now and then someone discovers some hidden stash. Even conservative estimates would suggest that there is still a lot to be found."

"I thought the Spaniards had taken it all back to Europe," Julia said.

"No, not all." Patricia sounded thoughtful. "What's left is very rare and priceless. Even a small cache would net someone millions."

"That's why the interest in the map," Julia said. "There's nothing to lose if it turns out to be a wild goose chase, but everything to gain if it isn't."

"Millions to gain," Patricia said.

There was silence as the car wove through the crowded traffic into the dark Lima night.

"That guy called me a MILF," Patricia said suddenly. "I don't know whether to be insulted or honoured."

Ed started laughing, and Joe shook his head. Julia looked up at him. "What's a MILF?"

"You really don't want to know."

And because of that, she really did. Discreetly, Julia pulled her iPad from her messenger bag and made a note to look it up later.

"This guy, Esteban," Julia said. "You recognised his name, Joe. Who is he?"

"Bad news," Ed answered for Joe. "Bad, bad news. I've had some dealings with him in the past. He's hard to avoid when you work in Peru."

"He's cartel." Joe's grip was white-knuckled on the steering wheel. "We ran into his army years ago when I was working an op here with the Marines." He glanced at Julia before turning his attention back to the road. "He's worse than bad news. He's ruthless, resourceful and relentless. If he wants something, he doesn't stop until he gets it."

"And he wants the treasure." Julia stared out into the black night as car lights flickered in front of them.

"Yeah, he wants the treasure." Joe reached for her hand.

Without thinking, Julia met him halfway. "We need to head to Bolivia."

"Book flights for the morning, baby. We need sleep."

"But Alice—"

"We're no good to anyone if we're dead on our feet. Patricia hasn't slept for a week. The morning is soon enough."

"I wish..." She looked into the night. She wished the whole mess was over. She wished Alice was safe. She wished her gran had never become a mummy hunter in the first place. Most of all, she wished she was braver and more capable.

Joe squeezed her hand and held it tight as they drove through the night.

CHAPTER 8

Callum McKay was in his office when Benson Security's resident computer expert rushed in. Callum and one of his three business partners, Rachel Ford-Talbot, looked up from their notes to frown at the blue-haired woman.

"I know." Elle held up her hand—the other one was clutching her laptop. "No interrupting, but this is serious stuff."

She plopped the laptop on the desk and her fingers flew over the keyboard.

"What's going on?" Lake Benson, the original owner of the company and ex-SAS soldier, demanded from the phone in the middle of the desk.

Elle gave it a guilty glance. "Were you having a conference call?"

Callum glared at her while he spoke to Lake. "Elle's got some important news."

"About?" Lake asked.

Callum cocked an eyebrow at his hacker.

"The situation in Peru," Elle said before looking back at her screen.

"We're calling it a situation now?" There was an unvoiced groan in Lake's words. "The London office isn't even officially open and you guys are on your second case. Second *unpaid* case. The building, which we were in the middle of renovating, already needs to be redone because the last *unpaid* case caused someone to set off a bomb in it. I'm beginning to regret expanding the business."

"Not as much as I regret being dragged into your expansion," Callum grumbled.

Rachel rolled her eyes with the sort of drama only a woman dressed in a designer suit and bright red lipstick could pull off. The gesture dripped sarcasm. "Do I have to remind you that all of the problems the new London office are dealing with have come straight from the original Scottish office? The office you head up. If you hadn't foisted these people on us in the first place, we wouldn't be in this mess."

"Who made you a partner again?" Lake asked.

"I did." Rachel studied her perfectly manicured nails. The woman was a trust fund darling with the personality of a bad-tempered cobra and the instincts of a shark hunting prey. When she'd decided that Benson Security needed a holistic personal protection section to care for the needs of women who wanted security, none of the three male partners had the guts to stop her buying into the company.

"Although this partnership dynamic is fascinating," Elle said, risking life and limb in the process, "I need to show you this."

She turned the laptop towards them. There was an image of a man, taken from a distance with a high-powered lens, on one side of the screen, and on the other was a long list of names.

"What are we looking at?" Callum racked his brain, trying to figure out if he recognised the face.

"You're looking at a list of people who were murdered

after dealing with Carlos Esteban," Elle said, and Lake sucked in a breath, making the hair on the back of Callum's neck stand on end.

"You know this guy, Lake?" Callum asked.

"I know of him." Lake's tone was deadly. "He heads up one of the more vicious South American cartels. It's smaller than some of them, but it's growing in power—mainly through violence."

Callum stilled. "Joe sent me a message an hour ago saying he thought the cartel might be involved."

"Oh, it's involved, all right," Elle said. "I remote-hacked the phone that was delivered to Julia's hotel room, and the call came from the heart of a compound owned by the Esteban cartel. Carlos Esteban is definitely holding Alice hostage, and he's serious about getting his hands on that mummy."

"Why wasn't I told about this?" Rachel fixed Callum with an icy stare. "As far as I was aware, Joe and Julia were on a personal trip to South America, in order to get a crazy family member out of jail."

"They were," Callum said. "The jail problem morphed into a hostage situation, which Elle here has been investigating."

"And now that hostage situation has turned into a clusterfuck involving a cartel," Lake said.

"Consider yourself informed," Callum told Rachel.

Her eyes narrowed in a way that made it clear she was plotting his demise.

"So," Elle said into the silence, "you want to know the rest?"

Callum broke his stare-off with Rachel to look at his hacker. The subject matter was at odds with her blue hair and bright pink Hello Kitty t-shirt.

"Spill," he said.

"Carlos Esteban is known for never letting a hostage live. Not only that, but he's known to wipe out anyone he does business with, after he gets what he wants from them. The last *business deal* he made ended in a hotel blowing up in Arequipa. All guests killed—including the three men Esteban had business with." She stared at each of them in turn, her blue eyes wider than usual. "There hasn't been one recorded instance of someone dealing with Esteban and walking away. They either become part of his operation for life, or they die. There is no middle ground."

A heavy silence filled the room.

"You have any luck tracking down help for them in Peru?" Callum asked Lake.

"Everybody I trust is tied up in something else and can't get away. I have one more option I can tap for emergency help, but that's it."

Callum and Rachel stared at each other for a moment. There were times when he could almost feel the witch read his mind. This was one of those times.

"I'll call Father and see if I can borrow his jet again." Rachel stood, pulling her phone from her designer bag as she did so. She started to talk as she strode from the room.

"I'll dig up everything I can on Esteban." Elle grabbed her computer and followed Rachel.

"You taking the whole team?" Lake said.

"Megan's still healing from the bullet to her leg," Callum said. An injury from their last unplanned op. "She can stay here with Dimitri and man the store." He didn't mention that Dimitri's traumatised sister would be there too. Both men knew that Katrina wasn't anywhere near ready to leave the security of the building. And neither of them would take her into another dangerous situation. Not after everything she'd gone through at the hands of her kidnapper. "Rachel can handle the interviews we have set up."

"So everybody else, then," Lake said. "Keep me posted. Let me know if I need to call in emergency help."

"Thanks." Callum stood, ready to shut the call off.

"Be careful," Lake said. "Elle only scraped the surface when she described Esteban. The guy is smart, ruthless and evil. Don't underestimate him. He is completely relentless when it comes to getting what he wants."

Callum felt a cold dread settle in his chest. "I'll call you on the other side."

With a click, he ended the call and went to pack—texting Joe as he did, to let him know help was on its way.

CHAPTER 9

There was no oxygen in Bolivia's capital city. None. The air was so thin that they may as well have been on the moon. After a sleepless night worrying about Alice and listening to her gran snore, the last thing Julia wanted to do was catch an early morning flight to La Paz.

And now, she was going to die on the runway, in Bolivia. Somehow, it seemed a fitting end to her rather pathetic life. By the time Julia had made it down the stairs from the plane to the tarmac, her head was spinning and she was fighting the urge to vomit. Just as her legs gave way beneath her, she felt Joe's arm around her waist.

"Altitude sickness." He kissed her temple before calling to someone in Spanish.

A minute later, Julia was riding in a golf cart with a flashing light, with a mask over her face and a bottle of oxygen at her side. If she hadn't felt so bad, she would have been humiliated. The whole thing was made even worse by the fact her grandmother was unaffected.

"Don't feel bad." Patricia reached over from the seat

behind her to pat Julia's shoulder. "I've been in South America for a while. I spent weeks in high altitude before going to Lima. You'll get used to it. The key is to move really slowly until your lungs adjust to having less oxygen. Coca leaf tea helps too. We'll get you some. It's going to be fine."

Julia groaned. She thought it had been quiet, but Joe must have heard. His arm wrapped around her and he pulled her tight to his side. She was feeling too ill to object. Joe was strong and warm and solid. And Julia was in no state to worry about the dangers of getting close to him, not when there were so many other worries vying for attention. The one uppermost in her mind was the fear of dying. She was pretty sure that if someone took the oxygen tank from her, she'd collapse and expire on the runway of the highest international airport in the world.

"It's going to be okay." Joe rubbed her arm.

Julia whined. It was pathetic, but she wished someone would knock her unconscious and wake her when they turned the oxygen back on.

Getting through the airport was a blur. All she remembered was handing Joe her passport and fighting nausea. The next thing she knew, she was in the back of a minibus, minus her oxygen tank which had to stay at the airport, racing through crowded streets into downtown La Paz.

"La Paz is the highest capital city in the world," she told Joe, aware that she sounded a little drunk and a lot disorientated, but unable to do anything about either. "Twelve thousand feet above sea level."

"Is that right?" There was a smile in his voice as he held her against his side.

Part of her thought she should probably fight his proprietary hold on her. The rest of her was too comfortable to care.

Julia rested her cheek on his chest, mainly because she

had no strength to hold her head up, but she found she liked it there. "Over a million people live in and around the city." Yep, every fact she'd read on the plane was spilling out of her mouth—whether she wanted it to or not. She lifted a weak hand in an attempt to point at the snow-covered peaks surrounding the city. "That's the Cordillera Real range. That peak there is twenty-one thousand feet. This city is more than halfway up that mountain. Can you believe it?"

"No, baby, I can't believe it." Joe's chest shook beneath her, and if she'd had the energy she would have glanced up to see if he was laughing at her.

She continued her rambling, unstoppable guided tour. "We're only forty-two miles from the highest navigable lake in the world. Lake Titicaca. That's Lake Titty-Kaka." She mustered enough energy to look up at him. "That name is all kinds of wrong, Joe. It brings to mind images that shouldn't be in my head."

"Baby." He shook his head. His grin was wide and he was definitely trying not to laugh.

"La Paz sits in a canyon that gives it some protection from the elements," Julia continued. "Although it's expanded quickly over the past few years and now reaches the high plains area of the Altiplano. That's where we just came from. That's where the airport is." She looked back up to Joe. "Does it mess with your head that we flew up twelve thousand feet to land? I mean, shouldn't you go up then come back down? Isn't it against nature to go up and then stay up?"

Laughter came from the front seats in the van, and Julia forced her head to turn to see who it was. Her gran and Ed were smiling back at her. Huh. Julia hadn't even noticed they were there. Her head felt too heavy, so she rested her cheek back against Joe, her focus on the view zooming past their window.

"There aren't that many Spanish-style buildings here," she said, more to herself than anyone else.

"There are in the older areas," Joe said. "Some of the government buildings and museums have great Spanish architecture."

"Not as many as Lima." Julia nuzzled against the warm cotton of his t-shirt. She could have sworn it helped with her nausea. "I wanted to go to San Francisco Monastery in Lima. It has an ancient library and a mosaicked courtyard. The ceiling is carved Moorish design, and there are catacombs underneath it." She felt wistful. All she'd seen of Lima was a prison, a bar and lots of bad roads. "Did you know that someone rearranged all of the bones in the catacombs in pretty patterns? There's a circular pit full of skulls arranged in matching concentric circles."

"Bones in circles, huh? You'll get to see it, baby. Once this is over, I'll take you sightseeing." Joe's voice rumbled through her cheek, making her melt inside. "We'll take the train from Cuzco to Machu Picchu village, then the bus up the winding mountain road to the old ruins. You'll feel like you're sitting on top of the world."

"Joe." Julia gave him what she hoped was a stern look. "I feel like I'm at the top of the world right now. Hello? Altitude sickness, remember?"

He laughed again, making her body shake along with his.

Julia's attention turned to the strange city around her. It seemed to be made up almost entirely of tall buildings crammed into small spaces, each one vying for the title of highest residence in the highest capital in the world. It made her dizzy looking up at them.

"I didn't realise," she said.

"What, baby?"

"I mean, I knew academically that we would be at a high elevation. But we're on the same level as the mountaintops, and if that wasn't high enough, I booked the presidential suite at the top of the hotel." She looked up at Joe. "I can't go any higher. I can't. You need to change the room. Get me something on the ground floor. Or a basement room. I can do a basement room."

"You're going to be fine." He kissed her forehead, making her shiver.

"I'm going to be sick, that's what I'm going to be." She'd been given medication at the airport by a sympathetic man with a medical bag and a big red cross on his vest. Seemed she wasn't the only idiot tourist who turned up in La Paz and instantly fell ill. The medication had helped, but she still felt like she was travelling inside a tumble dryer.

"It will get better. Some rest, taking things easy, some tea, and you'll be good as new."

"You think you can tell someone anything in that sexy drawl of yours and they'll believe it, don't you?"

His grin was smug. "You think I'm sexy?"

"I didn't say that." She felt her cheeks burn and concentrated on the view, instead of on the man she was draped over like a limp noodle.

"You booked the presidential suite?" Joe asked,.

"It was the only one with three bedrooms." She groaned. "I forgot to tell them we needed four beds. I'll get them to reconfigure the queen-sized one when we arrive. Gran and I will share a room." She gave him a hopeful look. The thought of another night listening to her gran snore was really too much. "Unless you want to share with Ed."

"We aren't that close."

There was more laugher from the front of the van. Julia ignored it. The van was pulling up in front of another massively tall building. She felt nauseated looking up at it.

"I can't go up there," she said.

"Sure you can." Joe climbed out of the car and reached in for her.

Julia had no option but to let him help her. Her limbs had turned to jelly. She felt like she was weighted down, and each step was taken through ankle-deep mud. By the time they'd made it the short distance into the marble and brass lobby, she was completely weak and gasping for air.

"I need to lie down." She hated saying the words, but it was true. And she didn't mean in a bed. She meant right there, on the lobby floor.

She heard Joe and her gran talking, and the next thing she knew, Joe had put one arm under her knees and the other around her waist, and then he was cradling her to his chest like a child. She was too disorientated to protest. She lay in his arms, shutting her eyes tight, and let him take her to their suite. The long ride up in the elevator didn't help her nausea.

"I feel silly that you're carrying me," Julia said as they entered the suite. She noticed nothing about it—she was completely captivated by the man who held her tight against his chest.

"And I feel honoured."

His words melted something inside Julia, and the wall she'd built between herself and Joe crumbled a little.

"I don't understand you," Julia mumbled as her eyes closed.

"You will, baby. You will."

Joe gently placed her on the bed. With her face against the cool cotton sheets, Julia felt the world stop spinning and sleep overtake her.

Two hours and several cups of coca leaf tea later, Julia felt much better. Not right, exactly, just less likely to vomit on the people around her. She still felt weak and exhausted, but she didn't feel dizzy. She wasn't sure if that was due to the tea, which tasted better than she thought it would—and according to Google, wasn't at all addictive—or the medication Joe shovelled into her. Either way, she was ready to go find Juan Pablo de Santos and, hopefully, the mummy.

The taxi dropped them off in one of the city's meeting areas, Plaza San Francisco, a concrete intersection with a grassy area above a busy underpass. The area was nothing special—lots of traffic and people waiting to catch buses, generic office buildings and large billboards. In the distance, behind the many high-rise buildings, were the suburbs that went up into the hills. They looked like sheer walls made up of houses built on top of one another. And above it all were the snowy peaks of the mountain range, so close you could almost touch them.

And in the middle of this industrial area was San Francisco Church.

The massive sandstone building, with its dominating bell tower and ornately carved stonework, was completely out of place.

"Eighteenth century," Joe told her leaning in. "I know how much you like facts and figures."

Julia cringed at the reminder of her earlier insanity, which made Joe laugh. Julia ignored him, looking around like the tourist she wished she was instead of a woman on a mission. A small market was set up facing the church, selling flowers and candles for worshippers who sat on the steps leading up to the colossal wooden doors.

"This isn't how I imagined South America would be," Julia said to no one in particular.

"South America is a mix of everything," Joe said, showing just how closely he paid attention to her. "It's as modern as anywhere on the planet, but at the same time it's steeped in the past like nowhere else." He pointed at a traditionally dressed Quechua woman, with her mass of coloured skirts nipped tight at her waist, a multi-coloured woven shawl around her shoulders and a black bowler hat on top of her head. Plaited black hair ran down her back, and her face was weathered by the sun. "See? You get the traditional with the new." He pointed at a woman in a business suit, complete with briefcase, designer heels and a phone at her ear.

"It feels more diverse than Lima." Not that she'd been in Lima for long enough to judge.

"More concentrated, maybe."

They rounded the corner of the church into a narrow street with smaller, older buildings. These ones looked more traditionally Spanish, their exteriors a combination of fading stucco and wood. Julia tried to avoid the mass of people and tripped on the cobblestone road. Before she'd managed to steady herself, Joe snatched her hand and held it tight.

When she tried to pry it free, he gave her a look of reprimand. "I don't want to lose you in here. It gets crowded." He looked back at Patricia and Ed. "Keep a hold of her," he ordered.

"My pleasure," Ed said before taking Patricia's hand.

Julia watched as her gran blushed and tried to act like it wasn't a big deal to be walking around a strange city holding a strange man's hand. It was hard, for a second, to remember that they weren't two couples sightseeing in Bolivia. They were there for a reason. Alice's life was on the line.

Plus—Julia shuddered—that was too close to going on a double date with her gran, and *that* was far too disturbing to contemplate.

They strode up the crowded street, mixing with locals and tourists alike.

"Does everything in this city have to be uphill?" Julia complained.

"You'll feel better soon and you won't even notice the incline," Joe said.

"I doubt it." Julia's idea of a workout was walking up the three flights of stairs from her office to her tiny apartment. "I don't work out like you do. I'm not fit."

"You look good to me."

She felt the blush heat her cheeks and snapped her attention away from the man holding her hand, to the market stalls against the buildings. Some of them were set up for the day, while others seemed to be an extension of the small shops behind the outdoor tables. She saw colourful woven ponchos, shawls and bags. Woollen sweaters and knitted hats with earflaps. Large woven blankets with hot pink stripes, hung from poles. Table tops were crowded with all kinds of clay work, from copies of Incan pots to the round-bellied figure of a woman.

Joe noticed where she was looking. "Pachamama. Earth mother. She's worshipped here."

"I thought Bolivia was Roman Catholic."

He shrugged. "They mix it up. There's a church where the old friars commissioned a painting of Mary done in the local style. They didn't realise the image could be read in two different ways—Mary or Pachamama. The locals knew they were looking at Mother Earth; the Spaniards knew they were looking at Mary. They both won."

Julia eyed him with admiration. "You know a lot about this place."

"Like I said last night, I spent some time here when I was in the Marines."

"Doing what?"

"Secret stuff." His grin was wicked, but it didn't quite make it to his eyes. Julia could only guess at the minefield of memories he had from his time in the service.

"This way." Patricia consulted the map in her hand. "I've

only been here once before, but I'm fairly certain De Santos has a shop around this corner."

They turned into an even narrower street. The buildings rose above them, balconies poking out into the street over their heads. There was graffiti scrawled on the walls, and the stalls seemed smaller and darker somehow.

"Mercado de las Brujas," Joe told her. "Witches' market."

Julia ogled the stalls and felt her eyes bug out. Hanging from the awnings were hundreds of dried creatures.

"Llama foetuses," Joe said. "They bury them in the foundation of buildings as an offering to Pachamama. For protection."

Julia jerked when she spotted jars of dried frogs.

"For Aymara rituals," Joe said. "The regional tribe."

There were dried snakes and turtles. Jars with strange concoctions. Statues that looked a lot like voodoo dolls. There were long pieces of string holding hundreds of feathers. Small packets of various powders. And bundles of cheap beaded necklaces, like the ones they handed out for Mardi Gras.

"See the things that look like toys or key rings?" Joe pointed at the kitsch objects. There was everything from baby dolls to fake money. "They're buried along with the foetus offering. They represent what people want Pachamama to bless them with."

"This is all very dark," Julia said.

"This is the tourist part, babe. People use this stuff, but it's the milder version of what's available up some of these alleys. Trust me, that you don't want to see."

Julia took a step closer to Joe. She was equal parts fascinated and frightened.

"It's so unhygienic," she told Joe. "All those dead, dried things. The bacteria alone must be shocking."

Joe burst out laughing and let go of her hand long enough to wrap his arm around her shoulders.

"What's so funny?" Julia was torn between removing his arm and letting it stay where it was. She hated that she felt a whole lot safer while plastered against him.

"Nothing, nothing's funny."

Julia frowned up at him, about to call him on his obvious lie when her gran stopped dead in front of them.

"That way." She pointed into a dark alley that was so narrow they would have to walk single file.

"You sure?" Joe said.

"Yes, I recognise the alley. And the stink." She scrunched her nose. "I'm fairly certain that smell is from the dried animals they grind into powder."

Julia stared at her grandmother in horror before looking up at Joe. "I need a mask."

She was grateful he didn't mock her. "Pull the neck of your shirt up over your mouth."

"That would look stupid."

"And wearing a mask wouldn't?" her grandmother said.

"Stop," Joe told Patricia. "You have your worries, Julia has hers. Keep your opinion to yourself."

Patricia's eyes went wide, but she nodded once at Joe. Patricia reached into her handbag and came out with a silk scarf. "Wrap this around your neck and you can pull it up to cover your mouth."

"Thanks, Gran." Julia gratefully took the scarf and did exactly that. All the while, her cheeks were burning at how stupid she was to do it. Nobody else seemed bothered that they'd be breathing in the dust of ground-up dead things.

"You good?" Joe said.

She nodded, but couldn't look at him.

"That's better than a mask." Joe leaned in until his mouth

was at her ear. "Although that silk scarf is giving me all sorts of ideas on other ways we could use it later. Private ways."

"Joe!" Her eyes sprang up to his and saw they were heated and amused.

"You ready?" he said without a hint of impatience.

She nodded. Joe kissed the tip of her nose. "That's my girl," he said before tugging her into the dark alley.

CHAPTER 10

Joe didn't like their situation one bit. The alley was only wide enough for them to walk in single file. Joe put Julia in front of him and brought up the rear. One look at Ed and he saw his friend was on the same page. Much to Patricia's disgust, Ed insisted on leading the way, which put the women firmly between the men, where they could best protect them.

Joe kept one hand on Julia's shoulder as he scanned their surroundings. There were no other access points in the alley, only straight walls on either side of them. This meant no one could come at them from the side, but it also meant that there were no clear escape routes if they needed one.

At the end of the long, dark corridor, the alley opened out into a tiny courtyard. And at the rear of the courtyard was a shop. The interior was black and unwelcoming, the wares spilled out into the space around it, with displays attached to the walls. Baskets filled with assorted dead things sat on the ground at the bottom of the three steps that led up and into the crooked little building.

"Will you let me pass?" Patricia demanded as she smacked Ed's shoulder.

He looked back at her, his face stony. "No. Not until we know what we're walking into here."

"And what are you going to do if we're walking into trouble? Sue somebody?"

Ed's eyes hardened, taking years off him and bringing Joe back to the first time they'd met—on a naval vessel off the coast of Yemen. Joe had just started his career and Ed was on the flipside. He'd had a reputation as a smart guy who could get the job done—no matter what it took.

"Before I was ever a lawyer, I was a marine," Ed said. "Believe me when I tell you there's a whole lot I can do if need be."

"God save us from Neanderthal men," Patricia said. "I know Juan Pablo. Move out the way so I can talk to him."

"No." Ed shut the conversation down with one word as he strode forward, clearly on alert.

As they approached the front of the store, three figures emerged from the doorway. Two of the men moved to either side of the shop, leaning against the walls, but clearly acting as sentries for Juan Pablo. The artefact smuggler came with his own little army. Marcus had failed to mention that.

Juan Pablo stood at the entrance to his shop. He was average height for a Bolivian, which put him a full head shorter than Joe. He was stocky, with a square face to match. His black hair was neat and parted to the left. He wore black dress trousers and a white dress shirt that was open at the collar. His arms were folded and his face was drawn into a scowl.

"This isn't a tourist shop," he said in heavily accented English. "Go back the way you came. There is nothing for you here."

"Juan Pablo," Patricia called. "We've met before. I'm Patricia Matthews. I've been to your shop and we talked at the mummy convention."

Joe couldn't see the black-market dealer's reaction to Patricia's words, but he did see Ed's. The ex-marine had tensed for a fight. Joe tugged on Julia's shoulder, pulling her against his body.

The hairs on Joe's neck were standing to attention. He wrapped his hand around the gun that was in the holster fitted to his belt, hidden under his shirt. He unsnapped the latch, ready to free the weapon.

"Patricia." Juan Pablo's tone was ingratiating, oozing fake warmth and friendship. "It is good to have you visit my small business again. A fellow mummy enthusiast is always welcome here."

The man stepped out of the dark recesses of his shop interior and into the subdued light of the alleyway. His gaze was calculating, setting off every single one of Joe's alarms.

"But where is your friend?" Juan Pablo studied each of them in turn. "I see you have brought new customers for me to meet." He inclined his head as though expecting an introduction.

"Oh, this is—" Patricia said, but Ed cut her off.

"We aren't enthusiasts like Patricia here, just some friends visiting with her for a while."

"Indeed." Juan Pablo's eyes narrowed before he smiled at Patricia. "What can I do for you, lovely señora?"

"We're here about the mummy Marcus Delaney sold to you. It was stolen and we need to return it. Of course, seeing as you had no way of knowing that, we're more than happy to reimburse any losses you suffer."

Juan Pablo stiffened slightly and then caught the eye of one of his sentries. The other man nodded. It was a slight movement, barely noticeable. And it set Joe's nerves on edge. Every instinct he possessed told him to get out of the alley.

"Ah." Juan Pablo spread his hands wide, flashing a smile

that didn't reach his eyes. "But I don't have this mummy any longer. There was a buyer waiting to take it from me."

Patricia let out an exasperated little huff. "Who did you sell it to?"

His eyes flickered to Joe and Ed, assessing, but the smile stayed in place. "I cannot remember, but I will look up the information for you." He paused. "For a price."

"Of course," Patricia said.

Joe's back was tingling now. He glanced behind him, but the alley was clear. He noticed that Ed was staring at the skyline above them, checking for any sign of trouble. One of the sentries pulled a cell phone out of his pocket and tapped out a short text. Then he went back to lazing against the wall. If Joe hadn't been trained, if his instincts weren't screaming at him, he would have thought nothing of the act. But he was trained and his instincts were screaming—they were telling him to get out of there. Fast.

"One moment, please." Juan Pablo disappeared into the shop.

"I don't like this," Joe said to Ed. "We need to get out of here. This is a bottleneck. We're trapped and there isn't even any cover."

A slight scuffling noise behind him made Joe turn. Men. Coming up the alley. Ed followed his gaze. The men were acting casual. Sauntering, almost.

"Into the store," Ed said.

It was their only option. "Go. Now." Joe urged them forward.

One of the sentries blocked their path.

"No persons in store." He held up a hand to stop them.

The other sentry leaned off the wall, suddenly alert.

Decision time. Adrenalin raced through Joe. Trust his instincts or do as he was told. At lightning speed, he assessed the smaller man. No weapon. Joe shot out a punch and caught the man before he fell to the ground.

"Inside!" Joe barked low. "Now!"

The men behind them hadn't yet realised what had happened, and Ed was blocking the other sentry's view.

Patricia gasped as the women rushed into the shop.

"They're still at the end of the alley," Ed said. "I can take out the other sentry."

"Do it."

Ed turned to the other guy, still blocking his view of Joe, allowing him to lower the man in his hold to the steps, arranging him as though he was sitting. It would buy him seconds at best. There was a grunt. Joe looked over to see Ed lowering his sentry to a spot behind the baskets. It was the best they could do.

"Inside," Joe ordered, and they hurried into the shop.

Juan Pablo was pretending to go through a handwritten ledger, line by line, when there was a laptop sitting on his desk. He was killing time, stalling them until his men made it to the shop. Joe felt a white-hot rage rush through him, focusing his mind, honing his actions. He grabbed the man around his throat and held him against the counter, bending him back until he lost his balance and the edge bit into him.

"Call off your men." He squeezed his throat. "Now."

"*¡No es posible!*" Juan Pablo croaked.

"Yeah, it's possible. You called them. You can call them off." Joe shook him hard, making him splutter and choke. Juan Pablo clawed at Joe's grip, trying to prise it from his throat.

A soft hand curled around Joe's forearm. He glanced down to see Julia peering up at him, and was relieved to see she wasn't afraid of him—or his actions.

"Maybe he'd be able to talk if you loosened your grip."

"Maybe," Joe said. "But I'd like to deprive him of air a little longer. In my experience, that motivates a man. Take his laptop, phone, any other records you can find. We don't have long before someone arrives."

She nodded and rushed to do what he said.

"Joe," Ed said from his position at the door, "they're getting closer."

"How many?"

"Three."

Joe looked back at the man writhing in his grip. "Call them off!"

Joe let go of Juan Pablo's throat, grabbed his shirt and shoved him forward so he could see through the door and down the alley. Joe dug the barrel of his gun into the guy's kidney. He whimpered and arched up onto his toes to avoid it. But Joe kept Juan Pablo in place with an arm wrapped around his neck. "Tell them now. Give the order."

"*¡No puedo!*"

"Why can't you?"

Juan's eyes rolled up to meet Joe's. "We work for the same boss. They are his men. Not mine. We were warned that Americans were coming to take over our operation. They are here to stop you."

"We don't want your smuggling business. Who the hell told you this?"

"Marcus Delaney."

Joe wanted to roar, but kept control. He should have killed that spineless bastard when he'd had the chance.

"He lied. Who did you sell the mummy to? This is the last time I ask."

"*No lo sé. Por favor. Es la verdad. Es un inglés pero no sé su nombre.*"

"An Englishman with no name." Like Joe believed that. Unfortunately, his time for wringing the information out of the dealer was over. "Bet you have contact details or bank details or something on the guy."

"*Sí, sí, todo está en la computadora.*"

"You got his computer?" Joe asked Julia. "He says the info is on there."

"I have everything," Julia said.

"Is there a back way out of this place?" Joe shook Juan Pablo.

"*No, señor, sólo la puerta principal.*" He pointed a shaky hand to the store's only door.

Joe cursed as he lifted his gun hand. With a sharp downward strike, he knocked the Bolivian out. He didn't bother to soften his fall. As soon as Juan Pablo crumpled to the floor, Joe stepped over him and went to stand with Ed.

"We've got two minutes at best," Ed whispered. "Less when they spot their colleagues."

"There's no back way out."

Ed stiffened. "Then we're gonna have to hit first."

Joe felt a tug at his shirt and turned to find Julia staring at him. "What is it, baby?"

"We can go up." She pointed to the rusted ladder halfway up the wall at the end of the alley beside the cluttered exterior of the shop. It was bolted to the brick. An abandoned fire escape for the buildings crowding in on them.

"Four men," Ed said from the doorway. "Make that five. Seven when the guys we knocked out come around."

Joe ran a hand through his hair. He'd never get the women past that many men. He looked at the ladder. He wasn't even sure it would hold their weight.

A voice rang out. The unconscious men had been spotted.

"Time's up." Joe scoured the store. They needed a diversion and they needed it fast.

Joe's eyes hit on some supplies near the door.

"Ed," he called. "It's time to go MacGyver on their asses." He pointed at the stock. Ed followed his gaze and smiled.

"Set it up, then get the women out of here. I'll cover you."

"We go together," Joe said.

"Sure, kid." Ed turned his attention back to the advancing men. "You've got a minute. Now get to work."

CHAPTER 11

Julia pulled her gran out of the way as Joe rushed around the dark little shop. He read labels and tossed items into a large basket.

"Don't fire unless you have to," Joe ordered Ed.

"They're almost on us," Ed said.

"Nearly there." Joe lifted the heavy basket he'd filled and dropped it in front of the open doorway.

"What can we do?" Julia asked him.

His eyes were warm when he glanced at her. "Just do what you're told. I'll get you out of here in one piece. Trust me."

Something passed between them, like an electric current riding on the air. "I do," Julia told him.

He nodded and turned his attention to the basket.

There was shouting outside. The sound of running foot-steps coming closer. Julia fought the panic bubbling up inside her. The sudden need to hide was almost too strong to resist. She looked at Joe and took strength from his calm, confident demeanour. He'd keep his word. She knew it. She did trust him—with her life. Her heart was another matter.

Joe swept everything off one of the tables. The table had been made from an old wooden door sitting on a couple of supports. Joe held up the thick wooden panel.

"It'll have to do," he said before spinning to Ed. "Everybody behind me. I'm going to light the basket and toss it out the door. Ed, you get the women up the ladder." Joe pointed at Julia and her gran. "You two get your asses up there as fast as possible. We'll bring up the rear."

Julia felt a wave of dizziness at his command. He didn't mean to leave them—did he?

"You're coming too, right?"

"Absolutely." It was a promise. She saw it in his eyes.

Without another word, he struck a match and held it against the string that trailed from the basket. Once it was sparking, Joe stood and kicked the basket into the alley. Fast as lightning, he grabbed the wooden door.

"Try to shield your eyes. This is going to give off powder. It will hurt like a bitch," Joe said. "Julia, use your scarf."

Julia yanked up the scarf as she grabbed his waist. Ed tugged Patricia in behind them. They cowered behind Joe, and the old wooden door, for the longest ten seconds of Julia's life. And then the night exploded. A multitude of sharp, deafening blasts, made louder by the echoing effects of the narrow alley. Men shouted. Lights flashed. A thick yellow cloud filled the air.

"Run! Run!" Joe yelled.

As a group, they charged for the wall with the ladder attached, trusting blindly that Joe could see the way. He'd unholstered his weapon again and crouched behind the board, shielding them from the alley and the explosions.

"Boost them up," he ordered.

"Already on it." Ed grabbed Patricia around the waist and thrust her up towards the ladder. She grasped the rungs and started to climb.

As the dark mustard-yellow cloud became thicker, Julia lost sight of her grandmother.

"Your turn." Ed pulled Julia to the ladder. Strong hands gripped her hips.

"Joe? You're coming next, aren't you?" Her voice trembled.

"Right behind you," he said, but he didn't look back.

"Up you go." Ed didn't give her time to prepare—he just lifted her high above his head.

Julia grabbed the third rung of the ladder and scrambled to get her foot on the bottom one. The cloud beneath her had grown too dense to see through. It looked like a war was raging in the alley. Lights flashed. Explosions burst and echoed through the narrow passageway. There was shouting and coughing. It was terrifying.

And Joe was in the midst of it.

Julia climbed, aware of the ladder shaking and creaking beneath her. She felt the sharp edges of the corroded metal bite into her palms. The scarf her grandmother had given her was pulled up over her mouth and nose, and still she felt her throat clog from the stinging powder Joe had released. It nipped at her eyes, making them water.

The ladder shook and shifted as someone climbed onto it beneath her. *Joe? Please be Joe. Please be Joe...*

"Hurry!" Her grandmother's voice came from above, and Julia looked up to find her leaning over the flat roof, her hand extended ready to help Julia climb over.

Julia grasped the offered hand and scrambled over the cool brick onto the concrete roof. There was an eerie second or two of silence before a different kind of banging rent the air.

Gunfire.

"Joe!" Julia leaned over the edge. She couldn't see anything. The alley was filled with dense yellow smoke.

"Get back!" Ed ordered as he scrambled onto the roof beside her.

He instantly leaned over the edge, a gun in his hand. "Joe. I've got your six. Move out now."

The ladder shook and Julia held on to the top of it, comforted by the vibrations, knowing it meant Joe was on his way.

Ed aimed into the middle of the alley and fired.

There was shouting. Julia didn't understand the words, but she understood the meaning. They were out to kill them. To kill Joe.

In the distance, sirens shrieked. The police were coming. Too late. Far too late.

There was a thud beneath them. The ladder groaned and then it stilled.

Joe wasn't on the ladder.

He was back in that alley. In the cloud. With their attackers.

No! No, no, no, no, no...

"Joe?" Julia leaned over, craning her neck to see something, anything. He had to be there. He had to be safe. He had to.

A strong hand yanked her back. "Keep down," Ed ordered.

"Joe!" She turned to Ed. "He isn't on the ladder. You have to do something. He needs help. Help him."

"He can take care of himself." Ed aimed into the alley and fired off two more rounds.

The sirens became louder. Julia strained her ears, desperate to hear something, anything that would tell her Joe was still alive.

Thudding. Gunfire. Shouting.

"Joe?" Ed's voice snapped through the chaos.

"Go!" Joe shouted.

Relief almost brought Julia to her knees, and then the

word penetrated. Her eyes shot to Ed, who was grim. "What does he mean? Go?" Her hands started to shake, and she could feel the blood drain from her face.

"Joe? You sure?" Ed called again.

"Get them to safety." There was a pause. A thud. A grunt of pain. "Go!" Joe roared.

Julia stared at the edge of the roof in horror.

Ed cursed and fired several shots into the alley. The sirens were on top of them now. Flashing coloured lights penetrated the thick haze.

"You heard the man." Ed grabbed her arm and spun her away from the edge of the roof. "We need to get out of here."

"No!" Julia struggled against him. They couldn't leave Joe. No. No. It wasn't happening. "No!"

"Julia, we need to leave." Her grandmother grasped her hand. "Joe wants us out of here. We need to do what he wants." Her tone was sympathetic but firm.

Between Ed and Patricia, Julia was dragged across the roof—struggling all the way.

"We can't leave him!" The sounds of fighting, cries of pain and intermittent gunfire were deafening.

There was a war going on down in that alley. And Joe was in the middle of it.

"We can't leave him." Julia fought to get back to the ladder.

"No!" Ed snatched her around the waist and lifted her, striding forward with Julia's feet dangling above the ground. "You can't do anything to help. You'd make things worse. Joe is doing this to protect you. Don't let him down."

Patricia jerked a door open. It led to a stairway. Julia barely registered it. Her eyes were still in the edge of the roof leading down to the alley.

Sirens. Whistles. Feet pounding the ground. Gunshots.

Wails of pain. Shouting. The sounds swirled around Julia until they formed one overwhelming cacophony of violence.

Ed carried her into the stairwell, holding her tight as he ran down the stairs.

"Joe!" Julia shouted.

All she heard was her own call echoing back to her.

CHAPTER 12

There were twenty-seven power sockets in their suite. Thirty-two light switches. Seven lamps…

"Julia," Patricia snapped. "Stop pacing."

Julia dragged her eyes away from the lamp. Seven. There were seven. She'd stopped beside the desk. The notepad didn't line up with the corner. The pen wasn't parallel to the pad. Julia fixed it. Still wrong. It was still wrong. No balance. That was it. She pulled open the drawer, took out a second pad and pen and placed them in the opposite corner to the ones that were already there. Better. She turned the pens so that the hotel logo faced upwards. Her fingers twitched to switch the lamp off and on. Three times. It needed to happen three times. She spun and paced to the window while she could still resist the urge.

She placed her palms flat on the glass and rested her forehead between them. Cool. Hard. Somehow soothing. With eyes closed, she rolled her forehead, feeling the pressure against the bone. It helped.

A hand rested on her back. Julia jerked out from under it and gave her gran a strained smile.

"I'm trying," she said.

"I know."

Patricia folded her arms, aware that Julia couldn't bear touch. Not right then. She felt like her skin had been sensitised. The air in the room acted like tiny knives against it. Even her hair rasped against her skin. Julia dug around in her bag, which was still across her body, and pulled out a hair tie. She tied her hair up in a messy bun at the back of her neck.

Her eyes drifted to the window. The canyon bowl La Paz sat in was lit up in the darkness. All around them were walls of blinking lights, stretching up into the night sky. Joe was out there. Somewhere. Pain speared through her stomach at the thought. They should never have left him. Never.

It was wrong. Wrong. Wrong. Wrong…

"Julia." Her grandmother's voice was firm, pushing through the tight band of panic squeezing Julia's chest. "I have medicine for the altitude sickness." She held up a pill and a glass of water.

Julia didn't know where the water had come from. She wanted to tell her gran, remind her that she needed the water in a bottle. A sealed bottle. Joe would have remembered. Her eyes drifted towards the lights again. Where was he? Was he still alive?

No. No. She couldn't think like that. No.

"Pill, Julia. You can't afford to get sick again."

Her eyes snapped to her gran. She was right. She had to stay well. To help Joe.

"Thank you." Julia took the pill and the water. But she walked over to the bar fridge and took out a bottle, leaving the glass on the bench.

The pill stuck in her throat.

"Still no answer." Ed's voice was grim.

They'd been trying to call Joe since arriving at their suite.

"I have to think," Julia announced, drawing confused looks from both of them.

What she wanted to do was sit in the closet while she did it. But that was one step shy of being completely insane, and she wasn't there yet. Instead, she pulled an armchair over to the corner where the window met the wall. She put the chair at an angle, so her back was facing the corner. Then she sat in the chair, her feet on the seat. She reached into her bag to get her iPad, and her fingers hit the laptop she'd taken from Juan Pablo. In her fear for Joe, the items she'd taken from the dealer's shop had slipped her mind.

"Ed?" She called over to the man who was busy whispering to her grandmother. Neither of them did a good job at hiding their worry.

"What can I do for you, *querida*?"

"Can you go through this computer? I need you to look for the sale of the mummy. If you start with transactions on the date Marcus sold it to Juan Pablo, that would be good. We're looking for a name, or a way to track down the person who has the mummy."

"Of course." Ed took the laptop from her and headed for the desk.

"After you've had a look, I'll see if we can set up a remote connection for Elle. If there's hidden information on that laptop, she'll find it."

He nodded and pulled out the chair. A moment later he was hunched over the machine, with Patricia looking over his shoulder.

Julia took out her iPad and started to go through the copious amount of notes she'd made since her grandmother called her for help. Patterns. She was good at patterns. Good at planning. Good at making things fit a schedule. Good at seeing details nobody else could see.

A thought. "Ed?" He instantly looked over at her. "Did you call the police? There were sirens. Maybe Joe is in custody."

"Of course." Ed reached for his phone. Then paused. "I'll try the hospitals too."

Julia focused on breathing. Slow in and out. She tapped out a rhythm against her leg. Three times through the rhythm. That was enough. Back to the notes.

Focus. She had to focus.

"IT'S GORGEOUS HERE." Elle was bubbling with so much enthusiasm that it hurt Callum's head.

He glanced over at the blue-haired tech as she rubber-necked out the car window on their drive from the airport into central La Paz.

"Why doesn't she have altitude sickness?" Ryan complained, clutching his stomach.

"Look at all the lights. They go right up the mountains. Oh, I can't wait to see the mountains in daylight. Can you believe how many skyscrapers there are here? Does Bolivia get earthquakes? If they do, those buildings wouldn't be good in an earthquake. Oh, look at the women in their traditional dress. I want a skirt like that."

"Make it stop," Ryan wailed, and Callum had to agree with him.

He turned the wheel and swung their car out into an even busier road. Half the cars on the road should have been sold for scrap years earlier. His phone buzzed, and Callum reached onto the dash for it, hitting the speaker option.

"I need help. Who do you know in La Paz that you can call now? Right now."

Joe.

"What's going on?" Callum snapped.

There was silence in their car. All attention on the call.

"Got jumped. Julia, Patricia and Ed got away. I hope. We got separated. The cops came. We scattered but I was chased. I'm holed up in a basement. I can't see a way out."

"Why the hell didn't you call Ed?"

"I lost my phone and stole this one. I can't remember Ed's number and I don't want to freak Julia out. Basically it was call you or Grunt. Consider yourself honoured. I called you first."

"Guess this means you two are going steady," Ryan said, earning a glare from Callum.

"What do you need?" Callum said as he navigated the traffic.

"I need somebody, anybody, to take out the assholes who've got me pinned. Tell me you've got somebody you can call. Hell, pick a name out of the yellow pages, I don't care, but I need someone now."

"Where are you?"

Joe rattled off an address and Elle typed it into the GPS on the dash. She gave Callum a nod once it was loaded.

"That's an approximate location," Joe said. "But these guys shouldn't be that hard to miss."

"Description?" Callum took the turns indicated by the GPS.

"Short. South American. Armed," Joe answered.

"Helpful," Elle muttered.

Callum turned a corner fast, making Ryan moan as he reached for the panic handle. They drove into a cobblestone road that seemed to head straight up the mountain. It was crowded, with everything from women selling chewing gum, to guys loitering for no reason at all.

"You made that call yet?" Joe sounded strained.

"No need," Callum said. "You already have somebody coming your way."

"Who?"

"Me," Callum said.

"And me," Ryan and Elle chimed in.

"How?" For once, the American sounded stunned.

"We just flew in on Rachel's jet—"

"Her dad's jet," Elle interrupted.

"—heading here to save your sorry backside," Callum continued.

"We just didn't know it'd need saving this soon," Ryan added.

Callum blasted his horn to get people off the middle of the street.

"Damn it, they've lost patience," Joe whispered. "Somebody's trying to sneak in."

"Don't hang up," Callum ordered. "I'm hitting mute; we'll hear you but you won't hear us. Tell me when it's safe to talk again."

"Copy."

Callum's attention was split between the narrow road, crowded with people, and the noises coming from his phone.

"I hacked the local CCTV," Elle said from the passenger seat, her fingers flying over her ever-present laptop. "There are literally no public cameras in the area Joe's holed up in." She snapped her computer shut in disgust.

"So we're going in blind," Ryan said.

"The end of the street he mentioned is up here on the left." Elle pointed to the darker end of the street where houses were smaller and the crowd had thinned.

Callum pulled the car over and climbed out. "You drive," he told Elle, who scooted across to take the wheel. He hesitated. "Do you know how to drive this?"

The car had been modified for disabled users, with the accelerator and brake as levers instead of pedals.

Elle gave him a look of disgust and revved the engine.

Callum left her to it and strode to the back of the car. He

popped the boot and took out their weapons bag. He handed Ryan a Beretta with an extra clip and took one for himself. He was just about to close the trunk when he realised that once Ryan and he had gone in to rescue Joe, Elle would be left vulnerable. He gritted his teeth. This was why he should have stayed with the military—no civilians to worry about during an op. But then the SAS hadn't wanted him when he'd lost his legs, so his choice of teammates had been greatly reduced.

"At the first sign of trouble," Callum told Elle when he climbed back into the car, "leave and head for the hotel where the others are staying."

Elle eyed the gun in his hand. "Why don't I get a gun?"

"Because you'd probably shoot yourself," Ryan said. "Or worse, one of us."

"What makes you think I don't know how to use a gun? I work for a security company."

Callum turned to stare at her. "Well?"

"Fine." She rolled her eyes. "I don't know how to fire a real gun, but I'm freaking awesome with one in Grand Theft Auto."

Callum turned to look back out the windscreen while Elle took the corner into Joe's street.

"Fantastic," Ryan said to Elle. "Next time we're in trouble in an online game, we'll call you for help."

"Slow down," Callum ordered.

For once, Elle did as she was told. They scanned the dimly lit street. Unlike the crowded area they'd left a moment ago, this was deserted.

"There." Callum pointed, and they craned to see.

Peeking out of a doorway about two-thirds of the way down the street was a huge guy. With a gun.

"I thought he said they were short?" Elle said. "How did he miss this guy? He's Goliath around here."

"He isn't even trying to blend," Ryan said in disgust.

"He doesn't need to." Callum scanned the street. It was shut up tight. "The locals have scattered. Ryan, you get out. Take this side. Elle will drive past and drop me at the other end. Then you park around the corner and wait. Got it?"

He got a round of agreement. Elle pulled over, long enough to let Ryan slip out before she was back in motion. As they passed the house Callum suspected held Joe, he spotted three men. Two flanking the building, hiding in doorways and aiming at the house. The third was sneaking along the perimeter wall, aiming for a window low in the building.

"There." Callum pointed to a particularly dark section of street.

Elle slowed for him to get out. "Don't die," she said cheerily before he shut the door and the car continued down the street into the darkness.

Callum wondered again what the hell he'd been thinking when he'd bought into Benson Security, then he put all of that out of his mind and made his way towards Joe.

THERE WAS one window into the basement. The one Joe had been forced to climb through when he'd been cornered. The interior door had been barricaded from the other side. Judging by the locks on the door, the barricading was a standard security habit of the homeowner. Great for the guy who owned the house; not so good for the idiot trapped in his basement.

This whole thing was one huge screw-up. He should never have taken Julia and Patricia to talk to Juan Pablo. He'd buried his damn primitive streak, the one that screamed he had to protect Julia, just so he wouldn't freak her out. And where had it gotten him? Yeah, he was trapped in an empty house, with a knife wound in his side and a busted lip. Not to mention the bruises that would hurt like a bitch in the morning. But the worst part, the part that was driving him insane, was that he didn't even know if Julia was safe.

He heard a scraping in the courtyard outside the window. Courtyard. He silently scoffed. It was a strip of dirt between the perimeter wall and the house. The guy attempting to sneak up on him wasn't trained worth a damn. Experienced, yes. Trained, no. A rookie marine would make less noise than this asshole.

Joe scanned the room behind him, looking for something to board the window, or to hide behind. There was a sink in the corner, piles of woven cloths and a tonne of rodent droppings, but not a whole lot else. He was a sitting duck.

He inched across the room and crouched beneath the window, aiming his gun upwards. If this guy had any sense, he'd hold steady at the window and let his friends creep in to cover him. That was the only way they'd get Joe, if they worked as a team. Otherwise, he planned to pick them off one at a time until Callum arrived.

A stillness overcame him as he waited for his prey. Unlike the men after him, Joe had been trained for this. Not only trained, he'd lived it. Day in, day out for over a decade. He felt emotion drift away and logic take its place. He was ready. He would get out. He'd get back to Julia, and then they were going to have a long talk about following orders in the field. He'd heard her shouting for him. Heard her fighting to get to him. Heard Ed drag her away. As much as her actions warmed his heart, they made the rest of him turn cold. What if she'd been hurt? No. He couldn't think about it. Not now. Later.

A noise above him. Joe looked up and saw the idiot's gun poke through the window. He almost shook his head at the stupidity. Reaching up, he grabbed the idiot's arm and, using all of his upper body strength, pulled his pursuer into the room.

His gun went off. There was shouting outside. A scuffle. Joe noted it in an academic sense. He had the guy disarmed and unconscious in seconds. Amateur.

"You all right in there?" Callum's deep Scottish brogue cut through the silence.

"Yeah." Joe looked up at the window as Callum's head appeared. "Took you long enough."

"Had to come all the way from London," the grumpy bastard said. He nodded at the guy at Joe's feet. "He dead?"

"Not yet." The asshole had tried to kill him. Worse, he'd tried to kill Julia. It was only a matter of time before Joe returned the favour.

"What do you want to do with him?"

That was the sixty-four-million-dollar question. "Probably a good idea to question him. Make sure more of Juan Pablo's crew won't come after us."

"Then he's coming with us." Callum turned and whistled. A moment later, Ryan appeared.

"You couldn't have got yourself in a mess at sea level, could you?" He looked a bit green around the gills.

"Lift your guy up and feed him out to us," Callum said.

"What about the other guys?" Joe said. "Can't we use them? This son of a bitch looks heavy."

Callum's eyes were flat. "That isn't possible." In other words, they weren't alive enough to talk.

"Damn it." This was going to open the knife wound in his side again, and it had just stopped bleeding.

He bent over and lifted the guy with a grunt, throwing him over his shoulders in a fireman's hold. Joe backed up to the window and aimed the guy through the opening. There was a thud. Joe looked around, but didn't see anything. He angled the guy at the window again and shoved. Two more thuds. This time Joe realised what it was. The guy's head had hit the wall. Hell.

Joe looked up at Callum, who was staring down at him as though he was completely incompetent. Ryan was trying not to laugh.

"I'm injured," Joe said. "One of you want to climb in here and heave him out the window?"

"You're doing great." Ryan choked the words out.

"Asshole."

Joe thought the guy's head had probably suffered enough, so he turned and tried to angle him out the window feet first.

"Somebody reach in and pull his ankles," Joe ordered as he lifted the guy's legs to the window.

It was too high. The angle was off. The guy slipped right off Joe's shoulder and landed on the concrete floor. Head first.

"Well, hell." Joe looked down at him.

"He still alive?" Callum said.

Joe knelt and felt for a pulse. Nothing. There went their informant. He stood, hands on his hips, and stared down at his now-dead attacker. When he looked back up at Ryan and Callum, Callum was shaking his head and Ryan was staring at the sky while biting his lip.

"We never mention this again," Joe said.

"Scout's honour," Ryan said.

Joe crouched over the man, rolled him on to his back and checked his pockets for ID. There was nothing. But he did recognise him as the guy who'd used a knife on him in the alley.

He stood and reached for the ledge, ready to pull himself up.

"Mind the walls," Ryan said. "Wouldn't want you to hurt your head."

It was late by the time they made it back to the hotel. When Joe threw the door of the suite open, he found Ed pointing a gun at him. The relief on the older man's face was palpable.

"Am I glad to see you." He put the gun away. "We tried calling."

Joe scanned the room behind him. "Lost my phone."

Patricia came rushing up and wrapped Joe in a hug. "Are you hurt?" She held him at arm's length and looked him over. The same way his mother had done when he was a kid.

"A bit beaten up, but good." He stepped around her. "Julia?"

Callum strode into the room behind him, followed closely by the rest of the team.

"Um, Joe?" Patricia asked nervously, backing away from the newcomers.

"My team." As far as Joe was concerned, that was enough introduction. "Where is Julia?" The demand cut through the chaos around him. Silence fell, all eyes on him.

Patricia stirred first. "She's fine, Joe. She's fine. She went into our room earlier, saying she needed some peace to think." Her face softened. "She's been very worried about you."

Joe was already striding towards one of the twin rooms. "She's staying in my room from now on," he called over his shoulder, uncaring as to what anybody thought about his declaration. All he could think about was getting to Julia.

As the volume rose behind him, Joe let himself into Julia's room. One small lamp let off a yellow glow beside a pristine bed. The other bed had a suitcase on top of it, with clothes scattered over the surface. It didn't take a genius to figure out which bed belonged to Julia.

Joe scanned the room. Somewhere small, that was where she'd be, if she was feeling insecure. The bathroom door was ajar, and he covered the distance to it. No Julia. That left the closet. He opened the door, saw the light from her ever-present iPad and felt something settle inside of him.

"Hey, you." He crouched in front of the open door.

Julia was sitting on the floor, staring at her iPad and hugging her knees. "Joe?" Her eyes went wide. The iPad fell to the floor.

"Hey, baby." He smiled at her, burying his need to grab her and hold her, in case he spooked her.

"Joe!" She launched herself at him, making him land on his backside.

Julia straddled his legs and wrapped her arms tight around him. She pressed her face in the crook of his neck, and he felt the wetness of her tears. He held her fast against him as a deep peace flooded his body.

"It's okay, baby. I'm okay."

Her sobs were quiet, as though she was afraid to be heard. Joe scooted them back until he was leaning against the end of the bed. The soft light wrapped around them like a blanket and everything felt right with the world. Joe was vaguely aware of the murmur of voices outside the bedroom door, but all that mattered was the woman in his arms. He cooed nonsense to her as she cried, soothing her with his touch, breathing her in and letting the warmth of her body ease his lingering tension. He let her cry it out even though he knew there were people outside waiting to talk to them. None of that was as important as Julia. Nothing was as important as Julia *ever*.

"I thought you'd been killed." Her words were a trembling breath against his throat.

He stroked up her back until he clasped her head. "I'm hard to kill."

"You scared me," she whispered.

"I know. I'm sorry." He pressed her closer to him, merging their heat.

"You can't die." It was a desperate declaration. Joe stilled, his instincts hearing something in her words that his brain told him was simply wishful thinking.

"Why's that?" he murmured.

It felt as though his heart was pounding hard enough to hear.

"Because you're Joe."

He would have been disappointed, but he heard something more in her voice, something she wasn't saying. Something he had to hear her say.

"Is that it? That's the only reason?" He kept his tone soft, a gentle tease.

She seemed to burrow into him and whispered, "No, it's because you're *my* Joe."

Joe wasn't sure he would have believed he'd heard it, if he hadn't felt the words against his skin. A surge of pure, unadulterated possession almost overwhelmed him. He wanted to roll them to the floor and show her just how much he belonged to her. He wanted to mark her as his, so that everyone would know. It took all of his will to control his urges. Instead, he gently coaxed Julia to look at him.

He fought a smug smile when she kept her hands flat on his shoulders. She even looked him in the eyes. Shyly, but without fear. Joe gently cupped her cheek. He used his thumb to wipe away the last of her tears.

"I am, you know," he said softly. "I am completely yours."

"Joe?" Her fingers curled in his shirt. Confusion, hope, need, fear—it was all there in her eyes.

"Always." He rubbed his thumb across her full bottom lip. "Always yours."

"Joe." She seemed to melt under his touch. Surrendering. Accepting. Hoping.

"Come here." His hand on her hip pressed her towards him.

Her eyes went wide but she didn't resist.

"Need you," he whispered against her lips. "Kiss me."

Her eyes fluttered shut and she pressed her soft, soft lips against his. The kiss was heaven. An intoxicating merging of heart, body and soul. Her sweet fragrance filled his mind. Her warm curves pressed against him. The gentle, seeking touch of her lips and tongue made him want to roar. She was perfect. She was home.

JULIA WAS LOST in Joe's kiss. Each touch of his lips against hers proved he was real. He was alive. He was there. With her. His kiss was a soft, slow seduction. A sensual tangling of lips and tongues that made everything else fade to insignificance. Being with Joe, breathing him in, getting lost in his confident touch, made Julia feel safe. Needed. Wanted.

And oh how she wanted him too. His lips were firm but satin soft. His musky scent was intoxicating. Addictive. Julia knew she would never get enough of it. Strong muscles flexed under her fingertips, reminding her of the strength Joe possessed. Not only physically, but in every way possible. He was an immovable force that persistently and consistently pressed towards his goal.

She wanted to luxuriate in his strength. To wallow in it. She wanted to crawl so deep inside of him that no one would ever get to her. She wanted Joe surrounding her, a barrier to the world, an anchor for her continuously spinning mind.

Joe slowed the kiss down, leaving Julia breathless and longing. He rested his forehead against hers.

"The natives are getting restless." His voice was husky as he stroked up and down the length of her back.

Julia felt like she was floating and Joe was the ocean. She flicked out her tongue to taste him against her lips, and he moaned.

"You're killing me. You're not ready for what I want, and if we don't go deal with the team, they'll come in here to get us."

The word slowly penetrated her daze. "Team?"

He leaned back and smiled at her. Somehow that smile felt as though it was unique, one he kept solely for her.

"Half the office flew out to rescue us."

She blinked hard as the fog lifted from her mind, and her cheeks began to burn for an entirely different reason.

"My work colleagues are out there while we're in here kissing?" Her voice became increasingly hysterical as the words rushed out.

"It's okay. Nobody cares what we're doing in here."

"Oh my goodness." Julia shot to her feet. "This is so unprofessional."

"Babe." Joe followed her. "You aren't working. This is a personal trip. You can't be unprofessional on a personal trip."

He tried to hide it, but Julia caught his wince when he straightened.

"You're hurt!"

"It's nothing. I'm fine." Joe was gentle as he tried to stop her from lifting his shirt.

"That's blood." Julia was outraged.

She'd thought the stain on his shirt was dirt, but it was blood. His blood. Joe was bleeding. She fought past his attempts to discourage her and pulled his shirt up and over his head.

"Joe!" She traced the gash on his waist. A knife wound. Someone had tried to stab him and skimmed him instead. It was shallow, but bleeding again. The horror of it hit her. He was bleeding because she'd climbed all over him.

"It's nothing. I've had worse." He covered her hand with his, pressing it flat against his side. His hot flesh seared her, but she didn't let herself think about the fact Joe was standing half-naked in front of her.

"That does not reassure me, Joe Barone." She knocked his hand out of the way to examine him. There were cuts and bruises everywhere. How could she have missed them? "I shouldn't have thrown myself at you like that. You're hurt. I was selfish."

"Hey." Joe cupped her cheek. "You can throw yourself at me anytime. Trust me, it isn't selfish when I want it too."

"You're impossible." She grabbed his hand and led him to the door. "We need to find a good first-aid kit. I only have a little one in my bag, and it won't be enough for your injuries. We have to get those wounds cleaned and treated."

He followed behind her, holding her hand, as though he was afraid to release her in case she disappeared on him. He didn't seem to care that she was bossing him around. In fact, he seemed oddly pleased about it.

"There's a kit in my room," he said.

"Of course there is."

She opened the door to the living area and stopped dead.

In her urgency to get Joe fixed up, she'd forgotten about the team. It felt like the room was packed, and every set of eyes was on them.

Joe reached for her waist, and she felt his heat at her back an instant before his body touched hers. Julia's eyes lowered to focus on the floor and she took a step back, pressing herself against Joe—her safe haven. The silence was heavy, and Julia desperately wished she was back inside the closet.

"I see you've all met," Joe said, walking her into the room.

"I see you two have done a whole lot more than meet." Ryan gave them a cheeky grin.

Julia's face must have been luminous, because the burn in her cheeks was painful. *Danger! Danger! Abort! Abort!* There was silence as Julia willed herself to become invisible.

"Come on." Joe stepped in front of Julia, still holding her hand. "Let's get that medical kit."

He strode across the living room towards his bedroom.

"Hey, Julia, glad to see you're alive," Elle said as they passed.

Julia dared to look up at the woman who was becoming her friend. "I'm pleased you're here." There was no amusement or judgment in Elle's eyes.

Elle nodded, making her blue bunches bob. "Eduardo gave me the laptop you lifted from the shop." She said Ed's name with a flirtatious lilt that made Julia smile. "He'd already worked through the Spanish and pointed out places to start searching for our buyer. It makes my job easier. I'm running a search on IP locations right now. Hopefully we'll get a name on the mummy buyer." She paused. "That sounds wrong. As in, really wrong."

"I know." Julia's smile widened.

"No way!" Ryan's voice cut through the room. "I just realised who you are. It didn't click until I saw you with your gran."

Julia felt every muscle in her body solidify. The atmosphere in the room was suddenly thicker.

"I think that's a conversation for another time," Patricia said in a tone that demanded she was obeyed.

Unfortunately, she was talking to Ryan, and the only thing he would stop for was food.

"You're Julia Collins," Ryan said, with no small amount of awe.

"It's the altitude sickness. Yes, she's Julia Collins. We work with her," Elle said slowly.

"And you're Patricia Matthews." Ryan pointed at Julia's gran.

"Seriously," Elle said to their boss, "he needs help."

"I should have put it together." Ryan smacked his forehead. "But you're nothing like your sister."

"Ryan." Joe's voice was a warning rumble.

Ryan was unaffected. He was far too excited by his revelations. "Do you know who your girlfriend is?"

At any other time, Julia would have freaked out at being called Joe's girlfriend. Not this time. This time, she couldn't speak at all. Her throat was solid. There was a reason she kept her past hidden. And she couldn't open her mouth to tell Ryan not to reveal her secrets. She couldn't do anything but stand there and wait.

"You're dating acting royalty, dude," Ryan told Joe. "Julia's mum is Libby Collins, as in three-time Oscar winner Libby Collins. Her sister is Belinda Collins. I can't remember how many Oscars she's been up for, but I'm pretty sure one of them was just for being hot. Daniel Collins, her young brother, does those superhero movies." Ryan looked at Julia. "If he needs a coach to help with the action scenes, I'm available. Then there's her dad; he's a director. He has an Oscar as well, or is it two?"

"Two." Patricia looked about ready to rip Ryan's head off.

Ryan didn't care. He was beaming widely now. "And Julia. Our Julia was a child star. She had her own TV show and everything. People were always going on about her voice. She was some singing genius or something." He frowned at Julia. "And then you disappeared. People thought you were dead, and all your family ever said was that show business wasn't for you and you're happy doing other stuff."

Julia waited, prepared for someone to mock her for going from child star to office manager. It didn't come.

"You about done?" Joe's voice was pure menace.

"No," the dense man said, oblivious to the rage emanating from Joe. "Why the big secret, Julia?"

Julia looked around at the astonished faces of the people who were closest to her. She didn't need to be a mind reader to know what they were thinking. She'd heard it all before. *You were famous? You want to run an office instead of performing? What's wrong with you? Why couldn't you cope with fame when everyone else in your family can?*

"This is why," Julia whispered to the silent room.

Joe tugged her hand. "I need medical attention."

"Five minutes," Callum called after them. "We need a debrief. In the meantime, I'm going to have a private word with my dumb-as-dirt employee."

"What'd I do?" Ryan said.

But the damage had already been done. Everyone would think Julia was an even bigger freak than they'd thought she was before Ryan had outed her and her family.

And there was no denying they were right. She was a freak. A freak who was incapable of living a normal life. She cast a glance at Joe. And that included normal relationships too.

"I need to..." She cast around for an excuse for leaving him to sort himself out. "I should show Elle what I've pulled up before the meeting starts. You can sort yourself out, can't you?"

She'd already disentangled her hand from his and was backing away from him.

Joe studied her for a moment. "We'll get back to this later." It sounded like a promise. Or a threat.

Julia didn't care which. Keeping her head down, she skirted the edge of the room back to her bedroom, where she'd left her iPad on the closet floor.

With her iPad in her hand and her messenger bag across her body, she felt more able to face her team. This was who she was. Not the child star everyone remembered, but the full-grown woman who needed her security blankets to make it through the day. She closed her eyes as the memory of the years she'd spent acting washed over her. The times spent emptying her stomach before each performance. The nights spent awake and worrying about the next morning. The fear of going out in public, where there would be cameras shoved in her face. It was a lot for any child to cope with, but for one who was naturally shy, well, it had destroyed what little confidence she did have.

It hadn't been her parents' fault. They hadn't pushed her. She'd wanted so badly to be the same as the rest of the family. And she'd failed spectacularly. But that was then. She wasn't that person anymore. She would never be that person. She would always be the freak who could barely cope around other people. The freak who was better off alone.

With a deep breath, she went out to face her team, prepared to run and hide if the questions started again. When she came back into the room, everyone was glaring at Ryan and he was rubbing his jaw. But there weren't any questions about her past.

CHAPTER 14

It felt all too familiar, meeting in a hotel room, talking about a woman being held hostage, planning a rescue.

"Anybody else got déjà vu?" Elle said, echoing Joe's thoughts.

"It's one in the morning." Callum helped himself to coffee. "I'm knackered. Can we get this show on the road?" He looked over at Joe. "Want to update us?"

Joe turned his attention to Julia, who was curled into a ball in the armchair over at the window. As far away as she could get from everyone else without leaving the room. She was busy scanning notes on her iPad, but Joe suspected it was purely to avoid looking anyone in the eye. She hadn't looked at him since she'd come back into the room. Thanks to Ryan's big mouth, they'd taken a step backwards. He should have punched him twice. Joe didn't give a damn who Julia's family were. There was something seriously wrong with their relationship if she thought he would.

"Joe?" Callum prompted, clearly losing what little patience he had in reserve.

Joe couldn't take his eyes off Julia. Every instinct he had, told him he'd stumbled onto her reason for retreating. He knew it, the same way he knew she belonged to him, on a cellular level. She thought they were comparing her to her famous family and finding her short. He'd bet anything she thought they considered her crazy for giving up her talents to work in an office. Couldn't she see that the talents and skills she used at Benson Security were important too? She was thinking less of herself again, and he wouldn't have it.

Joe turned to Callum just as he opened his mouth to shout. Joe could tell he was going to yell, because his face had turned red.

"I think Julia should update everyone. She's the one with the best overview."

"What?" came a horrified squeak from the corner.

Joe caught Patricia's eye as he turned back to Julia. Patricia beamed at him, and he knew he was on the right track.

"Jules," Joe called across the room. "Fill everybody in, will you?"

Part of him hated himself for making her the centre of attention when he knew she loathed it. But she could do this. She was the best person to do this. No detail got past her quick brain; no logical reasoning escaped it. The more he thought about it, the more he realised her skills were sorely underutilised, because everyone treated her as the scared rabbit she professed to be. But she was stronger than that. He was sure of it.

"I-I-I..." She looked like she was about to start hyperventilating.

Joe pushed himself off the sofa and sauntered towards her. He held a hand out to her. "You've got this," he said in a low voice, meant only for her.

Wide, panic-stricken eyes met his. Joe let her see his

confidence in her. He let her see that he absolutely believed she could do this and do it better than anyone in the room.

Come on, come on... He wasn't sure if he was praying or trying to communicate with her by telepathy.

"Do you need a data projector?" Elle called across the room. "Because I bought one of those mini laser cube things on the internet, and it's brilliant. We can connect it to your iPad and project onto the wall. Wait until you see the clarity of the images. And it can get so big. I love it. When I'm working alone in the office, I project my work all over the walls. It feels like I'm actually inside the programming. You've got to try it, Julia. It's super cool." She was practically bouncing on the spot as she gushed about her new tech.

Joe hid a smile. Bless Elle's geeky little heart.

"Looks like you're all set," he told Julia.

Elle came over with a tiny cube in the palm of her hand. "Gimme your iPad. I'll set it up. This is going to be brilliant." She didn't wait for a reply as she plucked it from Julia's hand. A second later, her fingers were flying over the screen. "Ry," she called to the man who was currently eating his way through Bolivia's food reserves, "how about we call for popcorn?"

"No popcorn," Callum growled as Elle handed Julia's iPad back to her. "This isn't a bloody movie screening; it's a meeting."

"In a hotel," Elle pointed out. "In the middle of the night. In South America. There *could* be popcorn."

"Julia," Callum snapped, but without his usual sting. "Get on with it. I want to go to bed."

With wide eyes and a look of confusion, Julia put her hand in Joe's. He could have fist-pumped the air with victory, but he didn't. He held Julia's hand as they watched the rest of the team rearrange the furniture to face the wall Elle had picked for Julia's presentation.

"I don't have anything prepared," Julia whispered up at him.

Knowing Julia, even if she'd had a month's notice, she'd still think she wasn't prepared. "Use your notes to illustrate what you want to say. If you don't need to show anything, put a photo of Elle on the wall. It'll keep her happy."

She almost smiled at that. Almost, but not quite.

"I'll get the lights," Patricia called as she headed for the switch by the door. "We should have popcorn. When we watch anything in Libby's cinema, we always have popcorn."

"Your parents have their own cinema?" Ryan's eyebrows shot right up his head, and Joe swore he'd smack them back down if the next words out his mouth were to invite himself over.

The room went dark, except for one small lamp over by the bedroom door.

"I'll stand back here and talk." Julia used the same tone she always used right before she ran.

"Do you need to stand?" Joe asked casually.

"No." She looked at him nervously.

"I have a better idea."

She squealed when he picked her up, making Patricia laugh. Joe settled into the opposite end of the sofa from Ryan and shifted Julia until he was comfortable with her in his lap. Then he clamped an arm around her waist to make sure she stayed there.

"I can't give an update in your lap!" She sounded so horrified that it took everything Joe had not to laugh.

"Start now!" Callum shouted. "I don't care where you are. Bloody talk."

Joe cocked an eyebrow at her. "You heard the boss."

Stunned, but cornered, Julia broke eye contact to stare at her iPad. There was silence in the room, and for a minute, Joe thought she wouldn't be able to do it. But then she cleared her throat and touched the screen, and a neat list appeared on the wall.

"See?" Elle pointed at the projection. "Isn't it fantastic?"

Joe nudged Julia, and she frowned at him.

He leaned in to brush his lips against her ear. "Talk, or I kiss you. What would you rather have happen in a room full of people watching you?"

He felt her go tense, and she pursed her lips as she glared at him.

"You know I would," he told her.

Her eyes went wide. She cleared her throat again and looked down at her iPad. "This is what we know so far," she said softly, but loud enough for everyone to hear.

Joe settled in to listen, feeling inordinately proud of the woman in his lap. Julia Collins may have thought herself a coward. Joe knew she was anything but.

"It all comes back to the missing mummy," Julia said as Joe stroked her back.

She sat up straight, trying to silently tell him to stop it. She thought she felt him chuckle.

She tapped her iPad. "This is Carlos Esteban. He runs one of the more notorious cartels in Peru. His main business is drugs, but that doesn't stop him from getting involved in other areas—prostitution, gunrunning, kidnap for ransom. He also runs quite a large legitimate empire, mainly real estate. And he has Alice." The screen changed to a shot of Patricia and Alice laughing together. "Alice is Gran's best friend."

"Hey, that's Alice Bridges," Ryan said around a mouthful of food. "She's a documentary film producer. Do you know anyone who isn't famous?"

"Me."

"Yeah, yeah, yeah," Ryan said.

"How do you know this stuff?" Elle said. "Do you spend all your free time watching TV?"

"You lot are just jealous because I figured out Julia's secret before you. Admit it. I have mad skills."

Callum leaned over and smacked Ryan on the back of his head. "Son, you need to learn to keep your mouth shut."

"Son? You're, what? Twelve years older than me."

"I'm talking about maturity."

"Oh, okay, in that case, I can't argue." Ryan settled back in his seat.

"Anyway," Julia said as loudly as her courage would allow, "Gran and Alice were after a mummy, but it was stolen and sold to a middleman, who then sold it on. If we're to get Alice back, we need the mummy."

"Who has it now?" Callum said.

"I'm working on finding that out." Elle pointed at the stolen laptop, which was hooked up to her state-of-the-art machine. "Tracing as we speak."

"We did find out that the buyer is local," Ed said from where he was sitting beside Patricia. A little too closely beside her, Julia noticed.

"Which means the mummy is still in Bolivia." Joe's arm tightened around Julia as he spoke.

"We hope so." Julia fought to ignore his touch and concentrate on business. All the while knowing that, at some point, she would have to deal with the trauma of conducting a meeting from Joe's lap. "All we know for sure is that we have two days to find it and trade it for Alice."

There was a heavy silence.

"Couldn't you lot use your ninja skills and break her out without trading the mummy?" Patricia sounded hopeful.

"Not enough people," Callum said. "Carlos' compound is

fortified and manned by an army. It would be a suicide mission."

"Why do they want the mummy anyway?" Elle asked.

"It's wearing a treasure map that leads to Incan gold," Ed said.

Elle's eyes lit up in the reflected light from the projection. "That is so cool."

Callum seemed to groan, but it was so quiet that Julia wasn't sure if she'd imagined it.

"There's another complication," Joe said, and Julia felt his voice vibrate throughout her body. "Seems Grandma is the only one who can read the map. It's written in some Incan code."

"Hey." Patricia threw a cushion at his head. It hit Julia instead. "I'm not your grandma."

"Not yet," Joe mumbled, his hand resting on Julia's knee.

Not yet. What did that mean? There was only one possible answer, and it sucked the air out of Julia's lungs.

Danger! Danger! Run! Abort!

"Breathe," the devil whispered against her ear as he stroked her back. "It was a joke."

She wasn't so sure. It didn't feel like a joke.

"Esteban isn't going to take the mummy without taking Patricia too." Callum rubbed his jaw. He did look weary, reminding Julia that the team had travelled halfway around the world to help them. "He doesn't want a swap. He wants it all."

"I figured he's probably tailing us," Joe said. "That's what I would do. Follow Patricia to the mummy; take it and the woman. Then off Alice. Everything tied up with a neat bow."

Julia turned and smacked his chest. "You can't talk about Alice like that."

"Sorry, baby." He captured the hand that had smacked

him and pressed a kiss to the palm. Julia sucked in a shaky breath.

The silence in the room was deafening as everyone watched their interaction with fascination. Julia fought the urge to burrow into Joe and hide until the attention focused elsewhere.

"I agree. Esteban has no intention of trading Alice," Callum said with absolute confidence.

The weight of his words pressed down on Julia's heart. She looked at her gran and saw her eyes turn glassy with tears.

"They'll trade her for me," Patricia said firmly.

"No!" Julia jumped off Joe's lap. "You can't do that. It's a death sentence. As soon as Carlos is finished with you, he'll kill you."

"But he won't do it until he has the treasure. It will give you time to get me out."

"Come here." Joe grabbed her wrist and jerked her back into his lap. "No one's trading Patricia to the psychopath."

"I don't know," Ryan said. "It sounds like a good plan to me."

That earned him another smack from Callum. At this rate, Ryan would have brain damage by the time they got back to the UK.

"That's because you haven't heard Julia's plan." Joe rubbed the inside of her wrist. "Tell them."

Plan? Was the man insane? She didn't have a plan. She didn't have anything. Most days she didn't have the will to get out of bed, let alone solve a mess like this.

"Julia?" Callum's voice brought her eyes around to him. "What's the plan?"

"Joe?" she whispered.

"I saw it in your notes," he whispered back.

Julia's eyes went to her iPad and she flicked through the

notes she'd made. Page after page of them, all neatly organised.

Ryan whistled as the pages appeared on the screen. "That is seriously impressive, Julia."

Her heart stuttered when she hit the page Joe was talking about. "This is the plan."

The team were quiet as they read her detailed notes.

"It could work." Ryan sounded impressed.

"It *will* work," Joe said. "If we find the treasure first, Esteban will lose interest in Patricia, and that eliminates her from the threat of kidnapping. Which only leaves Alice to worry about, and we can trade the gold for her safe return."

"I like this idea," Ed said. "I'd be much happier if we had the treasure instead of letting Esteban get his hands on it. Gives us more options. Plus," he grinned, "maybe we can skim something off the haul to make this worth our while."

Patricia frowned at him. "There will be no skimming. That treasure belongs in a museum." She looked at Joe. "I can see the merits of this plan, but what if Esteban kills Alice once he realises we have the treasure?"

"He won't," Julia said. "Otherwise we go public with the find and he gets nothing." At least, that was the theory. Julia's hands began to tremble as the consequences of her being wrong sank in. She was taking such a huge risk with Alice's life. "Everything I've read about him suggests he'll take the deal. It also suggests that he will probably try to kill all of us once the trade has been made. He doesn't like losing, and he'll see letting Alice go as a loss. Even after we get her back safely, we'll all still be at risk. I haven't thought of a solution for that part yet."

"That's because that part is our part." Joe looked over at Callum. "We know what to do, don't we?"

"Aye," Callum said. "Elle, get me a name for our buyer. I'm going to bed." He stood, and Julia realised he must have been wearing his prosthetics for far too long. She wouldn't be surprised if he was in pain. She felt guilty, having put him through this.

"He must be in pain," Julia whispered.

"He's a big guy. He can look after himself. It was his choice to come here," Joe told her as Callum strode from the room. Thanks to Patricia hiring the team and covering their expenses, they'd booked another suite on the same floor.

As soon as the meeting broke up, Julia scrambled off Joe's knee.

"Where you going?" Joe said as he hooked her hand.

"Bed. It's been a long day." She kept her eyes on the floor.

"You're sharing my room tonight."

Julia jerked her hand out of his and looked him in the eye. "No." Didn't he realise that things couldn't work between them? Didn't Ryan's revelations make him see how flawed she was?

She'd been foolish to hope, even for a minute, that she could give in to the pull she felt towards Joe. But she couldn't let it happen. She couldn't bear to look at him one day and see the disappointment he felt over her in his eyes. To feel his disgust when she didn't fit him. His anger when she failed to live up to his expectations. It would happen. It always happened.

"I'm going to bed." She turned from him and headed towards the room she shared with her gran.

When Julia looked over her shoulder, she saw his eyes on her and could almost hear his voice in her head.

You can run, but you can't hide.

He was about to learn that she was very good at both. She'd had a lifetime of practice.

CHAPTER 15

Thomas Hayes. That was the name of the British expat who'd bought the mummy. Elle had dug up the information before breakfast and woken everyone with the news. Not that Joe had been sleeping. Nope. He'd being lying in bed wondering why Julia wasn't there with him and trying to figure out what he could do to fix things. So far, he hadn't come up with anything yet.

"Who the hell is this guy again?" Joe said to Ryan, who was by his side, but also to the rest of the team through his comm device.

Ryan and Joe were sauntering down the street in front of Hayes' mini-mansion. They were decked out as tourists—small backpacks, easy-wash casual clothing, large cameras. Joe used his camera to snap photos of the glass and concrete monstrosity Hayes called home.

"I told you," Elle said through the audio link in his ear. "He oversees the South American representatives of the British Council."

"Like an area manager?" Ryan said.

"Exactly. His job is to see that British art and culture is promoted in other countries. It's a public-relations type job," Elle said.

"It's also a great position if you want to build your own collection of illegal artefacts," Joe pointed out.

"Yeah," Elle said. "The guy has a serious obsession with building his own collection."

"I don't get it." Joe pointed the camera, zoomed and snapped away. "What's the point in collecting stuff you can never show anyone because all of it's stolen?"

"Greed?" There was a snap in his ear, and he got a mental picture of Elle popping gum. "A sense of self-importance? A deflection from other things that are wrong with him, as in 'my art collection is big enough to make up for the fact I have a really small penis'?"

Ryan almost choked on the bag of chips he was shovelling down.

Joe spotted a white van coming up the empty street. "Got eyes on Ed."

He watched the van as he wandered along the street. There were no people walking or hanging around. After the crowded chaos of central La Paz, the wealthy suburb of Alto Florida was a little eerie. The houses were huge, if a little close together for Joe's taste, and there were manicured trees at regular intervals along the sidewalk. Every house was cut off from the street by a high wall or a spike-topped fence, but unlike Lima, there weren't any guards visible. It seemed the homeowners relied on their walls and security systems to keep the riffraff out.

The van stopped in front of Hayes' house and Ed climbed out. He was dressed in overalls with a clipboard in his hand. He nodded at Joe and Ryan as though they were strangers, before producing a ladder from the back of the van and propping it against the pole beside the walled house. According to Elle, that pole ran wires for everything from power to internet connection.

Joe and Ryan sauntered past Ed as he attached the disrupter boxes Elle had furnished him with, to the lines leading into Hayes' house.

"Tell me again why I came with you lot to La Paz?" Ed grumbled.

"You volunteered," Joe said. "You practically begged. You kept going on about wanting to find the treasure. No one twisted your arm to get you to tag along."

"That was before I got to play the workman because I'm the only South American in the group," Ed said in Joe's ear while he worked. "This is racist bullshit."

"Be grateful you aren't a woman," Patricia said. "If you were a South American woman, we wouldn't even let you do that much—we'd send you into the house as a maid. So please, don't talk to me about racial stereotyping."

Ryan thought that was funny. "Can you even comment on this, Patty? You're white, upper class and rich. You're a walking, talking example of privilege."

"And that means I can't have an opinion? That I can't stand up for my fellow woman?" Patricia asked coolly.

"Women of the world unite!" Elle called.

Joe groaned. "Can we focus on the job and start a march for equality later?"

"See?" Patricia said. "The fact you can say something like that as a throwaway statement shows how far we still have to go. Honestly, when I was marching for equality in the seventies, I didn't think I'd still be fighting for it over forty years later. Do any of you young people realise how pathetic that is? You're dropping the ball on this issue. You need to make more of an effort to put things right."

"Done," Ed said, and Joe almost kissed the man for stopping Patricia's rant.

"Elle," Joe said, "you in?"

"Give me a minute, Mr. No-patience."

Joe glanced back into the van as he passed, and saw Julia and Patricia sitting behind the work equipment. He kept his face blank when he really wanted to start shouting all over again that they shouldn't be in the field. He'd lost the argument because Patricia had pointed out that she was the only one who knew what the mummy looked like. And Julia had said that where her gran went, she went too. Then Ryan had argued that the mummy would be easy to spot because it was a dried-up dead body, and how many of them could be in the house? At which point Elle ruined that argument by saying, "Thomas Hayes is known to collect them. There could be dozens in there."

So Joe had lost the argument and the women were back in the field.

"Okay," Elle said. "I'm in. His security system was good, top of the line, but nothing fancy. He's only worried about burglars. Not people like us."

Joe shared a look with Ryan.

"Elle," Ryan said, "we're here to steal something, what does that make us?"

"Huh," Elle said, and then there was silence.

Joe scanned the area. It was quiet. "There's activity in the house on the left. Ed, you see anything from up there?"

Ed turned and waved at the neighbouring house. "It's a maid."

"You see anything else?"

"Are there any cameras on neighbouring houses, ones pointing at our house?" Elle asked.

"No," Ed said. "They're all focusing on their own properties."

"Will the maid be a problem?" Joe said.

"If she is, I'll handle it," Ed said.

"And how will you do that?" Patricia's tone was icy.

"Why, I'll use my considerable charm."

"Can we please, for once, focus on the job?" Callum snapped over everyone else. "No more talk unless it's to do with the operation. Keep your petty crap for your free time."

"Yes, sir," Elle said. It was unclear if she meant it sarcastically.

"The maid's gone," Ed said.

"The gates will open on my mark," Elle said.

"Out of the van," Joe told the women, and they scrambled out.

Joe and Ryan took up positions on either side of them, blocking them from view as they kept an eye on the quiet street.

"Three, two, one," Elle said, and then there was a clanking as the electronic gates opened.

"You sure this guy doesn't have any staff?" Joe asked as they rushed towards the front door and the gates clanked shut behind them.

"Doesn't trust them," Elle said. "They only come in when he's home."

"Street is clear and quiet," Ed said.

Ryan had his tools out and was busy picking the lock on the door. Joe kept his eyes peeled for trouble, all the while aware that Julia was back to avoiding eye contact again. It was a huge step backwards. One he couldn't afford to think about during an op. He needed to focus on keeping them safe and getting them out of there.

"We're in," Ryan said. The door opened and they piled into the house, closing it behind them.

The building was even uglier on the inside than the

outside. The walls were whitewashed cement or exposed brick. The furniture was minimal, to the point of there being rooms with only the odd, uncomfortable chair. The rest of the space was dominated by Thomas Hayes' art collection.

Ryan whistled as Patricia's mouth hung open. Julia's eyes were so wide that she looked like a meerkat. They were inside a private museum. There were huge contemporary paintings on the walls, and sculptures dotted everywhere. His taste ran from ancient artefacts to contemporary art.

"That's a Paula Rego," Julia said with awe. She looked at her gran. "I don't think he could afford that. I think it was probably intended to hang in the British Embassy."

Patricia pointed at the far wall. "That tapestry went missing from a Colombian museum two years ago. I wrote a paper on it when I was a grad student. It's worth a fortune. A unique piece of South American history."

"And Thomas Hayes has it." Julia pointed at some of the pieces in turn. "Antony Gormley, Jenny Saville, Rachel Whiteread, David Hockney. He's filled the house with work by famous British artists. This collection is worth millions, and I'd say most of it has been appropriated through his job or attained on the black market."

"By appropriated, you mean he stole it from the British Council?" Ryan said. "I don't know anything about art—you might as well be listing made-up names for all I know. But I recognise money when I see it in action."

There was a horrible pause. Joe and Ryan were suddenly very focused on the wires running from the artwork.

"You thinking what I'm thinking?" Ryan flattened his face to the wall and peered behind the painting next to him.

"Fuck." Joe's eyes shot to the corners of the room.

"I'll take that as an affirmative," Ryan said.

"Joe," Julia said, "there are other words."

For once he didn't soften at her gentle reprimand. "Elle. We've screwed up. Our information was wrong. There's a second security system inside the house. It's seriously high-tech and it's monitoring the artwork. I'm betting we've already triggered a silent alarm."

They could hear Elle tapping furiously. "No police call-out. Must be a private security firm. See if you can get me a company name."

"I'll look for one. The rest of you scatter," Joe shouted. "Find the mummy. We don't have much time. Minutes at best."

The women ran.

Joe followed the wiring, looking for a name, for anything at all that would tell them who'd installed the system and who was monitoring it. "Whoever this is, they're good," he told Elle. "Ryan, you got anything?"

"No."

He heard running. Doors slamming.

"I've got it!" Patricia shouted, no longer caring if anyone heard.

"Ryan, go help them. I'll keep looking." Ryan ran after the women. "Ed? Any activity out there?"

"Nothing. I'm going to get the van running and make friends with the neighbour."

"You think we can use their house to hide out until this is over?"

"It's an option, and we don't have many. I'll look into it."

"Callum?" Joe said.

"I'm on my way. I'm heading for the back of the property. There's a driveway leading up to the house next door."

Over his comm, Joe heard a car swerve. "Same house as Ed's flirty maid?"

"Yeah."

"Joe," Ryan said, "we've got a problem."

Joe started running. "I can't look for a name, Elle. We'll just need to see who turns up."

"I'll keep digging," she replied. "There are other things I can do. The clinic at the end of the street is about to have a fire alarm problem. I'm hoping it will cause enough chaos to hide your getaway."

Sure enough, Joe heard the wailing alarm as soon as Elle finished telling him her plan. He ran up a few short stairs to a mezzanine level that backed onto the manicured garden and endless pool. The wall at the back of the property was high, cutting them off from the neighbours and making sure the garden wasn't overlooked.

"What is it?" He skidded to a halt in the middle of a room full of dead people.

There were pedestals everywhere. Each had a large glass dome on top, and under the domes sat the curled figures of mummified bodies, each one with its knees up to its chest and its arms wrapped around it. Twelve—there were twelve bodies. Their time-leathered skin had taken on the colours of the desert, and looked tight, wrinkled and brittle over their bones. It was hard to believe the husks had once been walking, talking people. Now they looked more like the contemporary art dotted throughout the building.

Around the mummy cases, the walls were filled with vibrant contemporary paintings of nudes, as though Hayes was trying to contrast life and death. It was a strange art exhibition. Made even more disturbing because it had only ever been intended for an audience of one.

"The pedestal is embedded in the concrete floor," Ryan said. "The dome is sealed onto the pedestal with this welded bar." He pointed at the metal rim that encircled the dome.

"Smash it," Joe said without hesitation.

"We tried," Ryan said grimly. "Reinforced glass."

"We can't shoot it. It'll take several bullets, and someone would call the cops," Joe said.

As if on cue, there were sirens.

"Ed?" Joe said.

"Fire trucks," Ed said. "They're blocking off the west entrance to the street. The firemen are clearing the area. Wait a minute." They heard him enter into a fast exchange in Spanish. "The cordon ends at the other end of this street. I've been told to back off and clear the road."

"What about the maid next door?" Ryan asked, obviously looking for another way out.

"She won't open the door."

"So much for your charm," Patricia said.

Ed ignored her. "A black SUV just pulled into the east end of the street." They heard an engine rev. "I'm going to drive down and block them. See if I can buy you a couple more minutes—if it's the security company."

"Give me the plate number. I'll see if I can dig anything up on the car," Elle told Ed.

Julia suddenly placed a hand on Joe's forearm. "Inside the front door, there's a small sculpture. The Anthony Caro. It's concrete and iron."

"You mean the thing that looks like a bit of girder was swallowed by some cement?" Ryan asked.

"That's it. Can you get it?" Julia said.

Joe nodded his permission, and Ryan sprinted away. "Julia, that won't make a dent in this. You're talking several bullets in the same spot to get through the glass."

"I have an idea," she said. "I think it will work."

"If anyone can make it work, it's you. Have at it." He pulled his gun out of its holster at the back of his jeans. "I'll keep watch."

"Gran," Julia said, "I need your engagement ring."

"You aren't going to damage it, are you?" To her credit,

Patricia didn't hesitate in pulling it off her finger and handing it over.

"I promise, if there's any damage, I'll have it repaired."

Patricia's hand fluttered to her throat. She was clearly not reassured.

Joe could hear Ed arguing with another guy. A guy who wanted access to the street. A firefighter was taking Ed's side. The new guy was arguing that he was security and needed to investigate an alarm. Their time was up.

Julia rooted around in her ever-present messenger bag and pulled out a tiny first-aid kit. She took out two Band-Aids. Ryan jogged into the room, carrying the sculpture with him.

"This thing is heavy." He looked at it. "And ugly."

Julia taped the ring, diamond-side down, to the glass on the flat side of the dome.

"It's weakest here." She stepped back. "Ryan, pull down your sunglasses and hit that ring as hard as you can with the sculpture."

It said a lot about the faith the team had in Julia that Ryan didn't ask any questions. Instead, he did as he was told. The thud was deafening. The glass splintered.

"What the…?" Ryan said.

"Again," Julia ordered.

He hit the ring again. The glass shattered. Ryan dropped the undamaged sculpture.

"I don't like that thing," Ryan said. "But I can't argue it's well made."

Julia scrambled to get her grandmother's ring from the debris, while Patricia reached in for the mummy. She cradled it to her as though it were a fragile baby.

"They're in the driveway," Ed said. "I'll do what I can to distract them. Two men. Armed."

"Oh no," Patricia said. "I left the cloth for wrapping the mummy in the hotel."

"No time to worry about it. We need to get out of here." Joe grabbed Julia's upper arm, nodded at Ryan to take Patricia and then ran for the glass door that led out onto the patio.

"Gimme that." Ryan tucked the mummy under his arm like a rugby ball and ran.

"Don't squeeze, you'll damage it," Patricia said.

"If we don't get over that wall, we'll all be damaged." Joe looked at the smooth wall encircling the garden. The smooth wall with glass shards embedded in the top of it.

"I'm sitting at the back of the neighbour's house," Callum said. "You get over that wall, you're in their garden. Then there's a fence between you and your ride out of here."

"The security guys are in the house," Ed said.

"Corner," Joe snapped, and they veered to the corner. "Ryan, I'll boost you. Cover the glass with your backpack and mine, then we'll boost the women over one at a time."

"Mummy first," Patricia said.

"Mummy second," Julia said as Ryan handed her the dead body. "You need to be over the other side to hold it."

Joe boosted Ryan up, and he used the butt of his gun to flatten some of the glass. He took the camera out of his pack and tossed it over the other side, then used the padded material to make a seat. He pulled himself up, straddling the wall.

"I am seriously praying that nothing sharp is going to make it through this bag and damage the crown jewels," he said.

Joe tossed up his backpack, and Ryan did the same thing with it. Then Joe held his hands out for Patricia. "Let Ryan help you over."

She nodded and did as she was told. There was a tiny

squeak when she landed on the other side. "I'm okay. I'm okay," she called.

"Mummy." Ryan held his arms out for it.

Joe took it from Julia and tossed it up to Ryan, who instantly tossed it down to Patricia.

"You've snapped a bone! I can't believe you snapped a bone! This body has been perfectly preserved for over five hundred years and you break it the first time you touch it. As soon as we get back to England, I'm talking to your mother about you. You upset Julia, talk when you shouldn't and now you're damaging artefacts."

"Hurry up," Ryan said. "Patty's threatening to tell tales to my mum."

Joe made a cradle with his hands, for Julia's foot. "Get up."

Julia didn't hesitate. "What about you?" There was worry in her eyes as she reached for Ryan. "You can't stay behind again."

There was shouting in the house behind them. Time was up.

"Don't worry. I'll be right behind you."

She bit her bottom lip as Ryan fed her over the other side of the wall. "Get down," Joe ordered, and Ryan jumped down the other side.

Joe took a few steps back and ran at the wall, using the corner to climb up to the place where Ryan had left the bags. He threw himself over the wall, feeling the glass rip his jeans, but not the skin. He took the backpacks down with him to the grass.

The relief in Julia's face made him feel hopeful that he could get things back to where they'd been before Ryan had outed her. Later. After they'd made it out of this.

"Run. Get over the fence." Beyond the tall fence, Callum kept the van running.

Ryan clambered over the fence like a cat, deftly managing

to avoid the spikes atop it. There was shouting. The hired security guards were in the yard. Without having to be told, Patricia handed the mummy to Julia and let Joe help her over the fence.

"Don't put any weight on the spikes. Take your time. Go up and over them. Stand on our shoulders. Use us like steps to climb over. We'll help support your weight and keep you steady."

"Are you sure you can be trusted with this, Ryan?" Patricia snapped.

"Absolutely." He didn't even try to sound sincere.

"Move," Joe ordered.

Patricia had one foot on Joe's shoulder while he held her leg to steady her. She felt around and placed her other foot on Ryan's shoulder. Ryan reached up and steadied her as she got her other leg over, and then he slid her down his body to her feet.

Joe took the mummy from Julia and threw it over the fence, past caring whether anyone caught it. The voices of the security guards were getting closer. Time was running out. If they didn't get over the fence fast, they'd get caught.

"You next." Joe crouched to help Julia climb up his body. "Hold on tight to the fence, baby. I'm going to stand up so you can step over it.

"Joe?" Julia's voice was shaky. "Please don't look up."

He couldn't help the grin, in spite of the circumstances. "Nobody's going to look up your dress."

"Unless we have to," Ryan added with a smile.

"Not helping," Joe told him. The voices were near the wall now. "Elle, you still there?"

"Yup."

"I need a diversion. The security guys are almost at the back wall."

"On it."

Julia was astride the fence, one foot on Joe's shoulder and one on Ryan's. "That's it. Stand on Ryan and swing your other leg over. He'll grab you and help lower you down."

Just as Julia swung her other leg over the fence towards Ryan, the alarm on Hayes' house blared. Julia jerked. Her foot slipped. She lost balance. And toppled.

Right towards the spikes.

CHAPTER 16

The alarm went off. Julia startled. A second. That was all it took. And then she was falling. Joe shouted. Hands grabbed at her. She saw the fence spikes come at her. She twisted to the side and fell, barely missing the deadly points.

There was a ripping sound and then Julia's descent jerked to a sudden halt.

"No blood. No blood." She felt Joe's hands on her body through the fence. "No damage. You're okay. You're going to be okay." She could hear panic turn to relief.

And then she realised his hands were on bare skin.

In one crashing second, her predicament came into startling focus. Her dress had caught on the spikes and she was now hanging from the fence like a coat on a peg. Her dress was up around her armpits and the lower half of her body was on view for everyone to see.

"Joe?" Julia frantically waved her arms as she tried to cover herself. It was impossible. They'd been pulled up and to the sides by her dress.

"It's okay, baby, it's okay. We're gonna get you down from there." His voice had turned husky and kind of strangled.

Julia squeezed her eyes shut. This was not happening. It was a dream. A nightmare. One of those ones where you're naked in public. She opened her eyes and stared straight into the face of a grinning Ryan.

"Nice underwear," he said.

She froze, well aware that she was wearing beige granny pants. Although her gran wouldn't be caught dead in them. Julia had picked the underwear for comfort. Cotton, for the heat. Beige because... Oh, drat, there was no excuse. Her underwear was only fit to be burned. But to be fair, she didn't think anyone would ever see it. Let alone most of her team.

"Joe!" Julia began to thrash around, trying to get off the fence.

"Shut your eyes," Joe snapped at Ryan.

"How am I supposed to help you if I can't see?"

Joe growled, sounding half feral. Ryan shut his eyes.

"Hurry up," Callum shouted through the open window of the car. "Ed says the mall cops are back in the house, but they won't stay there long."

"This isn't happening...this isn't happening..." Julia chanted.

Her boss could *not* see her waist-high beige knickers. Her —yeah, she couldn't even think of a word for what Joe was to her—her Joe *wasn't* staring at her backside. It was all just a nightmare.

"The travel website said to pack practical cotton underwear." She was blathering excuses for her terrible knickers. This is what her life had come to. She was stuck on a fence, flashing her underwear to half of Bolivia.

"Calm down, baby." She felt the brush of fingertips over the curve of her hips. "Although I like the words on your rear. Cute."

She'd forgotten about the words!

"I didn't know they were there. I bought the underwear in a five-pack and I didn't see the rear until I unpacked them." Yes. She's just told them that. This was now beyond mortifying. The words *Sweet Cheeks* were emblazoned across her behind, and Joe could see them.

"Words?" Ryan's eyes sprang open and he stared at her underwear. "What words?" Something snapped inside Julia, and she did something she'd never done in her life before—she kicked him.

"No looking," she said.

Ryan stared at her in astonishment as he rubbed his knee. "Julia Collins, you are becoming wild."

"Shut your damn eyes," Joe ordered, sounding ferocious.

"I'm sorry I kicked you." Now Julia's emotions were overloading her with humiliation and guilt.

"He deserved it," Joe said.

"He's right." Ryan shrugged. He was still grinning.

"I can't get you off—" Joe started.

Ryan interrupted, his grin even wider. "I bet I could. I'm younger and I have more stamina."

"As soon as I'm over this fence…" Joe said.

"Hurry the hell up!" Callum shouted.

There was shouting in Spanish behind her. Joe shouted back. Ryan's eyes opened again. This time, they weren't looking at her. They were looking behind her. She craned her neck and got a glimpse of the man in the garden they'd cut through. He was wearing overalls and holding a rake.

"Don't shoot him," Joe said. "He's the gardener."

"Who's calling the cops," Ryan pointed out as the guy ran for the house.

"We'll be gone by then. Julia, we can't lift your dress off the fence to unhook you. I have to cut it."

She whimpered and felt Joe stroke the bare skin on the small of her back.

"Ryan, put your hands on her waist and take her weight. Don't. Touch. Anything. Else."

"Bloody hell, you think I'd molest her?" Ryan took a step forward, and she felt his big, hot hands on her skin. His wide grip almost spanned her waist.

His face was almost level with Julia's, and she could feel the warmth of his body. Suddenly, she was wedged between two extremely hot men. If it hadn't been for the fence at her back and the fact she was almost hysterical, the experience might have sent her imagination into overload.

Ryan's muscles flexed. Her body was raised slightly, and the tight hold her dress had on her, under her arms and breasts, eased. There was a cutting sound.

"Okay, lower her to the ground," Joe said.

Ryan did as he was told, but his hands lingered. Once she was on her feet, he leaned into her, lowering his head to speak against her ear. "If you get fed up with this guy, give me a call."

She gasped. Ryan stepped back, letting what was left of her dress fall to below her knees. He opened his eyes and winked at her. Julia stood there, stunned. She felt a rush of air, heard Joe land on the ground beside her and then watched in shock as he punched Ryan on the jaw. The younger man staggered back, but when he righted himself, he was rubbing his jaw and grinning.

"I deserved that." He jogged to the car.

"That and more," Joe called after him. He turned to Julia. "Let's go." His voice had softened.

She couldn't move her feet. "How bad is it?"

He glanced up at the material still hanging from the top of the fence and then back down at her. "It depends on your perspective."

She felt behind her, and her fingers touched skin. Her

dress was missing from her shoulder blades down. Her backside was bare for the world to see.

"Get in the car!" Callum revved the engine.

Police sirens joined the wailing house alarm. Joe grabbed her hand and ran for the car. They squeezed into the back seat beside her grandmother, who was hugging a dead person.

Patricia reached out to pat Julia's hand as Callum sped down the street.

"Julia love, women who want to have sex don't buy their underwear in multipacks. They wear silk. Or lace. And never have messages written on their backsides." Patricia groaned. "I need to have a serious talk with your mother when we get back. I blame her."

Julia hung her head as Ryan laughed raucously from the front passenger seat.

Joe wrapped an arm around her shoulder and pulled her into his side. He kissed the top of her head. They zoomed through the back streets of La Paz, until they hit the main street leading up to their hotel.

"I need something to cover this," Patricia said as they pulled up at the hotel's main entrance. "I can't walk through the lobby with a stolen mummy."

"Ryan, give her your shirt," Callum ordered.

"Why me? That means I have to walk into the hotel half-naked. This is a classy hotel. I don't think they'd like that."

"Give her your shirt."

"This is my favourite T-shirt." He stroked a hand down the *Grateful Dead* logo.

"Give. Her. Your. Shirt." It sounded like Callum was about to explode.

Ryan stripped off his shirt and tossed it to Patricia, who pulled it over the mummy's head.

"He's not the only one half-naked," Julia said to Joe. "I

can't walk in there like this. You'll have to go up to my room and get me something to wear. I'll wait here."

"Nobody's waiting here. We've got half of Bolivia chasing us after that screw-up. We need to get inside, get packed and get out of here." Callum looked back at Patricia. "You need to read the dead person and get us a location, because we're leaving La Paz within the hour. I don't care where we go, but we're getting out of here. Now, everybody, stop whining at me and get out of the damn car."

Ryan and Patricia scrambled out. Julia sat frozen in place.

"Don't worry," Joe said. "I know what to do. I'll cover your back. Stick with me."

Having no other choice, she followed Joe out of the car. As soon as they were out, he stood behind her and wrapped his arm around her body, beneath her breasts. He was plastered against the length of her, his front to her back.

"Okay," he said. "Step with me. You ready?"

No! she wanted to scream. She wasn't anywhere near ready. He took her silence as assent.

"Right foot, left foot," he said as they moved forward.

The bewildered doorman held the door for them as they passed him. A shirtless man, followed by an old woman carrying a mummy who was wearing a *Grateful Dead* t-shirt and then a couple who were joined at the hips—literally.

"Right, left, right, left," Joe said against her ear as everyone in the lobby turned to watch their procession to the lifts.

If Julia could have died from humiliation, it would have happened at that exact moment.

CHAPTER 17

They arrived in Cusco after dark, courtesy of Rachel's private plane. The capital city of the Incan Empire was a study in red-brick Spanish architecture, built on grey Incan stone foundations. At night, it was lit up in gold, the streets filled with tourists and locals, the mood welcoming.

Julia pulled her cardigan tight around her as she stood on the balcony overlooking the courtyard of their hotel. The building was over five hundred years old and used to be a monastery. The sandstone walls, with its red tile roof so ubiquitous in Cusco, had been built on top of the foundations of an Incan palace. So much history in one spot, and it was nothing compared to the rest of the city. They were in the centre of a cultural capital, the belly button of the Incan world, the staging post of Spanish domination and now a must-see destination for the international traveller. All that history; all those expectations from visitors. She wondered if the locals crumpled under the weight of living there.

"Take another photo of that piece."

Her grandmother's voice wafted up the stairs from the living room area of their small suite, to the bedroom mezzanine. She was busy going over the mummy's textiles with Elle. They were taking photos and scanning the information into Elle's laptop, where they could look at the images in more detail. They didn't want to miss a thing. All her grandmother had time to decode while they'd been in La Paz was their next destination—Cusco. Now the rest of the textiles had to be translated. And fast. Time was running out for Alice.

"Hey," Ryan, their current bodyguard, interrupted the busy women. "You want to go down for dinner or order in?"

"In!" the two women shouted.

They'd flown through dinnertime and it was late, though Julia still didn't have much of an appetite. Mainly, she was exhausted. She looked at the twin beds behind her with longing. Their soft, cool cotton sheets were calling to her. But with only a balcony rail between the bedroom area and the living area below it, there was no way she could get any sleep.

"Julia," Ryan called. "What do you want to eat?"

Another problem—she hadn't checked out the kitchens and wasn't sure if their standards met hers. She was just too tired.

"Nothing," she answered as she looked out over the flickering lights of the city to the darkness beyond, where she knew green hills surrounded them. "I think I'm going to take a walk down to the hotel chapel. I'll pick up something on the way."

"Stay inside the hotel. Don't wander." He thought about it for a second. "Maybe I should go with you."

"It's just down there." Julia pointed. "You can watch me from here."

"Okay, but if anything spooks you, come straight back."

Julia let herself out of their room and followed the long

corridor to the staircase leading down to the corner where the chapel was situated.

She crossed the courtyard, with its bubbling fountain and flagstone paving. All around her, the arched passageways of the building offered shaded spaces for guests to sit. Some of the arches were now part of the restaurant, and diners sat overlooking the courtyard as they ate. Julia could almost imagine monks scurrying about the place, tending gardens where the patio now stood, sheltering from the midday sun under the arches. It was like walking through history.

The chapel was small, but crammed full of gilt-framed paintings that ran from floor to ceiling. They came in all sizes, but were similar in style, having been painted five hundred years earlier. There were renditions of saints and Bible stories and church leaders. Julia sat in one of the wooden pews, her eyes towards the ornately carved pulpit, and wondered if it was wrong that the sacred space was now a meeting room for hotel guests.

"Is very pretty, no?"

Julia looked up to find a young woman dressed in the hotel uniform.

"Yes." Julia smiled at her.

"It is very popular for weddings," the woman said. "We have one booked this weekend. If you are still here, you might enjoy watching the ceremony. You will be able to see most of it from the courtyard."

"I wonder what the monks would think of their chapel hosting weddings." Julia was tired, and it loosened her tongue a little, allowing her to relax and chat with someone she'd only just met, rather than become tongue-tied and foolish looking.

"It's the nature of things, isn't it?" the woman said. "Before the building was a monastery, it was an Incan palace. In the basement, you can still see the stone walls they built."

"There's a basement?" Julia wondered if it was anything like the catacombs she'd longed to see in Lima.

The woman nodded. "We use only part of it for wine storage. I know the owners plan to develop the rest at some point. May I sit?"

Julia nodded, grateful for the diversion from her tense reason for visiting Peru. "Tell me about the history of the place," she said. "If you have time."

"I'd love to." The woman held out a hand. "My name is Maria."

And for the first time since coming to Peru, Julia felt like a normal person.

JOE FOUND Julia in the chapel, talking to one of the staff. He stood in the shadow of the doorway for a moment, watching her. Although still shy, she was smiling and laughing with the young woman. He knew she was taking a moment out of the trouble that swirled around them. She deserved more than a moment. This situation was stressful for anyone, but for someone like Julia, who struggled when outside of her comfort zone and routine, it must have been hell.

He was so damn proud of her. In her eyes, she was weak and scared, but in his she was courageous. The fact she was there, helping her gran, dealing with everything that was happening, was a testimony to her courage. Joe couldn't believe she was unable to see that for herself. Julia Collins was one of the bravest women he'd ever known.

He watched her stifle a yawn and noticed the darkening circles under her eyes. She was also exhausted. He pushed away from the door and sauntered towards her.

"I'd love to go to Sacred Valley," Julia was telling the young woman. "I read about it, and it sounds fascinating." The wistful tone in her voice broke his heart.

"I can arrange a tour for you," the woman offered.

Julia shook her head. "Maybe next time. Our schedules are very full."

"Si, next time." The smile was genuine. Yet another person enamoured with Julia's gentle heart.

"Hey, babe." Joe rested a hand on her shoulder, and she didn't pull away. In fact, she leaned into him a little. Yeah, she was tired. "I think it's time to get some food and sleep. You about ready to go?"

"Yes." She stood and smiled at the woman. "Thank you, Maria."

"My pleasure." The woman beamed and walked away.

"I swung past your suite," Joe said as he took her hand and led her from the old church. "It's full of people eating and staring at dead people. You won't get any sleep there tonight."

Her shoulders slumped. "I'll go past reception and see if they have another room."

"Or you could sleep in my room." She tripped over nothing, and Joe smiled. "Just sleep, babe, I promise. You're in no shape for anything else anyway."

Julia considered him for a moment, the warm yellow glow from the garden lights glinting off her hair as it shifted in the breeze. His fingers itched to touch, but he didn't.

"I need to stay away from you," she whispered.

Joe fought back the tension that surged through his body. "Why's that?"

"If I don't, you'll figure out how much of a freak I am."

Yeah, he wasn't going to let that go. He wrapped his arms around her and caressed her back. Her body softened against his instantly, showing him that her exhaustion had melted her defences.

"We're all freaks, baby. Haven't you figured that out yet?"

"Why are you so determined to convince yourself that my

freaky personality is normal? It's as though you don't care about all my weird habits."

"I don't." In fact, some of them were endearing.

Laughter rang up from the tables that spilled out into the courtyard. Soft music began to play. Nothing offensive. Elevator music.

"This is a strange place." Julia turned her face towards the gently bubbling fountain, her tone wistful, as though she was whispering secrets in the dark.

"How's that?" He nuzzled her temple, making her melt further into him.

"It was a palace for a king. Then it was a retreat for men who gave up everything to follow God. Now it's a tourist attraction where rich people pay through the nose to spend the night. They have business meetings in the chapel, surrounded by painted icons in gilt frames depicting saints. We sleep on beds worth more than the yearly income of some of the locals, and we do it beneath five-hundred-year-old paintings of Jesus."

Joe turned her in his arms as tenderness overwhelmed him. He cupped her cheek, revelling in her satin-smooth skin, and ran his thumb under her eye.

"You're exhausted."

"I'm okay." She contradicted her own words by resting her forehead against his chest and turning boneless in his arms. Even standing, she was fighting sleep.

"Come on." Joe tugged her back towards her suite. "Grab your toothbrush. You're sleeping in my room tonight."

"Joe…" She trailed off, obviously past fighting.

"I won't take advantage of you like this. I promise, I'll let you sleep."

"I know you will." She stood on tiptoe and he felt soft lips brush a kiss over his. The shock of her touch almost made him crumble.

Joe cupped her nape and pressed a kiss to her forehead before knocking on the door to her suite. Ryan let them in. The living area was a mess, food and paperwork everywhere. Elle and Patricia were poring over the mummy, while Ed and Ryan watched football on TV. Joe felt Julia cringe as she took in the chaotic sight.

"Get your things," he said. "I'll tell your gran you'll be with me tonight."

She nodded and headed for the stairs up to the mezzanine, slightly unsteady on her feet. As Joe filled Ryan and Patricia in on their new sleeping arrangements, Julia came back downstairs, her huge messenger bag across her body.

"Ready?"

"Yes. Take me to bed, Joe." Her sleepy eyes went wide and her cheeks flushed pink. "I mean—"

"I know what you mean." He was smiling when he placed his palm on the small of her back and led her out into the corridor.

"I got stuck on a fence today," Julia said out of the blue, sounding more than a little bewildered.

"Yep, you did." It was a sight he'd never forget—for more than one reason.

"Everyone saw my underwear." Her brow puckered.

"Not everyone. And those who did better not mention it or they'll have me to deal with."

"Thanks, Joe." With a smile, Julia leaned into him.

JOE KEPT HIS PROMISE. It was hell.

Even though Julia hesitated when she realised there was only one bed in his room, she'd still headed on through to the bathroom and came out a few minutes later wearing pink satin pyjamas, consisting of a camisole top and matching sleep pants.

She'd smiled shyly when his eyebrows had gone up at the sleepwear. For a woman who liked to live in grey and beige shapeless clothes, her sleepwear was something else entirely. The dichotomy fascinated him—like everything else about her. Julia was a complex woman who would keep any man interested for the rest of his life.

Joe motioned to the snacks he'd had delivered while she'd been in the bathroom. "I know you don't feel hungry, but have something small before you go to bed. You'll sleep better."

She nodded and headed for the tiny dining table set up by the window, overlooking the city. "What are these?"

"Bite-sized empanadas. They're deep fried, stuffed with vegetables and have minimal spices." He paused, wondering if he should tell her the rest, wondering if she'd be upset over his actions. He took the chance. "I asked what temperature they used for their oil before I ordered. I also asked about kitchen hygiene. They meet an international code. The manager said they haven't had even a mild case of stomach upset since they opened. He also told me the temperature they wash dishes in. That's okay, right?"

Her eyes shot to his, and she nodded. They stayed like that for a moment, lost in each other's gaze. The air became thick between them.

Julia blinked and picked up a pastry. "Thank you." She broke the spell holding them frozen in time. She nibbled at the pastry before gesturing to the food. "You having some?"

"Later." He came over to sit at the table beside her. "I've got some emails to go over and I'll eat while I do it. Unless it will bother you." Joe's room was a standard king; he had a tiny balcony and a bathroom, but no extra space to retreat to. Although the room was big enough that he shouldn't disturb her while she slept.

"I could probably sleep standing. In fact, if I was still hanging from that fence, I could have slept there."

He smiled at the memory. His heart had been in this throat at the sight of her hanging there. Every emotion had rushed through him one on top of another, making it hard to think straight. There was horror at her falling, terror that she'd be hurt, relief that she wasn't and then pure, unadulterated lust at the sight of her curvy ass.

Yeah, best not to think about that.

They fell into a heavy silence, their thoughts loud enough to make the room vibrate.

"Gran snores," Julia said suddenly, slicing through the thick air.

Joe's eyes snapped to hers.

"Loudly," she said. "And it's impossible to wake her. Or to sleep through it."

His lips twitched. He wanted to laugh. She was too damn cute. "Good you're in here, then."

"You don't snore?"

He thought about that for a minute. Surely someone would have mentioned if he snored? "I don't think so."

"I'll let you know if you do."

Her eyes went wide again at the reminder they were about to share a bed. She reached for the coca leaf tea he'd ordered for her. Although Cusco was still at high altitude, it was nowhere near the height of La Paz, but he knew she liked the taste of the tea. She swayed in her seat, and she'd only managed to eat half her pastry. It was better than nothing.

"Go to bed," Joe said.

Julia nodded and stood slowly, as though it was taking conscious effort to stay upright. "What side do you want?" Her voice trembled slightly as she pointed to the bed.

"Any side. I don't care."

"Okay." She went to the left side, threw back the covers and climbed into bed.

A strange sense of rightness flooded through Joe's veins at the sight of Julia in his bed. It was where she belonged.

"Night, Joe." She faced the edge of the bed and closed her eyes.

Joe turned off the lights, all except for the lamp beside the table. "Night, baby."

She was sound asleep within seconds. Joe sat going over emails about Carlos Esteban, while he polished off the rest of the food and watched over Julia. It was perfect.

An hour later, he stripped to his shorts and climbed into bed. As promised, he kept his hands to himself, content in the knowledge that Julia was beside him. She trusted him enough to share a bed, to sleep with him, and that was a gift he wouldn't squander.

Baby steps, he reminded himself as he felt sleep take him. Baby steps.

CHAPTER 18

Julia woke up to a warm, but empty bed. She heard water running in the bathroom. Joe. She remembered crawling into bed, but everything after that was blank. Obviously exhaustion had caught up with her and she'd slept like the dead. Typical. Only she would manage to go to bed with Joe Barone and have nothing to show for it.

The early morning light was soft against the pale yellow walls. The plaster was uneven in places, a chic decorating technique to make the place seem rustic and remind the guests of the history of the building. On the wall facing the bed was one of the many religious paintings in the hotel's collection. Julia knew that some of them were almost as old as the building. This one showed a warrior angel, and she was pretty sure the image in the clouds was supposed to be God. The painting reminded her of some of the Renaissance works she'd seen in the National Art Gallery in London. Although, to her untrained eye, it didn't pack the same punch as a Caravaggio. The massive, ornate gold-leafed frame gave the painting weight, though. She could imagine monks in centuries past, kneeling at the base of the artwork and using it to help them focus on God.

"What are you thinking about?"

When she looked over, she found Joe leaning against the doorjamb, drying his hands on a towel. His hair was sleep-rumpled, his chest was bare and his jeans were unbuttoned. Now that was a vision worthy of painting.

"The art." She pointed at the painting. "I was thinking that Caravaggio is better."

His lips twitched into a sensuous smile. "I don't know who that is, babe."

"Oh, he was a scoundrel, wanted for murder and unpaid debts. He lived the life of a party animal, and when he wasn't drinking, womanising and gambling, he painted. And he managed to paint some of the most powerful religious art ever made." She was babbling. Something she had a tendency to do around Joe. She'd learned long ago that people didn't want to know the facts that were stored in her nerdy mind, and yet Joe had a way of making her say them anyway. When he smiled at her, she felt the need to explain. "Gran was an art professor. Visiting with her was always a lesson of some sort. She'd take us to look at the Caravaggios in the National Gallery, amongst other things."

"Sounds like an interesting guy. Maybe you could take me sometime?"

"Gran would be the best one to go with. She knows all the wildest stories about the artists."

Joe's grin was dazzling. "Julia, I was asking you out on a date."

"Oh." Her cheeks flushed and she became intensely aware that she was in his bed. "A date seems kind of redundant, Joe, considering where I am right now."

That made him laugh, and the sound was like music. It made her blood rush faster.

"I kept my promise." Joe's eyes seemed suddenly darker. "I kept my hands to myself and let you sleep."

It was suddenly difficult to swallow. "Thanks."

He pushed off the doorjamb and sauntered towards her. The air in the room became charged, sending tingles across her skin. She flicked her tongue out to wet her suddenly dry lips.

"It's morning now," Joe said. "You're awake." He put a knee on the bed. "I think you should kiss me."

The words, along with the heat in his eyes, melted her reserve. She realised, in that moment, that her need for Joe now outweighed her fear of getting involved with him. And she badly wanted to feel his lips against hers. Only…

"I can't. I haven't brushed my teeth."

His eyes twinkled. "Do you have to do that before you kiss me?"

She nodded. Kissing was unsanitary enough without adding morning breath to the experience.

"Okay then, go brush your teeth." With a smile, he sat on the edge of the bed.

Julia threw back the blanket and scurried around the bed to the bathroom. Once inside, she splashed cold water on her face, then used Joe's toothpaste to brush her teeth. All the while, she examined her feelings and thoughts to see if she had any reservations. There were some, but they'd faded to insignificance. She needed to make a list. That was what she needed to do, but her iPad was in the room with Joe. She'd have to do it mentally. Inside her head she imagined a large whiteboard, and a black marker in her hand, and she began to write a list of her reservations.

1. She was seriously weird.

1a. Joe seemed to like that about her.

2. His alpha behaviour scared the life out of her.

2a. He only ever used his strength to make her feel secure.

3. She had very little sexual experience, and she was betting Joe had lots. The chances of humiliating herself were high.

3a. She'd already humiliated herself more in the past few days than she had in her entire life previously, and she'd survived. Plus, Joe made it clear he wanted her no matter what her experience. (Although it might be a good idea to mention it to him before they start.)

4. The chance of him getting tired of her freaky personality was high. Therefore, this relationship had no hope of being long term.

4a. Maybe, just maybe, she had courage enough to accept that they were only having a fling. After all, she'd had the courage to come to Peru. And to deal with a shootout and a burglary. So what if this thing with Joe didn't last? She'd survive. Although…

5. When their time together ended, she still had to work with him. That could be awful.

5a. She could get another job. She loved her job with Benson Security, but she could get a different one, if it meant she wouldn't have to watch Joe move on to other women.

By the time Julia had made her list, she'd rearranged everything in the bathroom to ensure they were in groups of three, with all their labels facing forward.

She groaned and she glanced at the closed door. She'd been in the bathroom a long time—Joe had probably given up on her. Even if she did walk out to be with him, he was most likely already gone.

That didn't change the one question she had to answer before she took this chance.

Was being with Joe worth the heartache that was bound to come after?

With a deep breath, Julia opened the door.

· · ·

JOE LEANED back onto his elbows on the bed, his feet still on the floor and his eyes on the bathroom door. He could hear muttering and things being moved around. He would bet his last dollar that she was either trying to talk herself into getting physical with him, or talk herself out of it. There was nothing he could do except wait for the verdict, but every fibre of his being hoped it went in his favour.

When the door opened, he found he was holding his breath. One look at Julia's face and he knew he'd won. A wave of relief, followed closely by urgent need, flowed through him.

He sat up slowly. "Come here." His voice had dropped an octave, and if it were possible, he would have purred.

Julia walked to him without hesitation, coming to a halt in the spot he'd pointed to, between his knees. She put her hands on his shoulders and looked into his eyes.

"I don't have a lot of experience," she said. It was so earnest that it made his heart ache.

"You don't need a lot." Joe curled his hands around the curve of her hips and pulled her to him.

She nibbled at her bottom lip. "I'll probably screw this up."

"What makes you think I won't be the one to screw this up?"

She blinked at him, startled. "I hadn't thought of that. It doesn't seem possible. You're...perfect."

Joe shook his head. "Jules," he said on a sigh. "I'm no more perfect than anyone else. We all have faults. Some of us are just better at hiding them, that's all."

Her nose scrunched in obvious disbelief. "I think you're humouring me, Joe Barone. Name one fault you have."

He tugged her closer, until their chests were pressed together and their lips were a hairbreadth apart. For once, he let her see the intensity he usually hid behind a veneer of charm. She sucked in a breath at the sight.

"You've seen Grunt with Claire," he said, of his Neanderthal best friend and his wife. "The way he does that possessive 'mine' crap with her?"

She nodded, and for once there was no gentle reprimand to keep his language clean.

"I'm worse than Grunt, baby. Always have been. When I see something I want, something I know belongs to me, I have to fight not to claim it and lock it up where no one else can get at it. I make Grunt's possessive streak look normal. The only difference is that the big bastard has never tried to hide it, whereas I'm very good at hiding what I need."

"Don't swear," she whispered.

His lip twitched. "Do you understand what I'm saying?"

"I'm not stupid. You're saying you have an obsessive and possessive streak."

He slid his hands under her camisole to caress the soft skin on her back. Smooth and warm. Her eyelids fluttered down before she lifted them again.

"It isn't a streak. It's all of me." He inclined his head and nuzzled at the crook of her neck, his lips touching golden skin as he breathed in her subtle scent of spring flowers. Delicious. She was delicious, and he couldn't resist a taste. He flicked out his tongue to swirl before he gently nibbled at the muscle. He felt her shiver under his firm hold. Her fingers dug into his shoulders as her breathing sped up.

When he stopped kissing her throat and looked at her face, her cheeks were pink and her eyes were slightly glazed. Beautiful. So incredibly beautiful.

"That's hardly a terrible flaw." Her voice was husky.

"No?" He cocked an eyebrow at her. "The need to possess. To own. It's a hunger. An all-consuming drive I have to fight every day. If I didn't, the things I wanted for mine would never see the light of day, would never be free."

"Things?" It was barely a whisper.

Of course she would focus on that word, when he was trying to protect her from the heart of him. The need in him that constantly raged like a consuming fire, and which he continuously fought to ensure it wouldn't take over completely.

"You should be worried." He felt the need to be honest with her. To give her this one last chance to escape—even though it almost broke him to do it.

"Why?" She searched his eyes, looking for the answer.

"Because"—he closed the slight distance between them and spoke against her lush lips—"I've never wanted anything more than I want you. This is your last chance. If you want out, go now. I don't think I can let you go if we take this further."

Her hands came up to cup his cheeks. "Yes. You would."

He started to disagree, but she shocked him by pressing a gentle kiss to his lips to silence him.

"I know you would let me go, because you aren't only about possession. You're about honour. And your honour would never let you keep someone against their will. Your honour is the reason you fight your need to consume. Your honour is the reason you're telling me this. You'll never cage me, because you'll always fight against the need. It's who you are."

Joe was in awe. To see himself through her eyes was to see a hero. If he hadn't been crazy about her before her earnest declaration, he would be now. Because he wanted nothing more than to live his life seeing himself through Julia's eyes. He wanted to tell her he loved her, all of her, but he knew the words would terrify rather than give hope, and she was right about one thing: he would rather die than hurt her.

"Kiss me again, baby," he said instead of declaring his love.

"Will you kiss me back?" Her timid smile told him she was teasing.

"Always." It was a vow.

This time when her lips touched his, Joe cupped her nape and splayed a hand on the small of her back. He pulled her flush against him. The minty taste of toothpaste did nothing to detract from the deliciousness that was Julia. She slid her hands off his shoulders to wrap her arms around him. The position lifted her breasts as they pressed against his chest. He felt her hard little nipples, heard her panting breaths around their kiss. Her lips were full and soft and lush. He wanted to nibble on them for hours.

Under his hands he felt her body grow languid. Their kiss deepened, becoming an intense dance of tongue and teeth. It was as though he'd been kissing her forever. When they broke apart, they were both breathing heavily. Julia's cheeks were flushed a deep, rosy pink, and her eyes were dark with desire.

"More?" His voice was husky with need.

"More."

Joe slid his hands down the pink satin of her camisole until he hooked underneath.

"Off," he said.

There was a slight hesitation before Julia lifted her arms to let him slide the material over her head. He removed it slowly, knowing that the glide of material over her skin would be a sensual delight. A tiny gasp escaped her when the satin tugged over her engorged breasts.

"Beautiful," Joe told her as he looked down at the rounded handfuls, with rosy nipples that matched the colour of her cheeks.

He tossed the top to the floor and ran his hands up and

down her back as he looked into her eyes. All he saw shining out at him was desire.

She cupped his cheeks and studied him. "You really believe it when you say things like that, don't you?" She sounded awed.

Joe couldn't believe her words. To be so stunning and yet never see it. How was that possible? But Julia was more than her beauty. There was a golden light inside of her. One that couldn't be hidden. Even if she wasn't gorgeous to look at, she would still *be* gorgeous, because of who she was. Her beauty was soul deep. The kind that would never fade or tarnish. She would always be stunning to him. Always.

"You," he said huskily, "are beautiful inside and out. You humble me."

"Oh, Joe," she whispered.

He could tell she was touched, but unconvinced. It didn't matter. He planned to spend a lifetime convincing her.

Joe lowered his face, nuzzling her throat and neck. She arched into his touch, angling her head to give him better access. Her little gasps of pleasure, as he licked and nipped and sucked her ivory skin, made his heart beat faster.

Joe felt her knees weaken and tightened his hold on her waist to keep her in place. Her skin was warm and soft, easily marked by his kisses. He gentled his touch, wanting to make sure he didn't hurt her.

"No." Julia clutched at his shoulders. "Harder."

"You'll bruise." And he wouldn't do that to her.

"I want to feel you. I want to know this is real and not another dream."

Her whispered confession made his hold tighten, and he fought to relax. "This is real. I promise you."

"Then make me feel it."

Her plea made his restraint snap. Holding her tight, he lifted her and twisted them both onto the bed behind him.

Joe lay at her side, his body flush against her, his arm supporting his weight above her head, while his other hand wandered.

Dazed eyes looked up at him as Julia threaded her fingers into his hair and tugged his mouth down for a kiss. He took her with a ferocity that left them both breathless. All the while, his hand shaped and caressed her breasts. Learning what she liked, feeling the weight of her. He pinched her nipple before tracing his finger around the areola. Her back came off the bed to press into his touch.

"More," she gasped against his kiss-swollen lips.

He felt dazed, out of control, lost in her. "What do you want, Julia? I'll give you anything you want."

"I want your mouth," she whispered somewhat desperately. "I want to feel your mouth on my b-breasts." She stumbled over the words, as though shocked she could say them out loud.

Joe didn't make her ask twice. Supporting his weight on both arms, he lowered his head and sucked one of her nipples into his mouth. He was relentless, sucking her deep, letting her feel the ferocity of his need, making her lift off the bed and claw at the sheet beneath them. When he rasped her nipples with his teeth, she moaned and suddenly clasped the back of his head. Her fingers tightened in his hair, tugging, keeping him in place.

"Harder," she moaned. "Oh, please."

He gave her what she wanted, sucking hard while he teased the neglected nipple on her other breast with his fingers. She went wild beneath him, all fire and passion. A raging fire that could easily be stoked into an inferno. She writhed with his touch, her gasps and moans a symphony to his ears. Her hips were undulating, seeking something that wasn't there, making her groan with frustration.

"Joe, I need you." It was a plea.

He released her nipple with a pop. "I know what you need." He crawled up her body and took her mouth with his. This wasn't a kiss. It was a possession. And the strangest thing about it was that it wasn't him who was doing the possessing. He felt taken over by Julia. Consumed by her.

And it was wonderful.

He felt hands on his chest. Nails across his nipples. Her fingers trailed back and forth in the hair between his pecs. He was swimming in her. Floating away on her taste and touch.

He ran his hand from her throat, between her breasts and over her navel until he reached the waistband of her pants.

Breaking the kiss, he supported himself on his elbow while he looked down at her. She was panting; the flush in her cheeks had blossomed out to touch her throat and chest.

"How far?" He didn't want to scare her. Didn't want her regretting this. Regretting them. He needed to know how far he could take it.

She tugged at the back of his head. Joe instantly understood. There were things Julia could only whisper in darkness. That wouldn't always be the way between them, but for now, if it made her feel more secure, he'd happily give her it.

He turned to give her his ear.

"I'm on the pill," she whispered.

Every muscle in his body went taut. He studied her face, looking for any sign that she might feel this was something she had to rush into. She didn't. Not with him. He would wait a lifetime for her. Her eyelids were lowered, her cheeks redder than seconds earlier. She was embarrassed by her own boldness.

"Baby?" When she looked at him, the depth of longing he found in her eyes was a punch that sent him reeling. Because it was for him. "You trust me that much?"

She sucked her bottom lip in between her teeth and then

gave him a jerky nod. He was about to say something when she opened her lips. He waited for her to speak.

"I'm not a virgin." Her face turned luminous. "And I know you would protect me if you thought you could harm me."

Hell! She brought him to his knees. He had to clear his throat to speak. "I've been tested. I'm clean." He brushed his fingers through her silky hair. "And I would die before I hurt you."

Her eyes turned impossibly dark. "Then take me," she whispered.

His eyes locked on hers, so he couldn't miss it when it happened.

He saw the moment Julia Collins gave herself to him. He saw her give her soul. Willingly. To him. Joe snatched it before she could take it back. He hid it deep inside of himself, where nothing could touch it. Where it would be safe. Where he could protect her. Because nothing would get through him to damage the precious gift Julia had just given him. Nothing.

She was his. Julia was his. She might not have realised what just happened, but Joe didn't care. He'd coax her along until she caught up. But this woman was his. Forever. To protect. To love. To keep.

He fell on her with a hungry kiss that stole his senses. All he could think of, all he could see, hear, smell, feel was Julia. This woman who humbled him with her courage and trust.

Joe dipped his hand under the waistband of her sleep pants, feeling the edge of cotton against his fingertips. He'd never felt anything sexier. A desperate need to see her naked almost derailed him. But this was about Julia. This was about building a future for them. And the foundation had to be perfect.

He slid his fingers under the cotton, feeling damp, silken curls. He trailed a finger through her wetness, making her lift her hips from the bed. She thrust her tongue into his mouth and groaned. Desperate—she sounded desperate. He circled the little nub of nerves that would drive her even closer to the edge, swallowing her gasps and moans. Her breasts pressed against his chest. Soft to hard. Nails dug into his shoulder as he drove her higher. She was so slick with wanting him that he had to fight the urge to rip her pants off and plunge deep inside of her.

Slowly, oh so slowly, he dipped a finger inside her, feeling her clench around him. A sweat broke out on his back when she forgot to kiss him, lost in sensation and unable to focus on anything else. Joe shifted lower to her throat. Her head went back as he rubbed circles around her clit. Her knees fell wide. Her hips pushed up to him and he moved his finger in and out of her, mimicking the action he'd soon enact. Short, shallow breaths, eyes shut, cheeks flushed, her lips parted as she gasped his name. He'd never seen anything so beautiful and knew he never would. This was it. Julia was the standard by which everything else would be judged, and he already knew he'd find it wanting.

"Joe." It was a slightly hysterical plea.

He felt her muscles tremble and tense. She tightened around his finger, making him ache to be inside her. He pressed his thumb to her clit and watched her explode. A second of tense nothing—no breathing, no noise, no movement—before everything in her shuddered and gasped and reached for him. Her thighs pressed together, keeping him in place. He didn't stroke her any more, knowing she was sensitive. Instead, he kissed her throat and soothed her with murmured words, telling her how beautiful she was and how wonderful she'd been.

With languorous movements, her thighs relaxed to release his hand, and she shuddered when his finger slid out of her. A slow, heavy flutter of her eyelids before she looked up at him. *No,* she looked *into* him. In that moment, he knew she could see his soul. He only hoped she knew what she was looking at, because his soul was tattooed with her name. He was hers. Forever.

Julia lay sated and pliant as Joe slid her sleep pants and underwear down her legs. He stood to take off his jeans, lost for words at the sight of her, naked on his bed. A second later, he was crawling between her thighs, pressing his body against hers. He stared into her eyes, wanting to tell her he loved her, terrified it would ruin everything if he did. All he could do was show her.

His kiss was gentle, slow, teasing as he pressed his hard length into her. She wrapped her arms around his neck and hooked her feet over his thighs, surrounding him. Grounding him. The world faded completely as he slid inside her. There was only Julia. He couldn't put what was happening into words. His mind was recording every sensation, every movement, every sound she made. He felt her wet heat grip him tight. Somewhere in the back of his mind, he noted how perfectly they fit, but it was a fleeting whisper of a thought. In this place, a place where only they existed, there was no space for thought. Only feeling. Knowing. Showing.

As he rocked his hips, he watched her eyes close in slow motion, as though it was too much effort to keep them open. Joe slid a hand under her rear, angling her the way he needed her, until he pressed against that secret part of her that sent shocks of wildfire dancing over her skin. She clenched around him, making him groan. He wanted this to last for hours but knew it would be over far too soon.

Their hips moved as one, in a perfect rhythm that had them gasping for air. Her legs tightened around him. Joe felt her nipples rasp against his chest. He leaned up to watch her face as he spoke to her with his body. As he told her she was it for him. She was his forever. And she would always belong to him.

He felt the tightening at the base of his cock. His legs tingled. His muscles clenched.

"Mine," he barked. "Mine."

He moved his hand out from under her, splaying his fingers low on her abdomen, aiming for that little button of pleasure, stroking it hard, making her tense with him. Making her fall with him. Together. Always.

Her head fell back, her neck flexed, she wailed her release and he felt her milk him with muscles deep inside of her. A second later, he followed, in an explosion of jerking muscle and blinding sensation.

It was over too soon, his muscles suddenly unable to hold his weight, but he wasn't ready to release her. So he rolled until Julia was spread on top of him and he was still inside of her.

She groaned her complaint, but otherwise didn't move. They lay there, boneless and worn out, sated for the time being. Joe stroked his hand down her back to the curve of her behind. So much more to touch, to do. He'd need a lifetime to learn her.

Julia wriggled a little, sending shock waves throughout his body.

"I can't believe we did that with an angel watching," she said with a husky voice. "That is so wrong."

Joe looked up at the painting facing the bed and started to chuckle. He held Julia tight as he rocked her body with his laughter. Which grew even more raucous when Julia grumbled at him. He wrapped his arms tight around her and felt her smooth, soft roundness against him.

Bliss. This was bliss. Now he just had to convince her that this was forever.

Because he wouldn't settle for less.

CHAPTER 19

The summons came as Julia was getting out of the shower. Five minutes later, the team were assembled in Patricia's living area. They were sombre and Patricia was shaking—Esteban had been in touch.

"Did you sleep at all?" Julia said as she hugged her gran tightly.

"No, but we're almost finished reading the textiles. We'll have an exact location soon."

"You need a nap first, and some food."

"No." Patricia kissed her head before stepping back. "First we need to watch Alice again."

"Did they say anything or just give you another internet address?"

"They said they wanted the mummy and I told them I needed more time. They said I could have more time, but they had a message from Alice first. That's when a text with another internet address came through."

"Elle?" Julia called. "Is it a different address?" In other words, was Alice still being held in the same location?

"Yeah." Elle stopped hooking her laptop up to the TV for a

second to hold Julia's eyes. Julia saw the same worry she felt reflected back at her. "I'm going to try for a trace while they broadcast. Hopefully, we'll get a lock on the new IP."

The computer genius was dressed in tiny red shorts and a white t-shirt with a red printed photo of Princess Leia wielding a gun and the words *A Woman's Place Is in the Resistance*. Julia was wearing shorts too. Ones she'd bought in La Paz airport after the dress fiasco. Unlike Elle's, Julia's were what her sister liked to call "mom shorts"—because they came almost to her knees.

"You about ready?" Elle asked Patricia.

"Yes. Of course."

But Julia could see her gran's hands shake.

"Will this be the same as last time?" Julia asked Elle. "Are we just watching?"

"I think so. I won't enable any cameras or sound at our end unless we have to."

Julia reached out to put a hand on her gran's back, offering comfort, as her eyes automatically found Joe's. He was standing by the door, talking in whispered tones to Ryan and Callum, but he didn't take his eyes from her. It was reassuring, and she somehow drew strength from his attentiveness.

"Right, I've typed in the address. I'm going to press enter. Pick your spot and settle down," Elle said.

Joe immediately came over to stand beside Julia. He didn't touch her, and she was grateful for that; it would have shattered the thin control that was keeping her sane while she waited to see Alice at the mercy of a madman. Julia felt someone else come up, and was pleased when Ed took her gran's hand in his.

"This will be over soon," Ed said to Patricia. "You'll feel better once you get back to work on the textiles. You're doing a great job, so close to finishing. Concentrate on that instead of this. It will help. You'll both be much safer once the gold is in our hands."

Gran gave him a weak smile.

The large TV blinked on, and they were watching another nondescript brick room. The room was mostly dark, the single bulb illuminating a cone of space beneath it.

Alice staggered into the light, as though someone pushed her. Julia folded her arms to stop from shaking. Alice was rumpled and dirty. Her hair was messy and there were dark circles under her eyes that made her seem gaunt.

"Patricia? Patricia darling, I'm sorry I haven't been in touch. We've been busy scouting locations for my new show."

Julia felt Joe tense at her side, his attention firmly on the screen.

"I met the new director." Alice's smile was wide and terrifyingly manic. "He's had a lot of experience making TV shows and he's very powerful within the industry. I'm lucky to be working with him. He's going to make me a star for sure."

Her act was fooling no one. She wasn't even putting any effort into it this time. The whole thing was desperate and a touch hysterical. It filled Julia with a cold sort of dread that seeped into her bones. She felt Joe's arms wrap around her and his front press against her back, before she even realised he'd moved. She'd been wrong—his touch didn't destabilise her. It made her stronger. And she needed his strength while she watched helplessly as the terrified Alice tried to be brave.

"The new boss, Mr. Esteban." Alice's voice faltered, and Callum cursed under his breath.

Julia felt Joe's arms flex and realised that Alice knowing her captor's name wasn't a good thing.

"Mr. Esteban"—Alice cleared her throat—"wants to remind you that you need to deliver his mummy." There was no joke this time. All attempts to play a part had vanished.

Alice's eyes kept straying off camera, and she visibly paled.

"H-he wants you to understand that time is running out." Suddenly her eyes went wide. "No," she said. "No." She backed away from the camera.

Julia stopped breathing. Joe's hold tightened.

Arms appeared out of the darkness behind Alice. A man with a mask. He held her upper arms and jerked her back into a chair.

"No! No! I did what you wanted. I told her." She looked at the camera, frantic now, tears streaming down her face. "I told you, Patricia. You heard me, I know you did. I told you." She started shaking her head frantically.

Julia curled her hands around Joe's arm and held on tight. The world stopped. Tilted. She became disorientated as she tried to make sense of what she was seeing.

"What are they doing?" Patricia was panicked. "What are they doing to her?"

Julia watched in horror as they strapped Alice's wrists to the arms of the chair. Alice was crying hysterically now, shouting nonsense, kicking her legs out. Struggling. Another man appeared in the frame and fastened her ankles to the legs of the chair.

The man behind Alice grabbed a handful of her hair and tugged her head back until she screamed. Julia recoiled, her nails digging into Joe's arm. Inside, she was screaming along with Alice. The masked man held Alice's head by her hair. The other man was holding her knees. A third masked man appeared on the left. He held something in his hand.

Julia saw a glint a millisecond before he used the object in his hand.

Garden shears.

There was no hesitation when he grabbed hold of Alice's hand and clipped off the small finger.

"Fuck!" Joe roared as Alice's blood-curdling scream filled the room.

Julia's knees gave out. She couldn't rip her eyes from the horror on the screen. Joe spun her, blocking her view with his body, but he couldn't stop her from hearing Alice's agonised sobs. Or the words of the man who spoke when Alice fell deathly silent.

"For every day we do not have the mummy, we will remove a body part. How much of your friend we return is up to you. I will contact you tomorrow."

Julia was shaking so badly that she couldn't stay upright. There was a commotion in the room. Noise. Voices. Shouting. All Julia saw was the blood. Red and pouring from Alice's hand. Blood. So much blood. Her ears rang with Alice's scream of shock and pain.

Her finger. Oh Lord. Her finger.

"Tea," Joe barked, and Julia felt herself being lifted.

Next thing she knew, she was sitting on Joe's lap on the sofa. She was shaking hard. No—the thought penetrated the grim loop in her mind—not shaking, shivering. Just as she realised that was what she was doing, someone placed a blanket over her and Joe tucked it around them.

"This is my fault. I did this." Julia rocked against Joe. "We should have handed over the mummy as soon as we found it. Alice would have been fine if we'd given him the mummy."

"Shh, baby."

She barely registered the words. "I thought I was so smart. Find the treasure; hand that over instead. I wasn't smart. I was arrogant. This is my fault. I hurt Alice."

"Where is that tea?" Joe barked.

"I hurt Alice. I did it. Me." She rocked harder.

Strong arms tightened around her.

"Stop it!" A barked order snapped through her rising panic. Her eyes shot to Joe.

"Joe?" she whispered.

His hand clasped in her hair. "This wasn't you."

She tried to shake her head. "My plan. It was my plan."

"No." His grip tightened, bringing her focus to him, forcing her out of her mind. "This is all on Esteban. Not you. Your plan is good. This is all on him. Do you hear me?"

She felt tears rolling down her cheeks as she clung to Joe —her lifeline.

"We should have given him the mummy."

"He would still have hurt Alice. It's what he does. You know that. You did the research. Think."

"Her finger, Joe." Her voice was a trembling mess.

"I know, baby, I know. But if we'd given him the mummy, he would have come after your gran and Alice would have died. At least now, she's still alive and there's a chance of saving her. This isn't on you. It's on him."

Julia buried her face in his chest and sobbed as his words penetrated. She knew he was right. But it hurt so bad.

CHAPTER 20

"Here, drink this." A cup was pressed against her lips. "Julia." Joe's voice was firm. "Sip the tea." She did as she was told.

She didn't know how long she sat there, cocooned against Joe, while he soothed her pain. Eventually she became aware of voices and Joe's firm chest under her cheek. The images in her head had faded, as though a gauzy veil was hanging between her sanity and the horror she'd witnessed. Self-preservation. Her ever-efficient mind was protecting her.

She felt wrung out. Her throat ached and her eyes were gritty and swollen. Deep inside there was acceptance. And guilt. Joe was right, this was on Esteban, but she'd played a part too. And she wasn't sure she'd ever get over it.

"You doin' okay?"

She looked up to find Joe's focus entirely on her. It was intense and comforting at the same time.

"Yes."

"Good girl." He kissed her forehead. "You're too strong to be knocked out by this."

She wasn't sure about that. "Gran?"

His arms flexed, but his voice was soft. "We had to sedate her. She's sleeping."

A million thoughts flitted through Julia's mind, ordering themselves, formulating a plan. "We can't decode the rest of the textile without her."

She glanced over at the mummy sitting on the coffee table in the corner of the room. Shouldn't it smell? The only scent coming from it was one of dusty old books. She made a mental note to ask Gran about it. Later. On some level, she was aware that her brain was focusing on the bizarre details around her to stop from thinking about Alice. For once, she was grateful for her weird ways.

"She needed sleep." Joe stroked her arm, making her melt into his strength. For once, she was completely uncaring that they had an audience for his affection. She needed it. His touch grounded her, reminding her that she wasn't helpless. She had her mind, her team and Joe.

"It could take days for her to decode the textile. Longer even to find the treasure." If the treasure was still there after all this time. "Gran seemed confident we would be able to get to it by tomorrow night. She said, from what she's decoded already, it's somewhere in the Sacred Valley. That isn't far from here."

She already knew what Joe was going to say, and prepared herself.

"Tomorrow might be too late," he said gently.

"Julia?" Elle said, coming over to them. She looked as shocked as Julia still felt. "What about the plan we talked about on the plane?"

Julia shook her head. "No more plans. They backfire and people get hurt."

"No." Joe put his fingers on her jaw to turn her face to him. "You can't think like that. In this business, we plan, we try, and sometimes we win, sometimes we don't. But we always try, because our chances of succeeding when people need us are higher than the failure rate."

"I can't…" She closed her eyes and saw Alice.

"Right now," Joe said, "our only option is to give him the mummy. You know if we do that, we may as well be signing Alice's death certificate. And Esteban won't stop until he has the only person on the planet who can read the map. If you have another idea, we need to hear it. You owe it to your gran, to Alice, to give us everything you have."

Julia felt her vision blur as she looked up at Elle.

"I thought it was a good plan," Elle said. There were tears in her eyes too.

"What if it gets everyone killed?" Julia whispered.

"What if it doesn't?" Joe said. He leaned in until his lips brushed her ear. "You're stronger than this, Jules. You had a shock, but you can do it. Tell us your idea. Let the team decide if it's a good one. Trust us. Trust yourself. *Trust me.*"

He leaned back then pressed a soft kiss to her mouth. When she opened her eyes, she saw the strength that was Joe.

"I'll get my iPad," she said.

His smile was beautiful—just like the man.

"Then I'll get Callum. He's making calls in his room." He lifted her and placed her on the sofa, the blanket still around her. "You need Elle's magic cube?"

Against all odds, he made her smile. "Yes, I do."

"Okay, you two sort out your notes. And don't forget to drink your tea."

"Yes, sir." She gave him a mock salute.

His eyes sparkled. "I like the sound of that. Use it often." And then he strode out of the room to fetch Callum.

"There's a team in the area who can assist if you're desperate," Lake said in Callum's ear.

Callum rubbed his thigh and looked out over the red roofs of Cusco. "We're past desperate," he told his business partner and friend. "They're chopping bits off their hostage."

"She knows who's holding her?"

"Aye."

There was silence for a fraction of a beat. "Then they're going to kill her."

"Aye. My guess, knowing Esteban's history, is that he'll tire of playing and get rid of her sooner rather than later. Then he'll wage an outright war to get Patricia and the mummy. It's Patricia he really wants. He isn't going to wait much longer."

"You said Alice is in a new location?"

"They moved her out of the compound. She's in a village up in the mountains. A village Esteban rules. It bothers me that he moved her. I can't see his reasoning. She was secure in his main complex."

"Unless…" Lake said, and Callum could almost hear his brain work. "Unless Elle triggered an alarm when she tracked the last IP address."

"I'll talk to her. Get her to backtrack, see if she missed something." Callum rubbed his chin, feeling the weight of the situation bear down on him. "She'll be devastated if she did."

"We all make mistakes. It's how we learn."

"Thank you, Master Yoda. I'll make sure to pass that on." He took a heavy breath. "Who's this team that can help?"

"You don't want to know."

The way Lake said it set off alarm bells in Callum's mind. This team, if they helped, would come in covert and leave the same way.

"Ghosts." CIA or MI6 spies—it was the only option Callum could think of. "How the hell do you know these people?"

"I have a chequered past."

"And a truckload of secrets."

"Some things are best kept secret, for everyone's sake."

"Tell me again why I went into business with you, you cagey bugger?"

The Englishman chuckled. "You'd be bored to death by now without me."

"Aye, right." There was a knock at the door, and Callum walked over to open it. It was Joe. Callum signalled him to come in and shut the door behind him. "How soon can this team get here?" he asked Lake.

Joe's eyes were laser sharp as he tuned in to the conversation.

"Six, seven hours."

"How many?"

"Four, but trust me, with the team you already have, it's enough."

"They got experience doing hostage extractions?"

"They have experience doing everything," Lake said. "It's your decision. Do I make the call?"

Callum stared at Joe as he thought it through. The chances of getting to the treasure—if there even was a bloody treasure—before Alice lost her life, were slim to none. They had no option but to go in and get her. Seven guns against a small army—and four of those guns were unknown entities to Callum. If he didn't trust Lake with his life, he wouldn't even consider it.

"Make the call," he said, and watched Joe tense. "Have them on standby. Whatever we do, we need to do it fast. I need intel on the new location, and I don't mean Google Earth. Can you pull some strings?"

"Consider it done." Lake's confidence flowed down the line.

"After this is done," Callum said, "you and I are going to have a wee talk about your mysterious contacts."

"That's fine, but bear in mind, if I tell you anything, I have to kill you."

"Arsehole." Callum ended the call and looked at Joe.

"That what I think it was?" the American said.

"Lake's found a covert team that can give us a few hours of their time, on the condition we ask no questions and forget them when they're gone."

"CIA?" Joe let out a low whistle.

"Hell, knowing Lake, it could even be Mossad. Who knows what contacts that cagey bastard has up his sleeve."

"So you're planning an extraction." Joe was no fool. It was one of the reasons Callum was pleased to have him on his team.

"You see another option?"

Joe shook his head grimly. Most likely, he had images of Alice losing her finger playing in his head too.

"Julia has another plan."

"It any good?"

He shrugged. "I haven't heard it yet, but it's Julia."

"Aye." Callum gave a wry smile. "That woman ever cottons on to just how smart she is, we'll all be in trouble."

"Yeah." Joe smiled. "We're working on it."

Callum felt a stab in the vicinity of his heart and dismissed it as quickly as it happened. Jealously. Loneliness. He had no room in his life for either.

"You're gone on her," he said, somewhat in awe that the man could give himself over like that.

Joe cocked an eyebrow, his smile wide. "What happened to not gossiping like silly wee lassies?"

Callum hung his head in shame. "Bloody Lake and his touchy-feely company. It's sneaking up on me." He looked up. "I apologise. I don't give a crap about your personal life."

"That's more like it." Joe slapped him on the shoulder as he passed. "Let's go hear what Julia's come up with."

They left the room together.

"ELLE and I had a chat on the plane ride from La Paz," Julia said as she looked at her teammates. Her friends.

They were scattered around the furniture in the living area of the suite her grandmother was using. It was a small space, but they made it work. The mood was sombre. So much so that Ryan wasn't eating his way through the meeting and everyone was conscious of Patricia, sedated and sleeping upstairs.

"Ah, this is why you two had your heads together for most of the flight," Ryan said. "I wondered."

"Don't let him distract you, babe," Joe said.

Ryan wasn't the one who was distracting her. Joe was sprawled in an armchair, his legs stretched out in front of him and his arms folded over his impossibly muscled chest. A flash of how those muscles felt under her fingers, her lips, her tongue, made her blush. She frowned at him, making him grin. There were times when she was sure he could read her mind.

"Anyway," she said to the rest of the room, "Elle and I thought we needed a backup plan in case there wasn't any treasure. Or in case we couldn't find it."

"*You* thought you needed a plan. I only did as I was told," Elle teased, and Julia realised she was standing at the front of the room, the focus of everyone's attention, and she hadn't even noticed until that point.

"Get on with it," Callum snapped.

Strangely, his usual grumpy attitude reassured Julia, breaking the momentary freeze her realisation had caused and forcing her attention back to the iPad in her hands.

"The theory is that we can cut out Esteban's need for my gran by handing him the treasure instead of the mummy.

And that we would hopefully retrieve Alice in the trade." Her voice cracked at the memory of what Alice was suffering. Her eyes sought Joe's, and he smiled with encouragement. "Elle and I decided that, even if there wasn't any real treasure, it would be best if we still had some to trade."

"You've lost me," Ryan said.

"No surprise there," Elle told him, and he tossed a cushion at her head.

"Elle has a friend who works in CGI—that's computer-generated imagery," Julia said. "They do special effects for movies."

Ryan sat up straight and a sudden awareness rippled around the room. She had everyone's attention now.

"We thought that if we could make a video showing Gran with the treasure, we could convince Esteban we had the real thing."

The silence was heavy, as the idea sank in.

"You have this video?" Callum said.

Julia nodded at Elle, and images appeared on the white sheet they'd hung as a screen from the mezzanine.

"This is amazing," Patricia exclaimed as she lifted a golden chalice. "I can't believe we're part of history like this. It's the greatest discovery to happen in a century." The camera panned to show a segment of an Incan cave in the low light of the portable storm lamps. It was thick with dust and dirt, but filled with ceramics, stone carvings and gold sculptures. "This is unbelievable. I wish Alice were here to see this."

The screen went suddenly blank, and Elle opened the curtains, letting light into the room.

"How?" Callum said, looking astonished.

"My friend had some footage he'd already designed," Elle said. "He tweaked it to look more Incan, and then I filmed Patricia while she was gushing over the mummy. I sent the footage to my friend and he inserted her in the stuff he already had. It's rough—it wouldn't stand up to examination of any kind. But if you sent it from one phone to another, it would look genuine."

"Just to be safe," Julia said, making the shocked faces shift back to her, "we thought it would be best if Gran could also produce a piece of gold as evidence." She took a deep breath. "So I went through her contact list and hit upon a local dealer. He has a small, genuine Incan gold statue we can use. He's holding it for me here in town."

"When did you arrange that?" Joe asked.

She blushed, thinking about how she'd spent most of her time since arriving in Cusco. "I called from my room, before I went to the chapel last night." She tapped her iPad and an image of a small golden llama appeared on the wall. "I can get Gran to dirty it up and tarnish it a little. Right now it looks too polished to have been living in a cave for centuries. Gran's an art expert; she'll know what to do to make it believable."

"The dealer sent photos and we inserted it in the video we made," Elle said. "That way we can point to it in the footage, to prove it's real."

"You borrowed a solid gold antique?" Callum was clearly sceptical.

Julia shuffled as she stared at her iPad. "I, um, bought it."

"What?" Elle snapped. "I thought this was some shady loan thing. I didn't realise you'd bought the thing."

"You have that kind of money?" Ed said.

Julia cleared her throat. "I called Rachel and asked her for a loan."

There was a stunned silence.

"Let me get this straight," Ryan said. "You called the Queen of Darkness and asked her to buy you a gold statue? One you intend to hand over to a cartel boss. And she said yes?"

"I told her Gran would reimburse her. I would have asked Gran, but I didn't want her in on the plan."

Ryan held up a hand. "Stop. I'm still stuck on the part where you dared to call the Queen of Darkness."

"Stop calling Rachel that," Callum said. "She's one of the partners, and that makes her your boss. Have some respect."

"Plus," Elle said, "she'll buy a voodoo doll with your name on it if she catches you saying it."

"Enough," Callum growled. "Let's get back to business."

"So," Julia said, "the plan is to use the film, and the statue, to lure Esteban into a trap. A trap where we take Alice and leave him with nothing. We figured he couldn't bring his whole army to a meet, and we would have a better chance of dealing with him outside his fortified compound. Basically, we were trying to even the odds and give you a chance to snatch Alice." She stopped talking and shuffled self-consciously as she waited for their verdict.

Callum looked at each of them. "What do you think?"

"I don't think we should do this. I think we should keep searching for the treasure," Ed said. "I know Esteban. This is too much of a risk. Too many things could go wrong if he finds out we're trying to con him. With the gold in our possession we have a much stronger bargaining position."

"But what if we never find the gold?" Elle said. "Alice doesn't have forever."

"Even as things stand, we're still in a position of power," Ed said. "Esteban wants the mummy, and Patricia, very badly. He's already put word out on the street of a reward for their whereabouts. We can use his desperation to buy more time."

Joe rubbed a hand over his face. "I don't know, Ed. You saw what they did to Alice and the fact she knows who her captor is, doesn't bode well for her. I think Julia and Elle's plan could work. It could take the pressure off Alice and divert interest away from Patricia." He looked at Elle. "What did Patricia tell Esteban when he called this morning?"

"I have the recording," Elle said.

Callum nodded for her to play it, and a male voice with a heavy Spanish accent filled the room.

"Do you have the mummy?" It sent chills up Julia's spine.

"No, but I'm close. I know where it is. We only need to get it." Patricia sounded every bit as anxious and afraid as she must have felt.

"Not good enough, Ms. Matthews. We agreed on three days." The voice was ice.

"I did the best I could. I can't go faster. I need more time."

"You do?" There was a calculated amusement in his voice. "I can agree to more time, but with each extra day you take to get me what I want comes a penalty. I'm sending you a link."

The line went dead as everyone in the room remembered the penalty. Julia put a hand on her stomach, feeling nauseated at the memory. Joe got up out of his chair and came to her. He wrapped an arm around her waist and tugged her into his side. She waited for embarrassment to hit her, but only felt relief. When she glanced around the room, she saw no one was interested in them and gave him a little more of her weight.

"It would be suspicious if we suddenly called now and told him we have the treasure," Callum said.

"Another reason why we should forget this plan and continue our search for the gold," Ed said.

Joe shook his head. "That isn't an option anymore. Our only option is to con the guy into thinking we already have the treasure and then we snatch Alice from him."

Callum pinched the bridge of his nose. "We need a location for this fictitious treasure. Somewhere isolated, but believable. Somewhere we can defend."

"I think you're making a mistake," Ed said. "It's insane to

hand over wealth like that to a man such as Esteban." He let out a sigh. "But this is your mission and I'll help with whatever you decide."

Joe gave him a chin lift in thanks.

"Do we really need an actual physical location?" Julia asked. "Couldn't we just trade the fictitious location for Alice?"

Joe answered, "A man like Esteban won't let his hostage go until he sees the actual location of the treasure."

"What happens if he goes inside the cave we pick and finds it empty?" Julia said.

"We don't let it get that far." Joe's words were steel, and Julia didn't ask how he planned to do that.

"Okay, does the location of the fake treasure need to be near Cusco?" Julia said. "It's really busy around here. The place is flooded with tourists." And the last thing she wanted was more people getting hurt.

"No," Callum said, "but it has to be somewhere Incan."

"And ideally somewhere that isn't too close to Alice's location. We need the time it will take for Esteban to get to us, to set up the trap," Julia said.

"Aye," Callum said with a strange look on his face. Almost as though he was seeing her for the first time.

"Where is Alice now?" Julia asked Elle.

"She's in a small town about eight hours east of Lima, up in the hilly part of the country where the jungle starts. The town they're in has an airstrip, but you're still talking hours for them to get to Cusco."

Julia looked at Callum. "What type of location is easier for you to set up an ambush? Should we pick the jungle, the desert, what? I take it reinforcements are coming, and you need to scout a location fast so that you and the team can set up."

Callum shook his head and looked at Joe. "You ready for a life where you can't get anything over on your woman?"

Joe laughed, but Julia was stuck on the word *life*. He didn't actually think they'd be together forever. Did he? She looked up at Joe, who was staring down at her. "Don't let him get to you. He's mad because you're smarter than he is."

"No kidding," Callum said. "Ideally, we need somewhere with plenty of cover and a decent escape route."

"If you're really going through with this plan, then I know a place," Ed said, drawing everyone's attention. "It's on the outskirts of Cusco, in the hills. My mother used to take us there when we were children. She said it was significant to the family. All I ever saw were a bunch of old rocks, tunnels and caves."

"This place well known?" Joe asked.

"It's not on any tourist map, if that's what you're asking. Some locals will know of it, but it's pretty much barren landscape and holes. I'll make some calls to ensure it's still the place I remember it being." He held up his phone. "One of my cousins will know a good spot for a fake treasure site."

"Make sure you can trust this cousin of yours," Callum said.

Ed smiled widely, "Don't worry, Amigo, I won't give away your secrets." He headed out of the room with his phone to his ear.

"We need to scope the place out." Callum stood and folded his arms over his grey Henley. "Ed and Ryan are with me. Joe, somebody needs to stay and guard the women."

"That is seriously sexist," Elle said. "The women can take care of themselves. And why couldn't we come with you anyway?"

Callum glared at the blue-haired woman who was half his size. "Do you know how to plan an attack? Can you fire a gun? Do you have any combat experience?"

"That's not the point. It's a sexist divide."

"It's a skill divide."

"I have skills."

"Not the right kind. Talk to me after you muster out of the army. Then I'll let you have a say."

"Nobody says muster anymore," Elle snapped.

"Nobody knows we're in Cusco," Ed said as he came back into the room, grinning at Elle's face off with Callum. "This hotel is very secure, and we'll only be a couple of hours. I think the women would be fine alone. Plus, we need all our military experience to plan and pull this off. I think Joe needs to come with us."

Julia stepped away from Joe. "I agree. We honestly don't need a babysitter. No one knows we're here; everyone still thinks we're in La Paz or Lima. Joe doesn't need to stay."

Joe clearly was still unconvinced.

"I promise we won't leave the suite," Julia said. "We won't even order room service. We'll hide, quiet as mice, until you get back."

Joe's jaw tightened, but he nodded. He put a hand on each of Julia's shoulders. "If there is even a hint of trouble, you run for the manager and call the cops. Got me?"

"Yes, sir." She saluted again, making his lip twitch.

"You have the gun I gave you and I'll have my cell phone. Don't take any risks."

"All we're going to do is research and plan. What can go wrong?"

Joe covered her mouth with his hand. "Never, ever say those words. They jinx everything. Let's hope the powers that be weren't listening."

When he lifted his hand, she smiled at him. "You worry me, Joe."

His answer was a toe-curling kiss.

CHAPTER 21

Patricia was awake, but she was subdued and seemed far frailer than Julia had ever remembered seeing her. They snacked on packets of chocolate chip cookies and drank mugs of tea while they waited for the men to return. Patricia and Elle continued photographing the textiles and feeding the information into Elle's laptop. Julia went over the notes she'd made on her iPad. And she didn't like what she was seeing. Patterns were beginning to emerge. Patterns with terrible conclusions. The more she read, the more worried she became.

When the room phone rang, Julia was preoccupied when she answered, realising too soon that she should probably have let it ring.

"Hello?" she said cautiously.

"Señorita Collins?" a female whispered.

"Maria?" The hotel staff member from the chapel.

"Si. There are men here asking for you. Bad men. You must get out of your room right away. Now, señorita, hurry." The line went dead.

Julia felt an unnatural stillness come over her and knew

panic would follow later. "We need to get out of here. Now." Julia spun on her gran. "Grab whatever is essential. Leave everything else. We need to run."

"What is it?" Patricia said.

"Esteban's men are downstairs looking for us."

Elle was already stuffing her laptop into her daypack. "Passports. Cash. Phones. Everything else can be replaced."

Patricia stood, flustered and hesitant in the middle of the room. "I can't leave the mummy."

"You have to." Julia rushed over to her and grabbed her upper arms. "They will take you and kill us. Do you understand?"

The colour faded from her gran's already pale skin, before she straightened her back. "The textiles—can I take the textiles?"

"Got her handbag." Elle ran back down the stairs from the bedroom area. "Where are your shoes, Patricia?"

"Elle has photos of every inch of the textiles. You don't need them," Julia said.

"What if I missed something?"

"Then you'll still be alive to figure it out. If they get you, they will kill Alice. She will be no use to them. And once you've led them to the treasure, they'll kill you. If we don't leave now, we lose both of you."

"Here." Elle thrust Patricia's shoes at her. "Put these on."

"Okay. You're right. You're right." Patricia tugged on the tennis shoes, but kept casting longing glances at the mummy.

Julia didn't bother checking her bag; she knew in detail what was in it. She grabbed her gran's arm and rushed through the door.

The terracotta plaster walls, hung with old religious art, seemed to close in on them. Patricia turned towards the main exit, but Julia tugged her in the opposite direction.

"We sneak out. We don't know who's down there."

They pushed through the fire exit at the end of the corridor and ran down the stairs. Behind them, they heard someone thumping a door. A voice rang out: "*¿Señora Matthews, estás ahí?*"

"We didn't register under my name," Patricia whispered.

"Through here." Julia pushed through the door to the kitchen, just as they heard a thud and a door crash open. "They're in our room."

They raced through the busy kitchen and out into the alley behind the hotel.

"This way." Julia pointed to the door leading into the chapel attached to their hotel.

"You want us to go back into the hotel? Are you nuts?" Elle almost shouted.

Julia opened the door and rushed inside. "The kitchen staff will tell them we ran out into the alley. They'll assume we headed away from the hotel. They won't think we came back in. Plus, I know a hiding spot in here."

"How?" Elle demanded. "How do you know?"

"I spoke to one of the staff about the history of the place. The same one who called to warn us."

They ran down the centre aisle of the small chapel. In the left-hand corner, halfway up the wall, was a decoratively carved dark wooden pulpit. The stairs to the pulpit were cut into the wall behind it. But what most people didn't know was that the stairs didn't only go up—they also went down.

Julia ran to the life-sized painting of St. John, complete with gilt frame, that took up the space next to the bottom step.

"You expect us to hide in the pulpit?" Patricia sounded hysterical.

"Quiet." Julia ran her fingers under the edge of the frame. A button. A pop. Pulling hard, she swung the frame out. "Get in."

A set of stairs led down to the cellars under the old building. Cellars that weren't used for anything but wine storage and were cut off from the public.

"Sit on the steps. I'm closing the door."

"Can we get back out if you do?" Elle asked.

"Yes." Maybe not the way they'd come in, but they'd get out.

They sat on the cold stone steps, the pitch blackness pressing in around them.

"I can use the flashlight app on my cell," Elle whispered.

"No—it's best we sit quietly in the dark and wait until we know it's safe to move," Julia said.

"How secret is this place?" her gran whispered. It seemed to echo off the bare confines of the stairwell.

"Not very, but it's not public knowledge either. It's mentioned in passing in the brochure, and Maria knew about it. I doubt more than a few of the staff know about the painting. Though the cellars under the building on the other side of the courtyard are used for wine. This side isn't used at all."

They fell into another nervous silence, which was suddenly broken with running footsteps and shouting. Angry male voices echoed in the chapel. Someone ran up the small staircase to the pulpit, cursed, then ran back down again. They heard doors slam. More shouting. Footsteps retreating.

They were being hunted.

Julia let a few minutes pass before she broke the silence. "We wait here until we're sure it's safe."

There were mumbles of agreement.

"What if I need to go to the toilet?" her gran said. "I drank a lot of tea this morning."

"We'll cross that bridge when we get to it."

Right now, Julia had more important things to worry about than her gran's weak bladder. She had to tell Joe about the patterns she'd discovered in her notes. She had to tell him what she suspected. That there was a traitor in their midst. That someone they trusted as a friend cared more about the gold than their lives. That they had been sold out to their enemy.

Julia reached into her messenger bag and pulled out her phone. But when she switched it on, she found there wasn't any signal.

"Elle," Julia said, "can you see if your phone has a signal?"

And her friend immediately dug out her phone.

CHAPTER 22

The men headed to a suburb high in the hills outside of Cusco. Joe could see the red roofs of the city behind them, but his focus was on the green hills in front of him. About two miles outside a tiny village that considered itself a suburb of Cusco—if the sign was anything to go by—Ed turned the SUV into a narrow dirt road.

"There only one road into this area?" Ryan asked from the back seat.

"There's another on the other side of the caves," Ed said as he negotiated the bumps.

"I don't like it," Callum said from the passenger seat. "We're further from the city than I thought we'd be. It means we'd be riding without cover for a good chunk of the journey."

"The other road is better," Ed said.

"Then why didn't we take the other road?" Ryan asked.

"Longer. This way is faster."

Joe kept his eyes glued to the windows while he dug out his phone. He switched it on and hit the speed dial for Julia. No answer. Joe felt the hairs on his arms stand to attention.

Julia would answer her phone. It was constantly with her, in that big, bottomless bag she hauled everywhere.

He tried again, but still no answer. He cut the call and rang Elle. He got voicemail. Now his sixth sense was screaming at him. Something was wrong. He knew it. He tried Julia again. Still no answer. He'd give it another couple of minutes, and if he still couldn't contact the women, he'd tell Callum they had to go back.

"The caves are up ahead, beyond that hill," Ed said. "It's said they were used during the Spanish-Incan wars. The Incas would lie in wait for the Spaniards in the crevices of the rocks."

Something in Ed's voice didn't sound right. The car swerved around a curve in the road, hugging a small hill. Large rocks appeared on the landscape. The grey stones jutted out of the earth at random angles, sharp and deadly in appearance.

"You said nobody comes up here?" Callum asked, his tone perfectly level, but Joe knew him well enough to pick up that he was worried about something too.

They were all getting edgy. One glance at Ryan told Joe he was alert too. Their trained senses were flashing alarms at them, telling them something wasn't right. But what? Joe scanned the barren landscape. If there was a threat, it was well hidden.

"Nobody comes here," Ed answered Callum.

A buzz from Joe's phone almost made him sag with relief, but when he looked at the text, it had come from Elle, not Julia. And what it said made his heart stop.

This is Julia. Ed's mother never left Lima. She couldn't have taken him to these caves. I think he called Esteban. There are men here looking for us. I think he sold us out. You are in danger.

Joe looked at his old friend as he drove them into the middle of nowhere. Was Julia right? Had Ed sold them out?

Who did he trust? Ed or Julia? There was no contest. Julia would never send him that message unless she was absolutely certain.

"Callum?" Joe kept his voice even and calm. "While I remember, you got a call from Stu Creek. He said to call him back ASAP. Sounded like he was desperate."

Joe glanced at Ryan. The man had transformed, his easygoing demeanour replaced by one of pure determination. He slipped his gun out of its holster and nodded to Joe as he did the same. They'd both gotten Joe's crude message—they were up shit creek; get ready fast; things were going to get bad.

"I'll give him a ring soon as I can." Callum kept his voice neutral.

Joe felt his body tense for action. "I'd do it fast. There's something about that guy I just don't trust."

"Maybe I'll give him a call now?" *Should we do something now?*

"That's a good idea," Joe agreed.

Fast as lightning, Callum reached out and grabbed the wheel, making the car swerve suddenly to the left. Ed pulled back his elbow and hit Callum hard. The Scot dodged the blow, and it glanced off his head. Joe cocked his gun and pressed it into the side of Ed's neck.

"How many?" he demanded.

"It's too late." Before they realised what Ed planned to do, he blasted the horn.

Joe used the butt of his gun to knock out the man he'd thought was a friend. Ed slumped over the wheel. Callum leaned over Ed and threw open the driver's door. He pushed Ed out.

Callum climbed into the driver's seat and gunned the engine as a dozen armed men emerged from the rocks. Joe ducked down as bullets flew. Ryan wound down his window and fired back.

"Um, I don't know if I should mention this, boss," Ryan said as he took out one of the men, "but should you be driving? On account of you not actually having any real legs and this car being a stick shift."

"My fake legs are going to kick your arse once we get out of here." Callum thrust the car into reverse.

"Sorry I mentioned it," Ryan muttered as he took another shot.

The car bolted backwards. Callum held on to the passenger seat headrest as he navigated by looking out of the back window. Joe held on tight. They were tossed up into the air and came down hard on a large clump of grass.

"How many?" Callum asked.

"At least ten, not counting Ed." The words twisted in Joe's gut.

"Put it out of your mind," Callum ordered. "Deal with it later. Right now we need to focus on the facts. We're outnumbered. Outgunned. And this car is crap."

As if to prove his statement, the car hit a ridge and went sailing through the air before landing with a crash against one of the huge grey rocks.

Joe shook his head to clear it. "Anybody injured?"

"Does a serious case of whiplash count?" Ryan scrambled out of his door.

"Whiney wee fart," Callum said as he climbed out and hunkered down beside the car. "Right, we're miles out of the city, but there was that wee village a ways back, the one Ed called a suburb."

"Not sure we can trust Ed's information anymore." Ryan peeked over the ridge.

"Like it matters if it's a suburb or not. Will you stop messing around and focus?"

Joe wondered if he should step between the two men. "Plan?"

"We head to the village," Callum said. "If we get a chance, we take one of their guys with us. I have a few questions for him."

Joe inclined his head towards Callum's prosthetic legs. "You gonna manage this terrain?"

"I bloody well have to, don't I?"

"I'll take point, you follow. Ry? You bring up the rear."

"No prob," Ryan said. "We've got incoming. They're still a distance away, but moving fast." He grinned at them. "Better run, boys."

They took off at a pace Joe knew must have been murder on Callum's damaged legs, but he never slowed or said a word of complaint. Joe led them into a maze of rock formations that looked like slabs of concrete reaching for the sky.

"Anybody else feel like they're an extra in *Planet of the Apes*?" Ryan said.

They squeezed through the narrow passageways and clambered over the boulders in their path. Without comm units, they had to rely on hand signals to communicate. Silence was the key. And although their pace was slower than Joe would have taken it alone, Callum didn't make a sound.

They heard men move through the natural maze behind them, getting closer. Scrambling over a series of rocks, they made their way towards a wide gap in the wall of stone. Through the gap were open fields and distant houses.

"I see a road," Joe mouthed.

"How far?" Callum mouthed back.

"Fifteen minutes' run."

Callum set his jaw. He grabbed the rock to his left to haul himself up over the boulders in their path. As he put his weight on the top of the stone in front of him, his foot slid. He fell forward. Joe was close enough to catch him before he hit the rock. But he wasn't fast enough to stop Callum's leg from getting wedged between two huge boulders.

Voices were getting closer. They were running out of time. Callum tugged at his leg, but it didn't move. Ryan tried to lever it out, but it was wedged tight.

"Leave me," Callum ordered.

"Don't be an ass," Joe said. "Unstrap the leg. We'll carry you."

"Too heavy. I'll slow you down. Can't risk it. Give me your backup ammo and I'll hold them off while you sprint for the road."

"To hell with that." Ryan produced a flip knife from his pocket and sliced through Callum's jeans. As soon as he saw the prosthetic straps, he sliced through those too.

For a second, Joe thought Callum was going to kill Ryan.

"We don't leave anyone behind," Ryan said. "We're all for one and one for all. We're the bloody musketeers."

Joe cracked a smile as he thrust his shoulder under Callum's arm. "Hold on. You've got one leg; you can still take your weight. I'll balance you out."

Grim and furious, Callum did as he was told. They ran as best they could, with Ryan watching their backs. If they were slow before, now they were crawling. But they made it through the opening in the rocks and into the field.

"Bushes," Callum said. "We have to go low."

They rushed for the first set of bushes that could cover them.

They were hidden just as Esteban's men emerged from the rocky maze.

"Is it safe now?" Patricia whispered into the blackness.

"I don't know," Julia said. "I haven't heard anything for a while, but they could be waiting for us. We'll give it a little more time." For once in her life, sitting in a small space in the dark wasn't a relaxing experience.

"Did you hear that?" Elle whispered.

They were silent, straining to hear. Julia was about to tell Elle she'd imagined it when she heard a scraping sound. They froze, each of them trying to become invisible in the dark stairwell.

"It's probably a rat," Patricia said hopefully.

"Big rat," Elle said. "Maybe we should go back out into the chapel."

It was time to confess. "I don't know how to open the door from the inside," Julia said.

There was a heavy silence.

"Get out your gun," Elle said at last. "Give it to me. You two sit behind me and I'll shoot anyone who comes at us."

"Have you used a gun before?" Julia whispered.

"No. Have you?"

"No. Gran, have you?"

"Do I look like Wyatt Earp?"

There was another pause. "Does anyone know how to switch the safety off?" Elle asked. "It won't fire with it on."

Julia and Patricia made muffled groaning sounds.

"If you don't know how to work a gun, why do you have one?" Elle was beginning to sound irate.

"Joe made me take it. He asked if I knew how it worked. I said yes, because I thought he meant the theory of the thing. I know how it works in theory, but I don't know how to handle one practically. Before I could explain that, he was gone."

"I'm going to talk to your mother when we get out of here," Patricia said. "Between this and your taste in underwear, you may as well have been raised by gorillas in the wild."

"Shh!" Elle said. "I think I hear footsteps."

They didn't have to strain to hear them this time. There were footsteps and they were getting closer. Julia held the gun tight. She wouldn't be able to fire it, but she could throw it at whoever turned up.

"Señorita Collins?" a female whispered. "Are you there? It is Maria, from management."

"Maria?" Julia stage-whispered, hoping it wouldn't travel through the painting into the chapel.

A beam from a flashlight appeared. The holder aimed it up the stairs before turning it on herself. Julia almost cried at the sight.

"Come." Maria motioned with her hand. "I saw you come in here and knew you must have been hiding. I will show you the way out."

The women didn't have to be told twice. They practically tumbled down the stairs in their eagerness to get to Maria.

"Thank you, Maria," Julia said. "For this and for calling to warn us."

"*De nada*. Follow me. Stay close—there are holes in the floor in some places. I will take you to one of the hidden exits. I have a key. It will take you out to a corridor inside the church of Las Damas De Nuestro Señor."

"Part of the old convent?" Julia said.

"Si. The monks and nuns used to meet up through this secret tunnel. There were many miraculous births in the convent. It was very famous for it." There was amusement in the brave woman's voice.

"Have the men gone?" Julia said. "The ones chasing us?"

"I think they have gone from the hotel, but they could have someone watching. That's why it's safer to go this way. These are not good men, señorita. They are well known for doing some very bad things."

"I know." Julia placed a hand on Maria's arm. "We can't thank you enough."

"It is the right thing to do." They'd reached a heavy wooden door that was centuries old and warped with time.

Maria produced a massive iron key and turned the lock. The door didn't make a sound when it opened. "We keep all doors in good condition," she explained. "You never know when you will need them." The door opened onto a dark passageway. "Take my flashlight. I can find my way out from here in the dark. It is not so far."

Julia gratefully accepted the gift.

"Follow this corridor to the end, where you will find stairs. At the top of the stairs there are two doors. Take the left one. It will take you through the back of the church to the outer door. You will be able to get a taxi on the street there."

"The rest of our group?" Julia's stomach clenched at the thought of Joe walking into another trap.

"We have people waiting to intercept them before they approach. And we will pack up your belongings and send them to your home address." Maria hesitated. "I don't think we can mail the mummy." She sounded so apologetic that Julia almost laughed.

"You might want to hand that over to a local museum. They'll find a good home for it."

"Si, this I will do."

"Thank you, for everything." Julia reached out and squeezed Maria's hand.

"I wish you well and hope you stay safe," Maria said.

Julia stepped into the corridor and waited for the others to follow. Patricia stopped at Maria and pulled her into a tight hug.

"Watch the mail, young lady. There will be a huge tip coming your way."

They closed the door to Maria's tinkling laugh.

The corridor was much longer than Julia thought it would be. They didn't say a word until they started climbing the stone stairs to the convent chapel.

"Anyone else thinking about those randy nuns and monks?" Elle said.

They pushed through the door Maria had told them to take and found themselves behind the pulpit in the chapel. The exit was on the left, and Julia couldn't help but notice that the women's chapel wasn't anywhere near as ornate as the men's. Maybe they didn't have as much money to decorate, seeing as they had all those extra mouths to feed? She tried to busy her mind thinking about living in a place like this, but it made no difference—it kept steering her back to Joe.

Had he gotten her message? Was he safe? Was he hurt? Her stomach spasmed at the thought, and she reminded herself that Joe knew what he was doing. He was trained, experienced and smart. She had to trust in him and believe he'd be fine.

Rushing across the chapel, they pushed through the exit onto a busy street. There was a line of taxis waiting, and they climbed into the back of the first one.

Once inside, the three women looked at each other.

"Where are we going?" Elle said.

"I don't know," Julia said. "I think the men will probably check the hotels."

"The central plaza," Patricia said. "It's always busy, and we can hole up in the cathedral, or one of the restaurants and bars."

When they readily agreed, Patricia told the driver to head to the Plaza de Armas. As soon as he drove into the traffic, the women ducked down to hide. Julia pulled out her phone. She had to make sure Joe had got her text. She had to make sure he was safe. Joe was out in the middle of nowhere with a man he thought was his friend, but who'd allied himself to Carlos Esteban.

She tapped his image on the screen of her phone as they rushed through the busy streets.

Joe, Callum and Ryan were hunkered down behind a copse of prickly bushes, their guns trained on the men who poured from between the giant slabs of rock. Seven, Joe noted. They'd reduced them by three and there was no sign of Ed. Whether that meant he was elsewhere or his new comrades had turned on him, Joe didn't know.

He felt a tap on his shoulder and turned to see Callum signal at him.

We hide. Wait.

Joe nodded his agreement. They sure as hell couldn't run for it. He watched as Esteban's men spread out, shouting out to each other, not even trying to keep quiet. They thought they had the upper hand. Joe liked to think they didn't. As some of the men made their way off in the opposite direction, the number who were close enough to be an immediate threat was reduced.

Things were looking up.

And then his phone rang.

He scrambled for it and shut it off, but it was too late. Esteban's men were running towards them.

"I'll hold them off," Callum said. "You two circle around. Take out as many as you can."

Joe and Ryan didn't have to be told twice. They ran, crouching low, in opposite directions, flanking their enemy, as Callum started to fire. Their boss was lying flat on his belly, firing with his arms out in front of him, making himself as small a target as possible.

Joe moved fast and silent, his breath eerily steady, his heartbeat calm. He was trained for this and he had confidence in his experience. He came up on the first man as he ran down a steep verge. Joe slipped his gun into the waistband of his jeans and pulled his knife out from a sheath strapped to his shin. He pounced on the man, attacking from behind, one hand covering his mouth as the other stabbed up and into his heart. A sharp, perfectly placed strike. He lowered the man to the ground and moved on to the next one.

Gunfire rang out. Esteban's men were focused on dodging bullets and getting to Callum's hiding spot. It never occurred to them that their prey wasn't waiting for them. It was clear this so-called army of Esteban's weren't trained. They might have been experienced in violence and blood, but they didn't think strategically.

Joe took out another two men, while Callum's bullets caught two more. One was writhing on the ground holding his leg. Joe crouched as he ran over to the man. He knocked him out and took his gun.

"Behind you!" The call came from the other side of the bloody field.

Joe spun and shot.

Hitting Ed square in the chest.

Ed looked down at the wound. The gun in his hand fell to the grass. Ed followed, his knees hitting the earth with a thud.

"Joe?" His eyes began to glaze over.

"Why, Ed? Why, dammit?" Joe caught his one-time friend and lowered him to the ground. He ripped off his own t-shirt and wadded it up, holding it to the wound. But he knew his efforts were futile. It was a lethal shot. "Tell me why, old friend."

Ed started to smile and then coughed. Blood trickled from his lips. "Money."

"Money?" Joe wanted to roar at the stupidity.

"You don't live here." Ed's voice was barely a croak. "It's hard here without enough money."

"Damn, Ed, you're a lawyer. You aren't selling trash from the city dump."

Ed tried to shake his head, but couldn't. "Corrupt. Everything corrupt. Need money to live well. Need money to buy…favours…to…be…happy…here…"

And then he was gone. Joe stared at the man he'd trusted, not only with his life, but the life of the woman he loved. A man who came from the same background as he did, who'd been trained in honour. A man who should have stood for something. Who *could* have stood for something. Instead, he'd sold himself for nothing.

"Joe," Ryan said flatly.

"I'm coming." Joe stood, feeling as though the air around him was pushing him back down.

Ryan was several feet behind Joe. There was blood on his hands. He gave Joe a look that was far too understanding.

"You had no choice."

Joe jerked his chin up. That didn't make it any easier. He looked down at Ed's body. It was wrong to leave him lying in a field. Every cell of his being wanted to carry him back to Lima for a proper burial.

"You can't," Ryan said, reading his mind.

With no vehicle, Callum incapacitated and who knew how many more of Esteban's men out there, they couldn't afford to take Ed with them.

"This wasn't him," Joe said. "The Ed I knew, back in the corps, wouldn't have sold us out."

Ryan clasped Joe's shoulder. "I liked him."

"Yeah." Joe ran a hand down his face. "He was the one who told me that honour wasn't a code for a marine—it was his soul."

He clenched his fists, angry at Ed. Angry at the choices

he'd made and the actions he'd forced Joe to take. Angry at the waste of a good man. A waste that would haunt Joe for the rest of his life.

"He lost his soul." Joe looked at Ed one last time. "I'll come back for you."

Ryan didn't say anything.

"Let's go." Joe would deal with his guilt and the ghosts that followed him later. There was nothing else he could do for Ed now.

They jogged to the bush where Callum lay flat on his back. "Out of ammo." He held up his gun.

"You okay?" Joe leaned down to help him up.

"No. The bastards shot my leg."

Ryan and Joe stilled, both of them looking down. There was no blood.

"Did they get the plastic part, Callum?" Ryan asked sweetly.

"Shut up."

Of course, Ryan didn't shut up. "I'd think you'd be happy that they didn't hit the bit that's still attached to you. The bit that bleeds. Remember that bit?"

"If I didn't only have one leg, I'd kick your arse."

"Yeah, yeah, yeah." Ryan put his shoulder under Callum's arm and took his weight. "Isn't there a really bad joke about a man with one leg?"

"Do. Not. Go. There."

"Maybe once this is all over we can stop off in the States on the way home and grab some dinner at IHOP?"

"You want to be fired, don't you?"

"I've just thought of something else," Ryan said with a wide grin. "Shouldn't a guy in your position have bulletproof legs? Oh! Wait! You could get them made with compartments and store stuff in them." Ryan looked awestruck. "Dude, you could be the Bionic Man. Or even better—Inspector Gadget."

"That's it, you're fired. Consider yourself out of a job." From the ferocity of Callum's growling voice, Ryan was lucky Callum didn't just shoot him.

"Boss, you fire somebody during every one of our ops. We consider it a sign of affection."

"This is only our second bloody op!"

"Yeah, and how many people have you fired and rehired so far? I'm the fifth." He patted Callum's chest. "You have issues. You might want to see a counsellor."

Joe tuned them out as they walked towards the road, leaving a field of death and a man who'd been a friend, behind them.

He dug his phone out to see who'd called. It was Julia. Joe put the phone to his ear to hear the voicemail she'd left. It started with, "We're okay, don't worry," and went downhill from there.

"We need to speed things up. The women were attacked at the hotel. They got out and they're hiding in plain sight with the other tourists. You two get a move on and I'll get us a car." He ran towards the dirt road and the small village beyond.

Nothing mattered to him more than getting to Julia. She needed him. And Joe desperately needed her.

CHAPTER 23

Julia, Elle and Patricia were sitting in a dark booth in the back of Cusco's Irish bar. The place was crowded with tourists who were seeking food from home and like-minded travellers. There was a soccer game playing on the massive screen behind the bar, and the patrons were very vocal in their support for each team. Through it all, the women sat with one eye on the doors and the other on Elle's laptop, where they were working to decode the last of the images on the mummy's textiles.

After listening to her gran and Elle talking about the decoding process for hours, Julia had come to a few conclusions. First, Patricia was never going to decode the map by the time Esteban called the following morning. Second, Ed had probably told Esteban about their plan to con him with fake treasure, rendering that option useless. And third, they no longer had a mummy to trade.

Basically, they were stuffed.

"Stop worrying," her gran said. "He'll be here soon."

"I know." Joe had texted her to say he was on his way, but had to get cleaned up first.

Julia hadn't shared the last part of the message because she feared that he didn't mean he had to wash off a little mud.

Her eyes drifted towards the door again, although it was getting hard to see the entrance now that the bar was filling up. They'd been watching for Esteban's men since they sat down, which was ludicrous, because none of them knew what the men looked like—except in the surveillance photos Elle had dug up online. But Julia figured that anyone who came into the bar and wasn't wearing Gore-Tex and fleece was probably suspicious.

She saw the door open. The crowd parted for the newcomers, as though a sea parting for Moses. And Julia knew. Her heart sped up, her nerve endings tingled and she knew. Then the bodies thinned and he was there.

"Joe!"

Julia was out of her seat and running to him before she could think. For once in her life, she wasn't afraid about being the centre of attention. All she cared about was that Joe was there and he was safe.

She launched herself at him, her arms going around his neck, her legs wrapping around his waist. He caught her without hesitation and held her tight.

"I was so worried," she said against his throat, breathing in the scent that was only Joe.

A large hand ran down her back. "We're okay, baby. You can rest easy now."

Julia leaned back to look up at him. "Ed?"

His face became stone, his eyes dark pools of pain. "He's dead."

"Oh, Joe," she whispered, devastated at the news of the man she'd grown fond of. The man she'd thought was a friend.

She wrapped her arms back around him, giving what

comfort she could. He stroked her back and nuzzled at her temple.

"Oi, lovebirds." Ryan appeared beside them. "You're blocking the path to the bar."

Julia looked around her and blushed. She was greeted by several smiling faces. And then she remembered she was supposed to be in hiding. "Oh, no. We were trying not to attract attention."

"Yeah," Ryan said. "Well, that's the way to do it. Come on. We need to get the other two witches."

"Hey!" Julia smacked him on the chest. Her eyes went wide, and she wasn't sure who was more astonished, her or Ryan.

He grinned wickedly. "Would you prefer I call you Charlie's Angels instead?"

"Next time," Joe said, "hit him harder."

When they got back to Elle and Patricia, Julia beamed. "Joe's okay."

"So I see." Her gran gave her an indulgent smile.

"So am I," Ryan said. "In case anyone was wondering."

Patricia looked behind Joe. "Where are Callum and Ed?"

Julia tensed and felt Joe do the same.

"Callum's back at the new hotel. We'll fill you in on everyone and everything when we get there." Ryan made a circular gesture with his finger. "The walls have ears. Pack up, ladies." He looked at Joe. "Have I got time to get some burgers to go?"

"No."

"You are a crap partner." Ryan pouted, his eyes on a plate loaded with a burger and fries that was being carried to a table near them.

"You can get food at the hotel," Julia said. For some reason, she wanted to pat him. As though he was a puppy.

"Bet it won't be as good." He let out a heavy sigh.

Patricia stepped out of the booth and tapped Ryan on the shoulder. "They deliver." She pointed to a sign over the bar. "Pick up a card on the way out and order from the hotel."

His grin was blinding. "If I were twenty years older, I'd run away with you, Patty." He headed towards the bar and the takeaway menus.

"Patty?" Joe asked, his lips quirking.

Gran shook her head. "That boy has the cheek of a teenager."

"Let's go." Still holding Julia's waist, Joe aimed them for the door. "Keep together. Follow our lead. The hotel's only a couple of blocks from here, and it's busy outside. We'll blend with the other tourists until we get where we need to be." He stopped beside a woman wearing a grey fleece beanie and spoke to her. As Joe dug into his pocket, the woman smiled and took off her hat. She handed it to Joe and he handed her money. In turn, he gave the hat to Elle. "Cover the blue hair."

Elle looked at the grey beanie in disgust. "What if she has lice?"

"What if you get dead because you're the only person in Cusco with luminous blue hair?"

Elle pulled on the hat.

The pub was facing Cusco's huge cathedral. The redbrick building lit up orange in the night, and there was a massive crowd gathered outside it.

"Festival," Joe said, answering Julia's unasked question. "Although most nights in Cusco are party nights."

Julia knew if they turned right, they were a short walk to their last hotel. Joe turned left and took them away from the crowded Plaza de Armas. The cobblestone street was full of tourists and locals. There were traditionally dressed women, their arms full of woven souvenirs, walking amongst the crowds, attempting to sell their wares. At the edge of the road, covered trailers acted as portable stores, selling everything from snacks and drinks to hand-crafted ceramics. Behind the trailers was the grey stone brickwork of the Incas. The irregular stones fit together like massive puzzle pieces. Somehow it fit perfectly to see the Incan stonework merge with the plaster and carved wood of the Spanish architecture that had been built on top of it.

"One day," Joe said in her ear, "I'm going to bring you back here so you can look all you like."

Julia blinked up at him, aware that the crowds moved around Joe and no one jostled them. "You mean when we aren't running for our lives?"

"Yeah." His smile was devastating. "Hard to be a tourist when you're running for your life."

"Hardly a relaxing vacation."

"Hardly."

They turned the corner into a narrower street. "The hotel's at the end of the block," Joe said.

"Isn't that a bit close to the last hotel?" Patricia asked.

Ryan had her and Elle wedged between him and the wall, acting as a barrier to everything in their path, as they made their way along the street.

"It's as safe as anywhere in Cusco right now," Joe said.

"That isn't reassuring," Patricia muttered.

"There it is," Ryan said. "The Marriott."

The high stone arches of the hotel came into view, and Julia read the plaque that said the building used to be a convent. "Do you think every hotel in Cusco used to belong to a holy order? Is anyone else bothered by that?"

"Nope." Ryan held open the door for them.

"The history of societal change from a religious paradigm to a secular one is fascinating," Patricia said. "You can see it in everything, not only the repurposed buildings, but art, literature, styles of government, everything. The questions are, is the building still sacred when it isn't being used for holy purpose? Is the art still divine when it isn't used for worship?"

Julia nodded along with her gran. At least someone was on the same wavelength. She glanced up to see Joe grinning and Ryan gaping at Patricia.

"You really were a professor, weren't you? I thought that was a nickname or something."

They groaned and passed him on their way to the reception desk. Joe got two keys and handed one to Ryan.

"Ryan, Elle and Patricia are in something called a mini-suite. We'll meet you there in an hour. Get cleaned up and have some food. Callum already has a room."

Julia tugged his hand. "What about me?"

"You're with me."

There wasn't time to process his decree before he was dragging her across the lobby towards the elevator. Julia glanced over her shoulder to see her gran and teammates smiling after her.

The lift door opened and Joe stalked in, taking her with him.

"You could have asked me to come with you." That was all Julia managed to say before she was pressed up against the wall and Joe was in front of her.

A second later, his mouth was on hers. His kiss was ferocious. It was a claiming. A taking. A branding. It left her weak and desperate for more.

The elevator stopped all too soon, and an older couple smiled at them knowingly as they exited. Joe dragged her down the corridor to their room. He had the door open in seconds. As soon as she was inside, he had her pressed against it.

He kissed her with a desperation that was almost brutal.

But somewhere, in the deep recesses of her mind, Julia knew he needed this, and she gave him everything he wanted. Her terrible tourist t-shirt came flying off, followed quickly by her white cotton sports bra.

"Beautiful," he growled as he fell to his knees and feasted on her breasts.

Julia could do nothing but gasp and hold on tight. He sucked and licked and scraped his teeth over her breasts, until she was ready to explode. The room was spinning. There were no thoughts in her head but Joe.

She was vaguely aware of the button on her shorts popping open. The zip lowering. He sucked her nipple hard, making her wail as he removed the rest of her clothes, tugging off shoes and lifting her feet to get rid of her shorts. Once he had her naked before him, he didn't hesitate—he lifted her knee and hooked it over his shoulder, and then his mouth was on her.

It was a ravishing. He didn't tease. He kissed her most private place with abandon. He was relentless, driving her as high as he could, as fast as he could. Julia lost the ability to stand and felt Joe's hands on her hips holding her up. Her head was swimming. Her only sounds were moans of surrender. She felt herself race towards climax. Too fast. Too hard. Too much. She couldn't get the words out to tell him to slow. And then it was too late. He pushed her over the edge. Her body spasmed with the agony of pleasure that overwhelmed her, and she collapsed—straight into Joe's arms.

Julia was gasping for air, fighting for reason, when she felt the cool cotton of the sheets against her back. A second later, Joe thrust inside her. Her back came off the bed with a desperate wail of pleasure.

"Need. You." Joe pressed his face into her throat and bit the muscle in the crook of her neck.

The sting of the bite, accompanied by the devastating

pleasure of him driving into her, sent her spiralling into another orgasm. Time suspended. It was as though she was outside her own body, yet completely aware of it at the same time. She was split. Soul and body. And then she came crashing back together, with one word on her lips.

"Joe."

CHAPTER 24

Callum was living his worst nightmare. In the years since he'd lost his legs, he hadn't let anyone, except medical staff, see him without his prosthetics. And now here he was, the butt of Ryan's jokes and a liability to his team. With one leg abandoned in a stone formation and the other sporting a bullet hole, he was officially out of the game. There was no way he'd be able to get replacements fitted in time to help—especially not while he was in a foreign country. He was reduced to letting the concierge in their new hotel find him a wheelchair.

A wheelchair. His team were going to see him in a wheelchair. How the hell could he expect them to let him lead when they saw how weak he really was?

They were staying in the Marriott, which was a couple of blocks away from the Plaza de Armas, where the women had been holed up all afternoon. Their new hotel was only two blocks away from their old hotel. They'd talked about that when they'd been in their stolen car, heading back to the city. They came to the conclusion that there were a lot of hotels around the Plaza de Armas, and a lot of tourists to hide amongst. Plus, the Marriott was the only hotel Callum was sure would cater to someone in a wheelchair. He was risking the team because of his failings.

He looked over at his bathroom with its extra-wide door. The shower was roll-in. There was plenty of space around the bed, and everything was at a height he could reach from a wheelchair.

He hated every single inch of it.

Picking up his phone, he put a call through to Lake.

"Benson," the taciturn man said.

"We're in a fucked-up mess."

"Details," Lake demanded.

Callum let out a sigh as he reached for the glass of whisky on the night table. He took a hefty gulp, rejoicing in the burn as it made its way to his stomach.

"Ed Sanchez, Joe's contact, the lawyer. The guy sold us out. Esteban bought him. He led us out of town to give Esteban's guys a chance to snatch Patricia and the mummy. They didn't get her, but only because Julia is a genius savant who stores information like a NASA computer. She knew a secret way out of the hotel and got the women to safety."

"I told you Julia was worth her weight in gold."

"Aye, you also told me she'd get over her need to hide behind office plants." He finished his whisky while he tried to remember the last time Julia had hidden from him. Hell, it had to have been back in England. Maybe she was adapting. "Anyway, Ed led us to what he said was a prime location for our fake treasure trove. Instead, he had the cartel men waiting for us. It was an ambush. A bloodbath. There are eleven bodies in a field outside of Cusco." He paused, hating what he had to confess. "Along with one of my prosthetic legs. The other one is sitting on my bed with a bullet hole in it."

"Injuries to the team?" It was the same voice Lake had used as operation commander during their time in the SAS.

"Unbelievably? None. The odd scrape and cut, but nothing major. Our worst setback is the fact I'm now confined to a chair." It turned his stomach to say the words. They were like bile in his mouth. Weak. He was so bloody weak. Half the man he'd once been. Literally.

"Even in your chair, you're worth more than most men in your situation."

The only reason Callum didn't take off Lake's head for placating him was because he knew his friend wouldn't dare try. If anyone was going to give it to him straight, it was Lake. He'd just have to quietly accept that on this one point, Lake Benson was completely delusional.

There was a knock at the door. "Concierge."

"Give me a minute," he told Lake before shouting, "Come on in."

The door opened and the man wheeled in a chair. It was to his credit that he hadn't asked what happened to Callum's prosthetic legs; instead he'd taken the request for a wheelchair in his stride—especially seeing as Callum didn't want to borrow or hire one. He wanted to buy one.

"Señor." The man positioned the chair in front of him, and Callum was relieved to see it was gunmetal grey and not some weird colour, like pink. "Can I help you with anything else?" He eyed the bullet-damaged leg, but his face didn't even flicker with shock or curiosity.

Callum handed him the leg. "Can you get rid of this?"

"Of course."

"I need clothes," Callum said. "In fact, my whole team will need everything. Clothes, toiletries, shoes—the works."

"If you could supply me with measurements and preferences, I'd be happy to supply your team with a basic closet."

Callum pulled out his wallet and took out five hundred dollars. "That's for you."

The man's eyebrows arched slightly. He took the money with a gracious nod.

"There will be fifteen hundred more when we leave. As long as there are no questions asked, and if anyone comes looking for us, they don't find us."

The man's eyes hardened. "The privacy of our guests is paramount in this hotel."

"Then we have an agreement."

"A pleasure. Please call with your team's details."

"I will."

The guy nodded and left the room, closing the door quietly behind him.

"I wish I could hire ten guys like the concierge here," he told Lake. "He does as he's told, he's discreet and he doesn't talk back."

Lake snorted, which could have been his version of a laugh. "What's the plan?"

"I'm calling in your contacts—apart from that, I'll need to get back to you with the details. Can you ask them to stay on standby?"

"Already done."

"When I get back to the office, there will be no personal time for anybody ever again. Don't fight me on this. I'm serious. I'm fed up with rushing into the chaos of our staff's lives without proper planning and preparation. This would never have happened in the service."

"And you wouldn't have made the money you're making now there, either."

Lake's words cut through Callum. He remembered Joe's emotionless recounting of Ed's last minutes. Money sure as hell wasn't all it was cut out to be.

"I need to go," Callum said.

"Stay in touch." The line went dead.

Callum tossed the phone onto the bed beside him, pulled the chair over and heaved his body into it. He needed a shower.

And then he needed to face his team.

In a wheelchair and powerless to help them.

He wondered what he'd see on their faces when they realised that their boss had turned from an asset into a hindrance. He bet it was nothing he'd want to see. Sometimes, on dark days, he wished the roadside bomb that had ruined his life had taken more than his legs. He wished it had taken all of him.

With a push of the wheels, he headed for the bathroom.

CHAPTER 25

They were lying naked in bed, in the room Joe hadn't even glanced at before he'd taken Julia. It hadn't been lovemaking. It had been something far more primal. Something he didn't quite understand, but had desperately needed.

Julia was lying on her stomach, her face on his chest, her arm across his abdomen. Joe trailed his fingertips down the smooth, creamy skin of her spine, to the luscious curve of her behind.

"Did I hurt you, Jules?" If she said yes, he honestly didn't know how he'd live with himself.

"Don't be daft," was the murmur against his chest.

Joe smiled into the darkness. He hadn't even turned on a light. He'd just fallen on her like an animal.

"I'm not usually like that..." He didn't know how to explain it.

Julia lifted her head and rested her chin on him. She looked him in the eye. "Don't. I like that it's different every time. I loved what we did. You can do it again." She paused. "Once I've had time to build up some energy."

She plopped her cheek back down on his chest, as though

even that small action had cost too much of her depleted resource of strength.

Joe couldn't help but smile as she eased his worry. She was too damn cute. They lay there for a few moments, enjoying the silence and the darkness. Enjoying the comfort of being skin to skin.

"Do you want to talk about it?" Julia asked softly. "You don't have to."

Joe closed his eyes, a futile attempt to keep out the images that were already inside his head. She waited patiently, no judgment in the silence, and he knew if he chose not to speak about it, she would understand. But that wasn't how it worked. The rest of the team would have to be told. The consequences would have to be dealt with.

"Ed sold us out." Joe's voice was strangely hoarse. As though he'd been crying, when his eyes were dry.

"I know." Julia squeezed him tight.

He thought of the text warning him about Ed. And then the call that followed. Her timing had almost been lethal—something she would never know. He'd already warned Callum and Joe not to mention the phone call that gave their position away. It wasn't her fault. It was his. He should have remembered to turn off his phone. It was a rookie mistake and they'd all paid for it. But not Julia. It wasn't on her.

"Esteban's men were waiting for us. It was an ambush."

She caressed his stomach. "Don't blame yourself. It wasn't you who decided to betray your friends. That was Ed's choice."

"Yeah, but I should have known something was off."

"Why? He was your friend. You trusted him. Why would you spend time suspecting him of subterfuge?"

Joe smiled and squeezed her tight. "Only you could use the word subterfuge in bed."

"This isn't exactly pillow talk, Joe."

"No." He sobered. "It isn't."

Julia's eyes softened. "It wasn't your fault," said his stubborn and beautiful woman.

"Maybe not, but it's definitely my fault he's dead." Images flashed in his mind. The gunshot. The blood blossoming on Ed's shirt. The life draining from his face. The glassy nothingness in his eyes when he breathed his last.

Julia shifted until she was leaning on his chest. She cupped his cheek and kissed him until the images retreated. Damn, but he loved this woman.

"It was either him or you. You did what you had to—what he forced you to do." It was said with such conviction that it was almost impossible to refute.

"How do you know?"

"Because I know you. You wouldn't have hunted him down as a traitor. You would only have hurt him if he was about to hurt you—or Callum and Ryan. It isn't your fault."

She kissed him again, sipping at his lips as though trying to take away his pain with her touch. Joe put his hands under her arms and pulled her until she was lying on top of him.

"I'm so sorry about Ed," Julia whispered. "I know you weren't close friends, but you trusted him. I don't know what made him act the way he did. He was a nice man around us—although his betrayal means I'll look at everything he did and said differently now. But I liked him and he was still your friend. A friend who forced you into a position where you had to do a horrible thing. I'm sorry he's gone, but it still isn't your fault. It's the choices he made. He must have known when he decided to sell us out that there would be consequences. He took the risk anyway. What a horrible waste of a life." Her eyes filled with tears as she looked at him, and Joe knew they were tears for Ed and for him. "It hurts, doesn't it?"

"Yeah, baby, it hurts." He clasped the back of her head and

gently pulled her in for a kiss. This woman who saw too much and felt too deeply. This woman meant for him. Slow kissing turned to slow touching, and this time, they did make love.

And they made it slowly.

CHAPTER 26

It was a subdued group who met in Patricia, Ryan and Elle's suite. The knowledge of Ed's betrayal was written in the red-rimmed eyes and shocked expressions of everyone present. None of them understood it. Julia doubted they ever would.

She stared out of the living room window, which looked out onto a close-up section of pristine Incan wall, and wondered what they were going to do next. They'd run out of options. And that meant Alice had run out of time. For someone who normally had a head full of ideas, her brain was horribly quiet.

A knock at the door drew everyone's attention, and Joe pulled the gun from his shoulder holster before looking through the peephole.

"It's Callum." He holstered the gun and opened the door.

Julia was surprised when Callum rolled into the room in a wheelchair, but she wasn't shocked. Everyone knew Callum had prosthetic legs. The fact they hadn't seen him in a chair before now was the part that was strange.

"We meeting, then?" he snapped as he rolled over to the window.

Julia automatically recoiled from his abrasive attitude. The fury emanating from him was almost tangible, and the room was suddenly thick with it. Her skin began to prickle, and without realising that she was even doing it, she took a step towards the bedroom and her escape.

"Everybody up to speed on what happened with Ed?" Callum said.

"Yeah." Ryan grabbed one of the seats at the dining table. As usual, there was a tray of food in front of him, but he didn't touch it. Instead, he kept a wary eye on Callum.

Julia scanned the people in the room and realised they were all acting the same way, watching Callum as though he were a bomb about to go off. She caught Joe's eyes from across the room and felt as though he could see inside of her. She watched as he noted her hands wrapped in the strap of her bag, and the distance she'd covered towards the bedroom. Julia lowered her eyes. She couldn't watch him and see the moment he realised that nothing had changed with her. She was still as much of a freak as she'd been when they first met.

"What's done is done," Callum barked. "We need to move on. If you can't do that, tell me now." His voice was a steel blade slicing through the air. There was silence. "Okay, in that case, what's the situation at the last hotel?"

"I did some recon," Ryan said. "Esteban's got men watching the place."

Julia studied her boss. He was coiled tight enough to snap. She glanced down at the beige alpaca wool blanket covering the space where his legs should have been, and it hit her—he was scared. Scared of what they would think of him. Scared they would think him incapable. A wave of empathy rocked her. She knew how that felt. She dealt with it every day. People thinking she was less than normal because she behaved in ways they couldn't comprehend. Her heart ached for him, even as she readied to run at the first sign of an explosion.

"Julia," Callum snapped, making her freeze in place.

A low growling noise came from Joe. Julia's eyes shot to his, only to see him glaring at Callum. Her warrior was ready to take on the boss for scaring her. Her heart reached for him at the sight.

"Yes?" she whispered to Callum.

"I spoke to the concierge. He needs clothing and shoe sizes for everyone and he'll kit us out for the rest of the trip. Toiletries too. Take care of it."

"Yes, sir." She flushed again at calling him sir, and before she could stop herself, she was looking at Joe for reassurance.

He was still glaring at Callum. "Tone," Joe said. "Wind it back."

The glare Callum gave him in answer was enough to make every hair on her body stand on end. Julia backed up against the wall and inched towards the bedroom. Emotion was pressing in on her. The lights in the room were too bright. The air was too prickly. It hurt to breathe in the tension. Everything within her screamed to run. To hide. To become invisible until the danger passed.

"Is Esteban in Cusco?" Callum asked Elle.

"Yes. He arrived about an hour ago. He's staying in a villa he owns on the edge of town."

"You're sure?" There was a dark, rumbling fury in the question.

Elle didn't flinch. "There are a lot of cameras in Cusco and I've managed to get him on several. I picked him up at the airport when he first arrived. He came in on a private plane with a mini army. I counted seven men travelling with him, with more waiting at the airport and at his house. About thirty in total."

Callum caught Joe's eye. "If Esteban is in Cusco, and he

brought some of his men with him, then we have an opportunity."

"You want to go in tonight," Joe said evenly.

Which meant Joe was going into danger again. Julia felt dizzy at the thought, and placed her palm on the cool wall behind her to steady herself. Joe was calm, controlled, capable. This was what he did. He would always be running into danger and leaving her to wonder if he'd make it out unharmed. If he'd come back at all.

If this thing between them, this wildfire of a connection, had a future, it would mean she was always going to say goodbye to Joe and would always be waiting to see if he came back in one piece. She wasn't sure she could handle a life lived that way.

"Lake has a team on standby in Lima. If I contact them, we can meet up in the town where they're holding Alice and get her out. But it has to be tonight. This is our best opportunity. They have less men guarding her." Callum looked at each of them, daring them to disagree. No one did. The weight of the situation wasn't lost on any of them.

"We can't take Rachel's plane," Elle said. "It's being watched. All the commercial flights are being monitored too. It's too far to drive to Alice's location. It would take days, not hours."

"Helicopters." Joe folded his arms across his wide chest. "There are a few tourist companies dotted around town. They do the sites from the air. They never go further than the Sacred Valley, but they could."

"We can't ask a tour operator to take us into a combat situation," Callum said.

Julia inched closer to the bedroom. She could feel it. The tension building, like gas filling the room. One spark and it would blow.

"Do I look stupid?" Joe said. "I can fly a copter."

Callum glared at Joe. Two cockerels getting ready to fight.

"We need weapons," Ryan said, drawing their attention. "We're almost out of ammo and we don't have any contacts in Cusco—at least none that wouldn't sell us out to Esteban."

"I can get the Lima team to supply us," Callum said. "But this is a solo op for Joe. We need you here to protect the women."

Ryan didn't like that one bit. He bristled in his seat. Julia felt behind her for the handle of the door. *Slow. Easy. Don't attract attention.*

"I need to back up Joe." Ryan stared Callum down.

Callum's cheeks turned a dark shade of red.

Oh no! Abort! Run! Hide!

Elle raised her hand, like she was in class. Callum narrowed his eyes at her, and she took that as permission to speak. "Two things. I need to go with Joe too. I'm the only one who can hack any closed-circuit security they are sure to have on the compound. They'll need me as their eyes and ears—unless the Lima team has a hacker. In which case, the scary hacker with the training and the gun should definitely go instead of me. As for the second thing, why does Ryan need to take bodyguard duty when you'll be here?"

Callum jerked back as though he'd been slapped, and then his mouth formed a tight line. Julia pressed a hand to her stomach as nausea rolled over her.

"I can't protect anybody. I'm in a wheelchair." Callum smacked his palm hard on the armrest.

The noise made Julia jump. Joe's eyes snapped to hers. She looked away. This was her. This was what she did. She ran. She twisted the handle behind her slowly, so as not to attract attention.

"Uh, yeah." Elle looked at their boss as though he'd lost his mind. "What's your point?"

"I don't have any fucking legs!" he roared.

And Julia was running. She barrelled through the door, as though the devil himself was on her heels. She frantically jerked open a closet. Too small. She ran for the bathroom and slammed the door behind her. And then she climbed into the tub and pulled her knees up tight to her chest.

Even through the walls she heard Callum shouting.

"How the fuck am I supposed to protect anybody from a fucking wheelchair?"

Julia flinched and pressed her hands to her ears. She scrunched her eyes shut tight. It would be over soon…it would be over soon…it would be over soon…

She rocked back and forth, counting her breaths in batches of ten, trying to block the overwhelming emotions riding on the air from seeping into her.

It's going to be okay…it's going to be okay…

"Jules?" A hand touched her hair, making her jump.

She looked up to find Joe crouched beside the bath. Worried. He was worried.

"Baby," he said gently, "what's going on? Callum is just being Callum. You've seen him shout before."

And every single time she'd felt the same way—as though wire bristles were scraping across her skin. He reached for her again, but she moved away.

"I can't," she said. "I can't bear touch right now."

"Okay, that's okay," he said, but she could hear the worry.

"It's not okay." She barked out a mirthless laugh. "I know it's not okay. But this is me. This is what I am. A freak." She nodded. "This is good. It's good that you see this now. It's good you know what I'm really like before things get too serious between us."

"You're not a freak and things are already serious between us."

She ignored him because she knew better. "I went to a clinic, years ago. Saw a psychiatrist and tried to get him to fix me." She looked at Joe. "He said he wouldn't. He said there was nothing wrong with me. That I was just built this way and no amount of therapy would fix it. Do you hear what I'm saying, Joe? I'm unfixable. This is it. Forever."

He shook his head. "I didn't hear that. I heard you tell me that a professional said there's nothing wrong with you. And he was right."

"Yes, I'm so normal that I'm hiding in a bath," she scoffed, fighting back tears. "I'm so normal that I can't bear it when people get upset. Anger is worse. I feel it in the air. It presses in on me, making me insane from the tension. Raw emotion makes my skin crawl. I feel it inside of me. It's loud and painful and I just want to run to get it to stop. My skin hurts. Touch is painful. Lights are too bright. Noise is too loud. Whatever you hear or see, I experience magnified a million times over."

"I didn't realise."

"Hypersensitivity, they call it. There's actually a name for it. No cure, but a name. Add to that my OCD problems and the fact I get paralysed with shyness and I'm just delightful to be around." She felt a tear run down her cheek as she cocked her head. "You still want me, Joe? You still think I'm normal?"

"Baby." His voice was agonisingly soft.

She shook her head. She'd been so foolish to hope for a future. To think she had a chance at normal. Normal was for other people. The best she could hope for was uneventful.

"I don't want to see you anymore," Julia said, her voice trembling. "I want this thing between us to be over."

He shook his head. "I don't accept that."

"Why? Do you think if we just try hard enough I won't be like this anymore? You think you can fix me, Joe?"

He reached for her again but stopped himself. "You don't need to be fixed."

"Right." She gave a brittle laugh.

"You don't need to be fixed."

Unfortunately, his decreeing it didn't make it so. Things didn't work that way.

"Leave me be," Julia said wearily. "I can't be what you want. All that would happen would be that you'd realise the same thing, sometime down the track. And then you'd look at me with such disappointment. I couldn't bear it. Not you," she whispered. "Not from you."

"Joe," Ryan called from the bedroom. "We need to head out."

A muscle in Joe's jaw throbbed. His fists clenched and unclenched on the edge of the bath.

"Give me a minute," he called to Ryan.

"Just go," Julia said as she closed her eyes.

"I have to, I don't have a choice, but hear this first." He gripped her chin. "I love you."

She jerked, but didn't shake off his touch. "You can't."

"I do." His voice was pure conviction. "Do you hear me, Julia Collins? I love you. The you who's brilliant and organised and caring. I love you. The woman who feels too much and can't process it. I love you. The woman who needs a man like me. A man who sees her. A man who can protect her. A man who believes, one hundred percent, that she's perfect just as she is. A man who loves her."

"Joe," Ryan called.

Joe gritted his teeth. "Think about this while I'm gone. Think about the fact that I see you, I think you're perfect as you are and I love you." His eyes were molten pools. "Give me a chance," he whispered. "Let me show you it's the truth. Let me love you."

"We need to go." Ryan sounded tense.

"You don't get to give up on us. You don't get to tell me what I think and feel, now or in the future. You don't get to do that." He stood. "I won't let you."

And with that, Joe strode from the room, leaving Julia stunned and alone, wondering what had just happened. And if she had it in her to believe he meant what he said.

CHAPTER 27

They were holed up in yet another hotel. This time in Lima. Julia was getting fed up with hotels, but even more tired of having people around her continuously. She needed to think, and she couldn't do it with the tension pouring off Callum. While she'd been hiding in the bathroom, the team had decided it was safer for Julia, her gran and Callum to wait out the operation in Lima. So when Joe had hired a helicopter to take them to the village where Alice was being held, another copter had flown the rest of the team to Lima.

Julia had arranged for an easy-access cab so that Callum's wheelchair wasn't an issue. The usually grumpy man was even more volatile than usual during the trip, which had all of Julia's senses working on high alert. She thought his temper was because he couldn't keep his disability hidden. He'd pinned the legs of his trousers up to stop them flapping about under his stumps, and it was clear his limbs were missing. What Callum didn't get was that no one was looking at his lack of limbs, because the rest of him was overwhelming. He radiated authority and danger, whether he was in a wheelchair or out.

Julia checked the time again. Four minutes since she'd last checked. The extraction team were maintaining radio silence. All Julia knew was that they'd arrived in the mountains where Esteban had a residence. Elle had reported that the town was tiny and empty. Everyone was either in bed, or in Cusco with Esteban. They'd acquired a vehicle once they were in town and had gone straight to the estate, where Elle hacked the security system. There had been no information on the team Lake sent to help them, which could only mean that the people who made up the team didn't want anyone to know they were helping out. Julia wasn't sure if that was a good thing or a bad thing, but she trusted Lake Benson's judgment.

Six minutes.

She walked over to the window and looked out over the bustling capital city of Peru. Even in the dead of night, the roads were filled with cars fighting for space. This time their hotel was right in the centre of the sprawling city. It was a modern tower block of glass and concrete, surrounded by the classic Spanish architecture of a bygone age. Normally Julia felt reassured in hotels that were the same the world over, but this time she wished she was in one of the brightly coloured adobe buildings with their ornately carved balconies. She could imagine spending a lazy day with Joe in one of those hotels. They'd lie on a bed made with white linen and laugh at nothing.

Joe.

Eight minutes. And still no contact.

She rested her forehead against the cool glass and tried not to think about what he might be doing. If he got hurt...

No.

She couldn't think about that.

She'd told him it was over between them. It was the sensible thing to do. Experience had taught her that the novelty of her personality wore off pretty quickly for people who got close to her. Julia didn't think she could live through another round of dealing with someone else's disappointment.

You're too needy. You're too weird. You overwhelm me. I can't be a crutch for you, Julia. You need help. This is your fault. You don't have a social life. I feel trapped with you...

Voices from her past crowded out her thoughts, but through it all there was still this huge, solid presence in her mind. Joe. He could even protect her from her memories.

Eleven minutes.

She felt her gran come up beside her.

"They're going to be fine," Patricia said.

Julia didn't say anything. Her gran didn't look like she wanted honesty, and anything she deemed acceptable would be a lie.

"I was trying to think of some family story I could tell you," Patricia said. "One to help you deal with your past and your feelings for Joe—before you sabotage your future, that is. Although breaking up with him while you were sitting in the bath has probably already done the job."

Julia squeezed her eyes shut. She was already aware that Ryan had blabbed about her conversation with Joe to everyone else in their suite. There was no end to Julia's humiliation. It was the gift that kept on giving.

"In the end, I couldn't think of one," her gran said. "I'm too busy worrying about Alice. Instead, I thought I'd give you the meaning behind the story I would have told. Saves time, anyway."

There was silence. Julia knew she was supposed to ask what it was. There was no way that was happening. She could out-stubborn her gran in a battle of wills, so she kept silent.

"Fine." Patricia rolled her eyes. "Here's the motto of the

story I would have told if I could have thought of one—get over yourself."

"Gran!"

"Don't you Gran me. I've been watching you blow hot and cold with that man for the past few days. It's obvious you're crazy about him, yet you keep talking yourself out of it. It's pathetic, and I'm fed up watching it. I never thought my granddaughter was a coward, but now I'm beginning to wonder."

Julia felt the words like a punch to her stomach, but she fought past it. She knew her gran meant well. She was also family, and it was really hard to get rid of family when they upset you. She knew—she'd tried in the past.

"Please, Gran, next time you want to give me a pep talk, don't."

"Oh, for goodness' sake. That boy loves you. We didn't need Ryan's gossip to figure that out. You can see it in everything he does. He just wants a chance to show you."

"And what happens when he starts to get irritated by the fact I'm shy and introverted and have many, many issues? What then?" She glared at her gran. "I'll tell you what. He leaves me in the dust. You've seen it happen. It happens all the time. I trust someone. I let him close, thinking he's the one who's going to accept me for who I am. Meanwhile, he's thinking he'll be the one who's going to fix me. Then when he realises he can't. That I'm unfixable. He runs."

Patricia folded her arms and glared. "See, that's where you've got it all wrong. The only person who thinks there's anything wrong with you is you."

The words echoed the ones Joe had thrown at her, making her heart clench.

"Rubbish. I can give you a list of the people who've sat me down over the years and told me I'm too much to handle. Or that I was disappointing. Or, my favourite, that I don't try hard enough to change."

Her gran waved a dismissive hand. "Well, they're all idiots."

"Thanks for clearing that up."

"I'm telling you right now, young lady, if you don't accept who you are and give that boy a chance to love you, you are going to lose him."

Julia seriously didn't want to hear it. "Gran, this isn't a long-term thing between me and Joe. It's casual."

Patricia threw up her hands. "And I thought you were the smart one!"

"Ladies," Callum interrupted.

Julia turned to him as her heart tried to escape through her ribcage. "Is there news?"

"No." He held up a phone, a look of utter disgust on his face. "But your mother is on the line. Who's talking to her?"

"Not me." Gran backed away from the phone as though it was a rattler.

Julia frowned at her. *Who's the coward now?* She took the phone from Callum and spoke before her mum had a chance to.

"Mum, guess what? I'm with Gran. Let me put her on the line." She stalked over to her gran and thrust the phone at her.

"Traitor." Patricia glared.

Julia turned away. So now she was a traitor on top of everything else. Family. There was a reason she limited her time with them.

"Libby, darling," her gran crooned into the phone. "I've been meaning to call you."

"She's lying," Julia called.

Her gran flushed and blurted, "Julia's got a boyfriend."

Callum groaned loudly. "I spent years in the special forces

only to come out and use those skills dealing with women who think they're still in high school."

"You're one to talk," Patricia snapped at him. "You won't even deal with your own issues. Talk about us when you're proud of who you are, legs or no legs."

Julia looked at the time on her phone. Only nineteen minutes had passed since she'd heard from Joe.

Nineteen long minutes. She looked back out the window and prayed he was safe. A world without Joe wouldn't be worth living in.

LAKE HAD SENT a four-man team to back them up. The men came prepared with weapons and comm equipment. They were dressed in black tactical gear, from bulletproof vests to side-arms strapped to their thighs. The men only gave their first names, and their accents were too generic to place— even as far as picking a country.

"David," the leader of the group said as he held out a hand.

Joe put him in his early thirties. He had the kind of standard good looks that made him blend into a crowd. His skin was a light brown, his hair a darker brown and his eyes almost black. It was hard to tell which nationality he belonged to. It could have been any.

Joe shook his hand and introduced his team.

Elle gave the ghost team a wide smile. "CIA? MI6? Mossad? Am I close?"

David's lips twitched. "All you need to know is that we're here to help."

"Would it be rude if I asked for some fingerprints?" Elle eyed his black gloves. "You know, just so I can do some investigating in my free time." She batted her eyelashes at him.

"Not rude," he said. "But not possible."

"DNA?" Elle asked hopefully.

David gave her a tiny smile before folding his arms and turning back to Joe. "We scouted the perimeter. There are fourteen active guards, more on rest. There's a blind spot in the southwest corner. We can go up and over the wall there, but we'll need to talk to someone first, find out where the woman is being held."

"She's in the basement," Elle said.

Joe smiled when sharp eyes zeroed in on the bubbly, blue-haired woman.

"Southeast corner of it." Elle beamed at David. "She's currently lying on a bare mattress. I don't know if she's asleep or unconscious. Thinking about any other options gives me the heebie-jeebies."

"You've got eyes in there?" David was fast reassessing his first impression of Elle.

"It's amazing what you can buy online these days," Elle said. "They even sell drones. Teeny-tiny ones that fit in the palm of your hand."

"A drone won't get you that information. Especially a commercial one." The guy wasn't fooled, though—he'd learned fast that all was not as it seemed with their resident hacker.

"No." She twirled one of her blue bunches. "But it did manage to locate the connector box for the internal security feed, and then Ryan there"—she gave Ryan a finger wave, and he saluted her—"climbed a tree, scaled a wall, did a bungee jump—who knows what he did—but he got the hardware I gave him inside the box. From there on in, it was child's play to hack their system." She smiled again. "And while I was doing that, I had my drone scope around. Did you know that there is a state-of-the-art warehouse about a mile from here that's loaded with weapons? Maybe, after we get out of here, you could call up your boss and get someone to drop a little bomb on the building, because I think these guys might be planning to sell those arms to other bad guys. Just sayin'."

David took a step towards Elle, as though fascinated by her. "You hacked a state-of-the-art closed system?"

"Like it's hard." She gave a snort. "Now, about that DNA..."

With a shake of his head, David looked at Joe. "Lake didn't tell us you had this kind of skill on your team."

"Lake Benson tends to keep a lot of secrets," Joe said drolly.

Elle jumped up to sit on the bonnet of the vehicle they'd liberated from outside someone's house. It was old, but Ryan had checked the engine and it was in good condition. It would get them back to the chopper. They'd been forced to land several miles outside of town, so as not to alert the compound to their arrival.

"Elle, bring up the compound diagram," Joe said.

Sitting tailor style, Elle put her laptop in the cradle of her legs, and her fingers flew over the keyboard. She turned the screen when she had what she wanted.

"I can give you a ten-minute window on security, but that's it," she said.

"How you going to do that?" David asked.

"I'm going to force their system to reboot, which will buy you the time you need to get Alice. During the reboot, the surveillance cameras will freeze on their last image before the system shuts down. You'll be invisible to the system for the duration, and all alarms will be disabled."

"You sure *you* aren't CIA?" David said with admiration.

"I eat CIA hackers for breakfast. Oh! That reminds me. Snack time." She reached into her pocket and came out with a Snickers bar. "Never thought you'd be able to get these in Peru." She held it out to them. "Want some?"

They shook their heads, but Ryan leaned in for a bite, because Ryan *never* turned down an opportunity to eat.

"We go in here," David said. "You and Ryan can take point. You get the woman out. We'll cover you."

They spend a few more minutes going over the plan before David's team opened a bag filled with weapons for Joe and Ryan to choose from.

"Can I get that gun?" Elle pointed to the biggest one.

"Do you know how to use it?" Joe asked.

"No."

He shook his head, reached into the bag and came out with a Taser. "Anybody gets close, zap them."

She looked at the weapon with disgust. "Why do I get the lame gun?"

"Because you know how to use it. With the other ones, you're more likely to shoot your foot."

"This is crap. I'm making Callum train me for combat when we get back to London. If I keep getting dragged into the field, I should know how to shoot things."

"You weren't dragged. You volunteered," Ryan reminded her.

Once they were kitted out, they looked at Elle.

"Wait for my signal before you reboot the security," Joe said, as Elle climbed off the car. They were stationed at an outcrop of rocks, a couple of miles from their destination. "You should be safe here, but if there's a problem, radio us and hide until we get back."

"Or electrocute the baddy," she said, making Ryan laugh.

"Okay, we're out of here." Joe tapped the comm unit strapped to her ear. "Don't forget to switch it on."

She looked so offended by his order that the men were smiling when they climbed into their vehicles.

Ten minutes later, they'd reached the spot where they had to leave their vehicles and continue on foot. When they reached the compound wall, David pointed to the blind spot.

Joe flicked his comm to speak. "We are go," was all he said.

A few seconds later, the reply came. "Clear."

Working as a seamless unit, the men were over the wall in seconds. David nodded at Joe and Ryan once, before he and his team blended with the darkness. The ghost team didn't make a sound.

Keeping their weapons at the ready, Joe and Ryan ran to the side door on the old adobe house. Actual physical security was lax now that Esteban was in Cusco. It was clear from the sounds of TVs and radios playing throughout the compound that the men didn't even consider the possibility of someone attacking.

Joe kept guard as Ryan popped the lock. They snuck into the building, checking doors for the entrance to the basement, sticking to the shadows and moving like ghosts. They found the right door on the third try and hurried down the stairs. A radio was playing. Men were muttering. Joe held up a fist, a signal to stop. Ryan guarded Joe's back, weapon up, as Joe peeked around the corner.

He tapped Ryan's shoulder and held up two fingers. Two men. With a few more gestures, they organised their attack. It went without a hitch. The men were too busy drinking cheap tequila and talking trash about women to notice Joe and Ryan. They were knocked out and tied up in less than a minute.

Joe signalled for Ryan to keep watch as he grabbed the key for the one remaining door. When it swung open, it revealed a large, dark cell, with a cot in one corner and a bucket in the other. There was one bare bulb, swinging overhead. And lying on the cot was Alice.

Joe placed a hand on her shoulder as he covered her

mouth with his other hand. Her body went rigid. "Patricia sent us," he whispered. "We're here to get you out, but you can't make a sound. Can you do that?"

She nodded, and Joe dropped his hand from her mouth. Struggling, she turned to look at him. Her hair was matted and dirty, her face was ashen, with dark circles under her eyes, and there was a bruise on her jaw. She cradled her damaged hand to her chest. It was wrapped in some equally dirty cloth, and there was blood on her clothes. Her eyes were wide with fear and hope.

"Do as you're told and we'll be out of here in a couple of minutes," he whispered. "Julia and Patricia are waiting at the hotel for you."

Her eyes became glassy and a tear ran down her cheek, but she didn't make a sound.

"Let's go." Joe took her arm and led her to the door.

She was tiny, shorter than Julia, and very slight. She stumbled on the uneven floor, but Joe thought she might have stumbled even if it was perfectly flat. She was weak from lack of food and broken down by the trauma she'd experienced. He wrapped an arm around her to give her support. Once they were out of the compound, he'd carry her.

They made their way up the stairs quickly, listening intently for the slightest sound. Ryan checked the exterior.

"Status?" Joe whispered into his comm.

"Clear left."

"Clear right."

"You're good to go."

He signalled Ryan and they ran for the perimeter wall. Joe supported Alice and Ryan watched their backs. With the help of the ghost team, they lifted Alice over the wall. Once they were on the other side, Joe picked her up and broke into a sprint towards their vehicles. All the while, the men around him protected them, and the woman in his arms sobbed silent tears.

Once they made it back to Elle, who hadn't had a chance to electrocute anyone and was annoyed about it, the medic on the Lima team saw to Alice. He gave her a shot of antibiotics and pain medication before cleaning and bandaging her hand. The whole process was done efficiently and was over in a matter of minutes.

"That feels better," Alice said as she looked at her hand. "Thank you." She looked at each of the team. "Thank you for coming to get me."

"No problem," Joe said. "Let's get you back to Patricia and Julia."

"Just one thing before we go," Alice said. "If I make a documentary about my ordeal, would any of you boys be willing to take part?"

Elle covered the grin that broke out as the men stared at the abused woman in silence.

"I'm an artist," Alice explained. "We suffer for our art." She looked at her hand. "And I bloody well suffered for this, so I'm damn well going to make some art out of it."

"Get in the car," Joe said with a shake of his head.

He could see how Alice and Patricia had managed to stay best friends for over sixty years—they were both completely mad.

"Are you sure you weren't hit on the head?" Ryan asked Alice with a gentle voice.

She gave him an incredulous look. "Were you expecting me to lie down and whimper? Was this traumatic? Yes. Will it ruin my life? No. Was it painful? Yes. But it still wasn't anywhere near childbirth. Don't even get me started on that agony. I'm a woman, son. We're strong. And now I'm bloody furious." Her eyes narrowed. "I'm going to make a tell-all exposé about Carlos Esteban and that pretentious American moron, Marcus Delaney. They think they're untouchable? Well, wait until the best documentary producer on the planet gets through with them."

Joe put the car in gear and headed for the chopper.

"Wait!" Alice shouted as she craned her neck to see the team from Lima. "Go back. We need more of the medication he gave me. That stuff is great."

CHAPTER 28

Julia ordered food for everyone's return and organised clothes for Alice. When her gran's best friend arrived at the hotel, she knew the clothes wouldn't fit. Alice had lost a lot of weight since Julia had last seen her. She looked gaunt and shaken. Her skin was a strange shade of grey, and her eyes were wider than any possum's. But her attitude was firmly in place.

"Julia." Alice held her tight. Physically she was a fragile shadow of her former self, but character-wise, she was still indestructible. "You came to get me and you brought an army."

"We're family," Julia said. "We're crazy, but we're always there for each other. How are you holding up?"

"As well as can be expected after being kidnapped and having a finger chopped off."

Julia didn't know what to say to that, but she made a mental note to get some sedatives from the hotel doctor, in case Alice needed them. She settled Alice gently on the sofa beside Patricia, who insisted on fussing over her best friend.

Julia felt a presence at her back that made her whole body tingle with awareness—Joe.

He placed a hand on the small of her back and leaned in to speak against her ear.

"Babe, I need a minute."

With everyone watching them, Julia couldn't exactly say no, but there was no way she wanted to be alone with him. She didn't trust her resolve. No matter how sensible her reasoning when it came to just how incompatible they were, her arguments crumpled under the weight of his sensuality when he touched her.

"By the window," she said as firmly as she could manage.

He didn't argue, leading her over to the corner by the window. Julia pretended that everyone wasn't watching them while they strained to listen in on their conversation.

"I'm glad you didn't get hurt." She stepped away from him, fighting the urge to touch him as a way to reassure herself he was fine.

"We need to work on your confidence when it comes to my abilities. But first we have some unfinished business we need to talk about."

"No, we don't." She backed up against the glass.

He put a palm flat on the window above her head and leaned into her. "Remember when you asked about my faults and I told you I was possessive?"

He seemed to expect an answer, so she nodded. Her mouth was suddenly dry, but she resisted the urge to wet her lips. He didn't need any encouragement, no matter how small.

"Well"—he toyed with a lock of her hair—"knowing that, do you really think I'd walk away from the woman I love, just because she's got cold feet?"

"Cold feet?" Her eyebrows shot up her forehead. He did *not* just say that. "This isn't cold feet. It's reality. You seem to think I'm some sort of Disney Princess and I keep telling you that I'm more like Jack Nicholson's character in *As Good As It Gets*." She placed her palm flat on his chest in supplication, realising too late that the heat of his body burned through her defences. Before she could snatch her hand away, he covered it with his and pressed it hard against him. Trapping her. Surrounding her. Making it hard to breathe.

She blinked up at him, wishing he was less handsome, less intense, less open about his feelings. Less everything. He overwhelmed her just by being him.

"This can't work," she said. "You must see that."

"What I see is a beautiful, interesting woman who's trying to throw away the best thing that's ever happened to her because she's scared."

Julia sucked in a breath. "Not scared. Realistic. We have no future."

He leaned closer, his musky scent enveloping her. "See, here's the thing: you're wrong. You aren't thinking straight because you don't see yourself properly. And to a guy like me, that isn't a deterrent, it's a challenge. I'm just gonna have to hound you until you see things my way."

"Joe! You can't ignore what I'm telling you."

"I can if you're talking garbage."

Julia wanted to stamp her foot and scream. He had to be the world's most stubborn and infuriating man.

"Jules." He leaned in to whisper against her ear, making her shiver. "I love you. I'm not going to give up on you, or on us. It's not how I'm made. I've got patience, baby. I'll wait however long it takes for you to believe that I see all of you and I love every weird little inch. Consider me your shadow until you see reason."

"That's stalking!" She pushed at his chest. Although admittedly it wasn't much of an effort.

"You say potato, I say potahto. I consider it perseverance."

"What am I going to do with you?" She wanted to lash out in exasperation.

His smile was sensually wicked. "Oh, I can think of a few things."

Julia felt her cheeks heat. "Stop it. Even if I somehow miraculously managed to believe that you wouldn't go running sometime in the future when you realise that I'll never change, there's still your job. You are the man who runs into a burning building. I'm the woman who runs away from it. I honestly don't think I can cope with watching you leave time and again and never knowing if it will be the last time I see you." She shook her head. "I can't do it. I can't."

"You know," Joe said, suddenly very serious, "this gig isn't forever. I never planned to work in the field long-term. It was one of the reasons I got out of the Marines. This kind of life is bad for relationships. For family." His voice lowered, making her heart race. "And I want a family, Julia."

She forgot how to breathe. *He couldn't mean...?*

"I talked to Callum about moving into a training and project management role once we have more staff on board. So"—he stepped even closer until their bodies were touching —"you don't need to worry about losing me every time I leave on a mission, because there won't be any more missions."

Her eyes went wide. "I can't let you give up your career for me."

"Babe," he said against her lips, holding her gaze with a look that was searing, "don't you know I'd do anything for you?"

"You'll resent me." Her words a whisper against his lips.

"Never." It was a vow. "I want you more than anything. I'm not giving up on adventure, baby—I'm just starting a new one. With you." He brushed his lips against hers. "If you'll let me."

"Why won't you listen to me? Why won't you see reason? You're driving me crazy."

"Good." And then he kissed her.

A slow, teasing, sensual kiss that stole her mind and left her breathless. When he pulled away, he rested their foreheads together.

"Mine," he declared. "You're mine."

And then he walked away, heading for Callum in the corner of the room and leaving her weak-kneed watching after him. He moved like a predator, all lean muscle and powerful grace.

"I remember that look." Her gran broke into her thoughts and made her aware that she was standing mooning after Joe.

"I do too." Alice sounded wistful. "It meant someone was going to get lucky."

"Alice!" Julia felt her cheeks burn as she said to her gran, "Why won't he listen to me?"

"Because you're talking rubbish, dear."

"No I'm not!" And she was seriously getting annoyed that no one would listen to her. "I know what I'm talking about. He'll get fed up with my weird personality and he'll hurt me. Why am I the only one who sees that?"

Ryan, Elle, Alice and Patricia shared a look before they all said at the same time, "Because you're talking rubbish, dear."

Ryan burst into laughter and Julia threw up her hands in disgust. There was no talking to any of them. They were all as pig-headed as Joe.

Alice smiled at Elle. "I can't thank you enough for coming for me."

"Anytime," Elle said with a smile that was quickly replaced by horror. "I mean..."

"I know what you mean." Alice smiled back. "And I will definitely call Benson Security next time I need rescuing."

"There won't be a next time," Patricia said. "We're going home to live staid lives, like two old biddies should do."

Alice gaped at her friend. "What about the treasure?"

"To hell with it! Look at the trouble it's caused."

"Exactly," Alice said. "I lost a finger over it." She held up her bandaged hand. "The least I should get in return is some Incan gold."

"What happened to giving away the treasure and publishing a paper on reading Incan textiles?" Julia asked.

Alice waved her undamaged hand. "That was before I was butchered. I liked that finger. It was thinner than the rest and it had a nice nail. Now I have a gap in my hand where it used to be and I'll never be able to look at garden shears again. In fact"—she turned to Patricia—"when I get home, I'm putting the house on the market and buying a flat on the Thames. One that doesn't have a garden. But that's beside the point. I need the treasure money to buy a new finger. I want one of those bionic ones I saw on TV."

"You saw bionic fingers on TV?" Ryan could barely keep the laughter out of his voice.

"It's a computerised prosthetic," Alice told him, managing to look haughty even in her bedraggled state. "It connects with the nerves and takes messages from the brain. And it comes in an assortment of colours." She looked back at Patricia. "I want blue, like Elle's hair."

"Now that sounds like a fun replacement for your missing digit," Patricia said, with her eyes on Callum as he whispered with Joe in the corner of the room. She turned back to Alice. "How about we talk this over after you've had a shower? You smell like the city dump."

She got to her feet and helped Alice up with her.

"You'd smell too if you'd been living in a cell for about a million years. I had to pee in a bucket. Do you know how easy it is to miss the damn thing? My knees aren't up to squatting all the time. There were days when I got into position and thought I'd never get out. Don't even get me started on my bowels. I think I have hysterical constipation. You know, like hysterical blindness, where people go blind due to stress. Well, my bowels stopped working for the same reason."

"I really don't need to hear about your bowels," Patricia said as she held open the door to the room she was sharing with Alice.

"You'll be hearing all about it in the middle of the night if we don't get it sorted now." Alice looked over her shoulder at Julia. "Julia, pet, can you order some prunes? And laxatives. And papaya juice."

"Papaya juice is for an upset stomach," Patricia said.

"You think my stomach isn't upset?" Alice said as the door closed on the two of them.

There was a moment of silence before Ryan said, "I need to get them together with my granddad and his brother. All they talk about is their bad hips and their toilet problems."

"If that's me in forty years," Elle said, "shoot me."

Once Patricia and Alice had disappeared into their room, Joe and Callum joined the rest of them. Joe's look was a challenge. A dare for Julia to take him seriously. To take a chance on them. Julia looked away. She ached, torn as she was between trusting him and taking a chance, and the fear of being devastated all over again. Because she knew that getting over Joe Barone would be impossible. If he hurt her, she would remain broken for the rest of her life. How could he expect her to take a chance on that?

Callum positioned his chair in the middle of the room. He was wearing a muscle shirt that flashed biceps, the likes of which should be illegal. But there was still a blanket covering his legs.

"The member of the Lima team who took the copter back

to Cusco for us, also took a message to our pilots. They're going to bring the plane to an old military airfield outside Lima. It's too risky to fly out of the international airport. Esteban is sure to be watching it. We've got about five hours until we need to be at the airport."

"I checked the surveillance cameras in Cusco," Elle said. "Esteban and his mini army are still there."

"That doesn't mean we should relax," Callum said. "Esteban has people everywhere." He looked at his team. "You did a good job—now get some sleep while you can."

"And showers," Elle said.

"Food first." Ryan was already dialling room service.

"You coming?" Joe held a hand out to Julia.

"I can't."

"I'm not going anywhere," he told her. "You know where to find me."

With one last, wicked smile, he turned towards the room they should have shared. Julia's heart actually hurt to watch him go.

As he passed Elle, Joe stopped. "Before I forget, I have a present for you." He dug around in his pockets and came out with a tiny Ziploc bag. "It's from David. He said to give it your best shot."

Elle grabbed the clear plastic bag. She was bouncing in place with delight. "Is that what I think it is? It is! It's a hair. With the root attached. DNA, here we come." She gave Joe a hopeful look. "I don't suppose he gave me a fingerprint."

"Not this time, crazy girl." With a shake of his head, Joe headed into his room—but not before casting one last challenging glance over his shoulder to Julia.

CHAPTER 29

Julia lasted a whole hour before she gave in and crawled into bed with Joe. His scent and warmth engulfed her as she snuggled up to his side. She was weak. Plus, she was giving him mixed messages—telling him she didn't want him one minute, getting into bed with him the next. Julia knew that made her a terrible person, but she honestly wasn't playing with him. She was confused. She knew she should run from Joe, but she wanted him so very badly. It was an impossible situation. One with which he wasn't helping at all.

"Hey, gorgeous." The sleepy huskiness in his tone was perfection.

He rolled them to the side and pulled her back into him, spooning her—his front to her back. A heavy leg was thrown over her thighs and his arm fed around her waist. He nuzzled at the crook of her neck. She was surrounded by him. Trapped in his embrace. And she'd never felt safer.

"Now this is the way I want to wake up every morning."

"It's afternoon." She didn't even want to get into the thought of forever. It was too big, too scary, too risky.

"Still feels like you belong here. There's only one thing wrong. Why are you dressed?"

"Because you need to get out of bed and I don't need to get into it."

"Ah, but you're already here." He nudged her hair out of the way and nibbled at her shoulder. "Too many clothes, but I can work around it."

Julia got the impression he was talking more to himself than her. His hand slid under her t-shirt, up her stomach, to cup her breast. That was all it took for her to forget her objections to their relationship.

He rubbed his thumb back and forth over her nipple as he made his way up her neck to her ear. The feeling of his breath against it sent her desire for him soaring. He teased her earlobe with his teeth.

"You getting hot, baby? Something you need?" Oh, that seductive voice in her ear.

Julia moaned her answer and pressed her hips back into him, feeling his hard length against the seam of her behind.

"You know this can't work between us." Her voice was hoarse.

There was amusement in his. "Seems to me it's working just fine."

"You know what I mean. We have no future."

"Then this is what? Goodbye sex?"

She couldn't think straight. Her mind was overloaded with the messages coming from her body.

"Yes," she gasped, and he chuckled against her skin.

"Tell me what you want."

The arm her head rested on moved, curving around her to play with the breast his other hand vacated. That hand moved slowly down her body to her jeans. He undid the button and pulled down the zip.

"Please," Julia said.

Her eyes were shut tight. Her world had reduced to just this man and how he made her feel.

"I'll please you, baby. Tell me how to do it."

She felt his tongue trace the shell of her ear and almost lost her mind. She'd never known, would never have guessed, that she was so sensitive there.

His hand dipped lower into her jeans. He found the elastic of her underwear and stopped.

"Joe," she said.

He was tormenting her with his slow caresses. A devil. He was a devil. His leg moved so that his knee was wedged between her thighs. Julia held on to the arm that crossed her body as though it were an anchor.

"Say the words. I want to hear Julia Collins say dirty words in that proper English accent of hers. Tell me what you want. Tell me in detail and I'll give it to you."

She groaned her frustration. He was asking her to step right outside her comfort zone. Her cheeks were burning at the thought.

"You can do it," he whispered against her ear. "It's only the two of us here. There's no shame. I want you to do it. It will make me hot. You want me hot for you, don't you?"

"Yes!"

His fingers slipped under the elastic of her panties, but stopped there.

"Joe!"

"Say it."

He pinched her nipple. Julia arched her neck, pressing her head back into him. He bit her shoulder muscle.

"Please, please pet me. Please touch me with your fingers."

"Where?"

"M-my clit, please, Joe."

With a growl, he slid his fingers lower. "You are so wet."

All she could think about was the feeling of his large

fingers stroking her, coaxing her closer to the oblivion of ecstasy with every touch.

She heard gasping and desperate moans. The sounds were so unfamiliar that it took a second for her to realise she was the one making them.

"Need you." His hand was suddenly out of her underwear, and Julia wailed in complaint.

The next thing she knew, her jeans were being pushed down her legs, along with her panties.

"Kick them off."

She did as she was told, managing to free one leg. It was enough. A strong hand on her thigh, bringing her leg up and back over his. She instinctively arched her bottom back into him. She felt his hand guiding his hard length into her, and then he was filling her slowly. Inch by achingly solid inch. The hand on her breast slid into the cup of her bra to hold skin. His other hand spread low on her abdomen as his fingers found her clit.

And she was lost for him.

There were no coherent thoughts in her mind. There was only Joe and what he made her feel. His slow movements in and out of her seemed to fuse more than just their bodies together. He was breaking through all of her anxiety, all of her fears, everything she held back. He was tearing it all down, demanding all of her. Giving all of him in return.

She heard his pants. Felt his muscles tense behind her. She was gasping now. Clawing for release. Moaning and begging. But he held her in place, his strength just another agonising tease for her senses.

Close. So close.

"Please!"

"You want to come, baby?" he growled against her skin.

She nodded. Desperate.

"Then tell me you'll give me a chance."

"Joe!" Was he insane?

He nuzzled the side of her throat. "Tell me you'll stop breaking up with me and give us a chance. Tell me and I'll let you come." He moved his hips, too slow to push Julia over the edge.

She couldn't think. She wanted it so badly, and he was using it against her.

"Tell me," he ordered with a nip of his teeth to her neck.

"Fine! I'll give us a chance. Now, please make me come!"

He pinched her clit and she exploded, milking him for everything he had, feeding off the groans he made as he found his own release. In that moment, there was no Joe and Julia. There was only them. The kernel of hope that Joe had planted deep inside of her months earlier began to bloom, and she felt her fears fade.

She wanted a future with this man. She wanted it so badly that the need overwhelmed the fear.

And in that moment, a burst of absolute clarity flowed through her. She'd never had a choice when it came to a future with Joe. She just hadn't realised it until then. It was never about what her mind decided. It was always about her heart. And her heart had made its decision months earlier.

Her heart belonged to Joe. Without him, she would break in two. He was it for her. There had never been another option. There was only ever Joe.

Her Joe.

CHAPTER 30

Joe found it hard to relax on their uneventful trip to the airport. After days of being on high alert, it was difficult to switch off. Although, when it came to Julia's safety, he wasn't sure if he'd ever be able to stop being vigilant. If anything happened to her, he'd lose his mind. He'd known months ago that she would be special to him. What he hadn't realised at the time was that she would become *everything* to him.

He ran his hand along Julia's thigh as she chatted with Elle, who was in the back seat. Joe kept his eyes on the road, aware he was the navigator for both their vehicle and the one behind him, which held Patricia and Alice.

They made their way out of the city, past the grand old Spanish buildings towards the beige shanties with their unfinished brick box homes. The grey tarmac roads turned to hard dirt, and everything in sight became a different shade of red and beige sand. Dirty-faced children played at the side of the roads. Chickens ran around between the houses. Crisp white laundry hung on lines strung outside houses with dirt floors. Rebar poked into the sky from the brick homes, waiting for another level to be added when the owners could afford the bricks. Most windows were without glass. Some buildings were painted bright pastel colours, making them stand out like gems in the desert.

In the distance, further up the hills around Lima, were houses made out of straw matting. Hundreds of them that blended seamlessly with their sand-coloured environment. Dented cars sat outside houses that acted as grocery shops, bottles of soda being sold through the bars on the glassless windows. Every now and then they'd pass a massive, steaming pile of garbage. Each one had children scrambling over it, looking for items they could reuse or sell on.

"I never knew it was like this," Julia said. "I thought Peru was full of rainforest and Incan temples."

"Some of it is, but these huge shantytowns sprang up in the nineties when the Shining Path terrorists were at war with the government," Joe said. "People ran from the rural areas, where they could grow their own food, to the safety of the city." He had run missions in Peru long after the guerrilla war ended, but still remembered the fear in the shantytowns. People who'd lived through terrorist attacks and police raids. People caught in the middle of a conflict they didn't fully understand and would gain nothing from.

"They keep it so tidy." Julia watched a woman sweeping the ever-encroaching sand out of her house.

"Proud people. Hardworking. They're good people to know."

"I wish I'd had a chance to get to know some of them. This whole trip has been one short hit-and-run experience."

They passed a tiny church crowded with people. They were laughing, music playing, food being cooked over open fires, ready to share.

"Had one of the best meals of my life in a church like that," Joe said. "Aji de gallina. It was a creamy chicken stew thing served with rice. Although it might not have been chicken. It could have been guinea pig. I didn't care. It tasted like heaven."

Julia smiled at him. "What temperature was it cooked at?"

There was a twinkle in her eye that made it clear she was making fun of herself, and Joe laughed. After their lovemaking, and the fact she'd come to his bed, Joe felt hopeful. They had a future together. He knew it. And he was beginning to think Julia might come to know it too.

They rode out past the shanties, into the flat desert, the mountains a distant blur through the heat haze that constantly shrouded the city. They passed a small house further from the rest. A tiny child was sitting in the dirt, playing with a stick. Joe glanced over to see Julia's face soften and then a look of pure determination replace it. He would bet his life that the shanty dwellers of Lima had just gained a powerful advocate in Julia Collins. With her soft heart, her contacts and her organisational skill, she could change the world. Joe grinned with pride, as he planned to be by her side while she did it.

He turned into the long road leading to the old military airport. They could see the hazy white building in the distance, their plane easy to spot on the paved runway, as it was about ten times the size of any of the others. Although, to be fair, there were only two other planes sitting beside the hangar. The ex-military airport was used for the odd chartered flight and for some cargo runs. Joe suspected that most of those cargo runs were less than legal, because the airfield was perfect for smuggling. It was isolated enough to be private and open enough to see cars coming for miles.

The last mile of the road was suddenly tarmac again, and ended in a turning loop outside the airport office building. A building that had definitely seen better days. Someone had thought painting it pink would brighten it up. It didn't. There was one man, sitting in the shade of the office doorway, watching them as they approached. Joe lifted his hand in greeting, but there was no response.

On their right was a large hangar with a worrying dip in the middle of the roof. There was a sign on the turning loop that pointed to the dust-covered area beside the hangar and gave permission to park there, which was entertaining because vehicles seemed to have been abandoned and left to rot in random spots all over the airfield. There was another shed on their left, with two more four-seater planes sitting beside it—between the shed and the runway. A runway, he was pleased to note, that wasn't filled with potholes. At least something around the place was maintained.

"This place gives me the creeps," Elle said as Joe parked the car beside the hangar.

The rental company had promised to send someone out to get the vehicles later that day. Joe hoped the cars would still be there when the company man turned up.

"We'll only be here a matter of minutes." He saw Ryan's vehicle coming a distance down the road, kicking up dust behind it.

He'd received a disgusted call from Callum twenty minutes earlier, saying they would be delayed because the two women needed to go to the toilet. A pit stop for the female bladder was another one of those things that Callum insisted never happened during his military career.

"I should have slept instead of trying to find out more about the mysterious David," Elle said as she climbed out of the car. "I feel terrible and my head is thumping. I'm going to sleep all the way back to England, and if anybody wakes me, they'll have all their accounts mysteriously frozen."

They started walking towards the steps that led up into the startlingly white plane as Callum's vehicle pulled up beside theirs. Joe scanned the area, but apart from feeling slightly uneasy, he saw nothing out of place. Two men in overalls were working on a small plane inside the hangar. Joe's glance in their direction confirmed they weren't a threat. Although Julia stared at them a moment longer, with a look of confusion on her face.

"Problem?" Joe said as the pilot appeared in the doorway of the plane.

"I think I'm imagining things," she muttered.

Joe stopped and placed his hand on her arm. Julia didn't imagine things. She noticed and remembered things.

"What?" He studied the men as he held her in place, then scanned the rest of his team.

A door slammed and Ryan climbed out of the other car. The women were busy getting their belongings together in the back seat, and Callum was still in the passenger seat, waiting for Ryan to get his wheelchair.

"I could swear that one of those engineers is the double of one of the men in Elle's photos of Esteban's army. See the blond streak at his temple? There can't be two men with hair like that, can there?" Julia's eyes were wide with worry as she looked up at him.

"Back to the car," Joe snapped.

He'd damn well check everything before they set foot on that plane.

"I'm probably wrong." Julia seemed embarrassed.

"Better safe than sorry. I've learned the hard way to trust my instincts. We'll check the guys out before we board."

She nodded, but still bit her lip, second-guessing herself.

"What's happening?" Elle whined. "Why am I not on that plane sound asleep already?"

"We're going to do a check first." Joe motioned to Ryan, who saw his signal and stopped retrieving the wheelchair from the boot. Instead, he lifted out their weapons bag and headed back to the driver's seat.

"Mr. Barone," the pilot called. "We're ready to leave."

His voice wasn't right. A little too tight. A hint of strain.

"Didn't Rachel say that one of the crew always waited at the bottom of the steps to help the passengers?" Elle wasn't concerned about her headache any longer.

"Yeah." Joe guided them back across the dirt to the car. "She did."

"Mr. Barone, I must insist that you board. We have a schedule." No, they didn't.

"Don't run, but hurry. Get in the car." Joe pushed the women forward.

And then he heard it. A gunshot. He glanced back in time to see the pilot crumple and topple down the stairs.

"Run!" Joe shouted as he grabbed his gun.

Esteban appeared in the doorway of the plane, weapon in hand. "*¡Persiguelos!*"

Get them, he shouted. The men in the hangar pulled guns out of the engine cavity and ran at Joe. Julia scrambled into the front of the car.

"You drive," he snapped at her.

She didn't hesitate in climbing over to the driver's seat. Elle slammed the door as she got in the back. Joe was in the passenger seat a second later. That was when the men started firing at them.

"Go!" Joe rolled down his window and shot back at the men.

Ryan was already speeding forward, towards the tiny planes on the edge of the runway.

Joe's phone rang. He tossed it at Elle, who put it on speaker.

"Where are you going?" Joe barked.

"We're surrounded." Callum's voice was even. Calm. "Two more came out the office, one from the front of the hangar. There's another in that shed to your left."

"Still better to make a run for it." Joe shot at the men chasing them as Julia sped after Ryan's car.

"Can't," Ryan said. "They blocked the road behind us."

He didn't need to say that they weren't in all-terrain vehicles. Their cars would never make it over the pothole and shrub-laden landscape surrounding the airport, and then they really would be sitting ducks.

"We'll pull up at those two planes and use them and the shed for cover," Ryan said. "Callum has the sniper rifle the Lima crew gave us for him. He'll pick them off while we go hunting."

"What about us?" Julia asked. She sounded afraid, but was keeping it together.

"You'll stay with Callum and follow orders." Joe didn't have time to soften it.

And Julia didn't argue. Bullets hit the back of their vehicle, making a hollow pinging sound. The car swerved.

"Sorry," Julia said. "First time driving while people shoot at me."

"And the last." Joe took aim and managed to hit one of the guys in the leg. It was a lucky shot; no one could hit anything deliberately when they were in a moving vehicle.

"Park beside Ryan," he ordered as Julia pulled a sharp left behind the shed.

Ryan was already out of his car and running towards the man who'd been stationed behind the shed. One bullet and Esteban's man crumpled.

"Oh my goodness, he's dead." Julia came to a screeching halt beside the body of the man.

"It was him or us," Joe said.

"I know. I'm okay." She wasn't freaking out, and that was good.

"Callum, I'm sending the women your way. They can hunker behind the cars and shed. You got a line of sight."

"Enough," his boss said. "You take Ryan. Finish this."

"You heard the man," Joe said. "Get to your gran and keep her and Alice as sheltered as possible."

"Be careful." Julia's wide eyes pleaded with him. "Come back to me."

Joe ran his knuckles down her cheek. "I'll always come back to you, beautiful girl."

With one last look, Julia was out of the car and running around the other vehicle.

Joe didn't have time to think about Julia. The only way he could keep her safe was to eliminate the threat. He climbed into the driver's seat as Ryan got into the passenger seat.

"Plan?" Ryan asked as he reloaded his gun.

"Mow them down, get out and shoot the ones that are left." He revved the engine and set off towards the men attacking them.

Esteban's men were shooting wildly. They also had more firepower than Joe's team.

"Hold on." Joe aimed the car at two men, clipping one and sending the other flying.

Ryan fired a shot out his window as two more bullets hit the side of their car.

"Esteban is still in the plane," Ryan said.

"How many men?"

"I count six still mobile, two injured and two dead."

There was the unmistakable sound of rifle fire. "Make that three dead," Callum said through Joe's phone.

Joe swerved across the sand, aiming for another two men. A burst of heavy fire hit them from the left, taking out their tyres. Joe lost control of the car. He fought with the steering wheel as they hit a shrub, managing to get them back on four wheels. Another hail of bullets took out the back window.

"You hurt?" Joe shouted as the car careened off course.

"No, but they've got automatic weapons."

More gunfire hit them, making smoke billow from the engine.

"That isn't good," Ryan said.

"No shit. Buckle up, because this is going to get rough. I've lost the brakes and we're heading for the plane. I'm going to try to slow us by shifting down gears, and then I'll have to pull the handbrake."

Ryan's head snapped to the front. "Aim for the sand. It'll slow us."

"Too far away from the rest of the team. I'll spin us on the runway and hope the lack of gas and the handbrake are enough to stop us. Hold on."

The car screamed as Joe forced it into a lower gear. Another burst of gunfire made the vehicle shudder.

"They've broken through the gas tank casing," Ryan said.

Another gear shift.

"One more down," said Callum's steady voice.

Another burst of fire took out their last two tyres, and all hope of controlling the car disappeared.

"Fuck!" Ryan shouted.

Joe pulled the handbrake. It was their only option.

The car spun, turning three-hundred and sixty degrees with a screech. The metal rims ripped at the tarmac, making them spark.

"The sparks are going to ignite the fuel," Ryan said.

They tilted and then there was an almighty crash. Joe ducked, but the car came to a halt.

"You okay?" He looked behind him to find the roof crushed where the car had wedged under the carriage of the plane.

"Yeah."

Without another word, they shoved at their doors.

"Mine's wedged, too warped to open," Joe said; he caught sight of flames in his mirror. "The petrol's on fire."

"Over here. Mine's open." Ryan scrambled out, and Joe followed.

The car had been flattened from the boot to the back of the front seats. It was pure luck they hadn't hit the plane front end first. The line of petrol from their damaged tank was burning on the ground. It was only a matter of time before it spread to what was left in the tank.

"Time to go," Joe said.

"Left," Ryan called, and took off at a jog, weapon up and crouching for cover.

Joe took the right. He'd lost his phone somewhere in the car during the crash, so there was no way to check in with Callum. Not that it mattered now. All he could do was what he'd been trained to do. Find the enemy and eliminate the threat.

"They're okay. I see them."

Callum's words made Julia's hands shake. Her gran placed her hands over Julia's to keep them steady. The four women were kneeling behind the car, which was shielded by the shed. Callum was firing from the passenger seat, and Esteban's men couldn't get close enough to stop him.

Julia had been peeking through the car windows when she saw Joe's car hit the plane. She hadn't been able to look after that. The women jerked as Callum took another shot.

"Three down," he said.

"How many does that leave?" Alice whispered. She looked like she was going to pass out at any second.

"Two injured," Julia said. "Three alive, and Esteban."

"I won't go back with him," Alice declared. "Kill me if he takes me, because I won't go back." She cradled her injured hand to her chest and rocked back and forth.

"Nobody is going anywhere with that son of a bitch," Callum said evenly. "This ends today."

"What does that mean?" Alice had a panicked look on her face.

"It means," Callum said with ice in his voice, "that Esteban will die today. I can promise you that."

"I can't go back," Alice whispered as silent tears fell down her cheeks.

Julia leaned forward and cupped Alice's cheek. "Believe in Callum. He knows what he's doing. He's done this before. All the men have. They won't let you get taken. It's a promise. The Benson Security team are experts at what they do."

Patricia shifted to wrap her arms around her friend. Alice leaned into her.

"Does it bother anyone else that the guys are out there fighting and we're cowering behind the car?" Elle looked down at them from where she was kneeling, watching the gunfight. "Doesn't that seem sexist to you?"

"It's got nothing to do with sexism," Callum said. "It's to do with training. If any of you had combat experience, you'd be out there with Joe and Ryan."

"I need combat training," Elle said. "Because I really want to shoot someone right now."

A staccato burst of gunfire rang out, followed by two distinct shots.

"Joe got another one," Callum reported.

More gunshots. It was never-ending. Julia didn't dare ask Callum for a status report on their ammunition stores, but she knew what they'd started with and that they had to be running low.

"The car's on fire." Elle actually sounded a little worried. "That isn't good, is it?"

No, it wasn't good that there was a burning vehicle wedged underneath a multimillion-dollar plane.

"Maybe we should move back," she said to Callum. They were awfully close to the plane.

He didn't answer; instead he aimed and took another shot. "One of the injured men is now out."

Another death.

"How many left?" Patricia asked.

"One injured, two uninjured and Esteban," Julia said.

"Who was hiding in the plane until he noticed it was sitting on top of an inferno," Elle said.

Julia couldn't *not* look anymore. She went to her knees beside Elle to spy through the windows of the car. Esteban was running down the stairs, gun in hand.

Another burst of gunfire to their left caught their attention. Julia gasped. Ryan was hit. She watched blood blossom on his leg before he dove behind a pile of junk.

"He's fine," Callum said tightly before they could ask.

Julia wasn't so sure, but she didn't argue. Instead, her fingers curled around the door handle in front of her and she held on tight enough to make her knuckles turn white. She saw movement to the right and watched as Joe crouched as he ran up the airplane steps. A minute later, he appeared again and ran for the hangar.

One of Esteban's men saw him and opened fire. The bullets sprayed the side of the plane, barely missing Joe.

"Elle?" Julia whispered with growing horror. Things had just gotten a whole lot worse. "That's the plane's fuel tank, isn't it?"

"Yeah, the idiots hit the tank," Elle said in the same tone.

Julia fought the urge to run towards Joe, screaming a warning. The plane's fuel was trickling towards the fire beneath it. And Joe was much too close. Her mind threw up every fact she'd ever learned about aviation safety. She was grateful that her freaky need to make sure she was secure before she travelled had given her the data.

"Planes rarely explode," she said, more to herself than anyone else. "The fuel usually burns and the body of the plane goes on fire. There might be a fireball, but they rarely explode unless there's been a build-up of fumes in the tank." She looked at Elle. "But the tank was full, right? The pilot refuelled in Cusco, didn't he? There's no space for fumes to occupy."

"No," Callum said. "We didn't want to tip Esteban off that we were leaving the country. We planned to refuel over the border before carrying on home."

Her eyes shot to the plane. "So the tank has plenty of space for fumes to build up. We have to warn them," she said to Callum, aware of how hysterical she sounded.

"How?" he said.

She had no answer. Joe was out there. Close to the plane. With men shooting at him. And his phone was dead.

"We need to move back," Callum said. "Everybody in the car. Julia, you're driving. Move it. Now!"

As Julia clambered in behind the wheel, another thought made her stomach heave. "Where's Esteban?"

Callum's expression was tight. "The bastard is in the hangar."

"With Joe," Julia whispered as she put the car in gear and drove around the building, away from the blaze.

CHAPTER 31

Joe spotted Esteban running for the hangar, and took a minute to check inside the plane. All three members of the crew were dead. Assassinated by Esteban's bullets. As he ran through the cabin, he stumbled on two large crates and his heart stopped beating for a second. The crates were marked as full of ammunition. Esteban had obviously thought to kill two birds with one stone when he'd hijacked their plane in Cusco. He'd planned to use it to get Patricia and the treasure, and to transport his illegal weapons one step closer to Lima.

Now, those weapons were sitting in a plane that was resting on a burning car. And there was nothing Joe could do about it. The crates were too big, and the priority was protecting the team.

Protecting Julia.

With one last glance at the crew members who'd been brutally slaughtered for doing their jobs, he ran down the stairs and headed for the hangar.

A burst of gunfire came at him from the left, almost hitting his head before he threw himself to the tarmac and fired. Three bullets. He'd hit the guy's arm. His attacker retreated, but the damage to the plane was already done. There was fuel leaking from the tank. And it was heading straight for the fire beneath it.

It was past time to end this thing.

Joe ran for the hangar, hugging the wall at the side of the gaping doors, all too aware of the heat at his back telling him time was running out fast. Esteban wasn't even trying to hide; he was over at the door on the opposite side of the building from the entrance the planes would use, and was shouting at his last remaining men.

"Get the woman," he told them. "Stop fighting the men and get the woman."

It was too late. Esteban had lost. He just didn't know it yet.

In the corner of the hangar, the man Joe had shot in the leg when he was still in the car, sat pressing a cloth to his wound and moaning for help. Esteban walked up to his man, who was stupid enough to look hopeful at the sight of his boss. Esteban shot the wounded man in the head.

"Weak," he spat.

Joe inched further into the cavernous space, making sure he kept the two-seater plane between himself and Esteban. The noise of gunfire covered any sound he might have made.

Esteban pulled out his phone, and Joe sneaked closer, looking for a good shot.

"We need reinforcements. Now!" Esteban didn't even wait for a reply. In his arrogance, he assumed his people would jump to fulfil his wishes.

He spun, catching sight of Joe as he rounded the plane. Esteban's gun came up, and he fired. Joe dove for the tatty old sofa someone had put in the corner at the back of the hangar. There weren't many options in the way of cover inside the space.

"Give it up," he called to Esteban. "Your men are dead.

You have nowhere to go. You can't get out of here alive. Surrender and you keep your life."

A burst of machine-gun fire erupted outside and echoed through the room.

"Does that sound like my men are dead?" More shots hit the sofa as Joe ducked down low and tried to make himself as small a target as possible.

He peeked out and saw Esteban was slowly making his way to the wide open doors and his escape. Joe fired. Two shots. He'd emptied his spare clip. He was out of ammunition. He chanced a glance at the dead man on the other side of the hangar. A gun lay beside him. If he could get to it…

"This is my treasure. Mine! You dare to come into my country and take what belongs to me? This is my country. I am the power here. You are nothing." Two more shots hit the sofa, one perilously close to Joe's head.

He had no option—he had to make a run for the dead man's gun. Mind made up, Joe sprinted for the other side of the hangar, bullets spraying the wall behind him. He glanced at Esteban. That was when he saw a line of fire race up the fuel that leaked from the plane. It was heading straight for a tank full of fumes.

Joe abandoned his attempt to get the dead man's gun, and veered to the left instead. He bolted for door at the back of the hangar. Shots rang out. He felt a bite to his shoulder. He barely noticed. He was out the door in record time, running for the low concrete wall that ran around the hangar. There was an almighty blast. Joe felt a full body punch hit him in the back. He was flung into the air, as the sky over the airfield turned black.

"Joe!"

Julia didn't care about bullets or gunmen or danger. All

she cared about was Joe. He'd been in the hangar. The hangar that was now a blazing pile of rubble and twisted metal. She was running around the car, heading for the blaze before anyone could stop her.

A man with a gun, dazed and dangerous, staggered towards her. A shot rang out and he crumpled. Callum. The horror of seeing the man die wasn't enough to stop her from running straight at the fire. She waved smoke out of her eyes, but it made no difference. The thick black plume was being carried over the area by the breeze.

"Stop her," someone shouted. Callum, she thought.

A strong arm hooked around her waist. "Don't be dumb," Ryan said as he held her tight. "You can't run into a fire."

Her eyes were fixed on the mass of debris that used to be a building. Jagged pieces of warped metal. Remnants of walls that now lay crumpled. And parts of the plane that had exploded. She struggled against Ryan's hold.

"We need to get Joe!"

"I saw him run out." Ryan's words made her stop.

Hope was a flame that burned hotter than the blaze in front of her.

"Where?"

"Come on." He tugged her towards the road side of the building.

Part of the plane's wing was in their path, and they skirted it. What looked like the remnants of an old sofa lay propped up against a low concrete wall, dropped there by the blast.

And behind it all, lying on his back, was Joe.

Julia shrugged out from under Ryan's hold and ran for Joe. She fell to her knees beside him and cradled his blackened cheeks. There were cuts and scrapes all over him.

"Please be okay, please be okay, please be okay…" she chanted as she leaned in to kiss his cheek. "Oh God, please don't let him die." Her vision blurred and she realised she was crying. Again.

Joe stirred under her touch and groaned.

"Damn, my head hurts," he said.

A surge of elation, and Julia's lips were on his. Joe. Her Joe. Always her Joe. How could she have thought of leaving him? How could she have let her fears take him from her? Never again. She'd never let her lack of courage stop her from trying with this man. Never.

"Baby," he said against her lips as his hand threaded into her hair. "I'm fine. It's okay."

"It's not." She gave a hiccupping sob before she kissed him again. "I can't cope with this. You can't die. And you keep trying!"

He choked back a laugh. "Babe, trust me, I really don't try."

"When we get back to England, you're going to make Callum give you a training job, Joe Barone, do you hear me?"

His hand tightened in her hair. "Does this mean you're giving us a chance?" His voice was flat, as though he was afraid to let her hear what he felt.

"No," she said against his lips, "It means I'm giving you all of me. Every freaky part. And you can't complain when I start to annoy you, because I told you it would happen."

He growled and pulled her in for an all-consuming kiss. He smelled of smoke and dirt. And Joe. Julia clung to him as she sobbed tears of relief. He was here. He was alive. He was hers.

"I love you," she said into his kiss. "I'm sorry I tried to make you go. I'm sorry I was scared." She looked at him, letting him see the truth. "It will probably happen again." And again, knowing her.

"Don't worry. I won't let you screw things up."

She almost laughed at his audacity. Like he could stop her. Crazy man.

"You're mine," she told him.

"Forever," Joe told her. "That's what we'll have. Forever." He looked into her eyes, letting her see that intense, possessive nature of his. "I won't settle for anything less."

"Forever," she agreed, because there was no other answer.

"This is great stuff," Ryan said from beside them. "And I'm touched to be included in your moment. But you're lying in the middle of Armageddon. There has to be a more romantic, and private, spot for this kind of thing. Think we can keep the lovey-dovey crap to a minimum until we get out of here?"

Elle came running up. "Holy hotcakes, Batman, did the world end?"

"Looks like it from here, doesn't it?" Ryan said. "Rachel is going to be pissed that we blew up her dad's plane. I vote we let Callum tell her."

Joe struggled to sit up, and Julia helped him. Her hand came away bloody.

"You're hurt!"

"Flesh wound, shoulder."

He was moving slower than normal, and Julia wondered how many other injuries he had from the blast.

"In case you were wondering," Ryan said, "I took a bullet to the leg, and I think it's still in there."

"Ryan!" Julia reached for him, because there was no way she was leaving Joe's side. In fact, she might have to keep her hands on him every minute of the day for the rest of her life.

Ryan held up his hands. "Too little, too late. I know where your priorities lie."

"I was about to ask if you were okay," Elle said.

"Thanks," Ryan said. "It's nice to know someone cares."

"I care." Julia was distraught that he would think otherwise.

"He's yanking your chain," Joe told her. "He's fine. He's still standing, isn't he?" Joe struggled to get up, and Julia helped him.

"Callum says we need to clear the debris from the road so we can get out of here," Elle said.

"Wait." Julia was shocked. "Shouldn't we stay until the authorities get here? There has to be an investigation. Rachel will need to claim insurance on the plane. What about the plane crew? We can't just leave them here."

Joe put a hand on her cheek as Elle shuffled in place and Ryan became stony-faced.

"Babe, if we hang around we'll be tied up in a police investigation for months. That means months sitting in a cell while we wait for someone to sort through this mess. I don't think your gran or Alice could handle it. You've seen what the prisons are like."

"But we can't walk away." It was wrong. It felt too much like running. And the plane crew? What would they tell their families? That they'd abandoned their bodies in Peru?

"The crew," she said.

"They're in the middle of that." Joe pointed at the blaze that was sending a thick plume of dense black smoke into the air. A signal for everyone for miles around that disaster had struck. It wouldn't be long before the police arrived.

Elle brought out her phone, pressed a key and held it up for everyone to listen on speaker.

"Julia doesn't think we should leave without dealing with the police," she told Callum.

"Get that bloody road clear. I want out of here in five minutes, tops. Julia, I understand your sentiment and I know it's the legally correct thing to do, but it isn't the wise thing to do. Lake has a contact in the British Embassy that will forward all of our findings here and keep our business out of it."

"What about Rachel's plane and the crew?" Julia said.

"It will be dealt with later."

"But—"

"No buts! Get the road cleared!"

Elle shut the phone off. "He's touchy because he can't get out of the car—it isn't set up for a person who doesn't have legs. He has to wait for someone to drive him." She looked at Ryan. "We need to get him new legs, and fast. He's going to be hell to deal with if we don't."

"You know those curved blade ones that runners use?" Ryan said as he started to clear a path. "I think he should get a set of those. Very cool. Did you see the movie with the woman who wore a set and they doubled as swords?"

"I can see Callum chopping people up with his prosthetics," Elle said.

"Joe?" Julia didn't like this situation one bit.

"I know it's hard," Joe said. "But this is the best for everyone. Lake and Callum will make sure justice is done here and that the remains of the crew are sent back to their families. You know if there was an investigation we'd eventually be cleared. But it's the 'eventually' that's the problem. It could take years and a helluva lot of money to sort this out. It's better to give the Peruvian government Esteban's head and strike a deal that leaves us out of it."

"It doesn't feel right," she whispered.

"I know, baby, I know. We'll get them home. And we'll make sure Ed's buried in Lima too."

"I hate this," Julia told him.

He kissed her forehead, and together, they went to help clear a space for the car.

"Joe?" Julia had another worrying thought. "How are we all going to fit in one car?"

He grinned at her. "Either we cosy up, or we see what we can hot-wire."

"And now I'm a thief too." She let out a sigh and carried on clearing the road.

"I'll pay someone to bring it back here. Does that make you feel better?"

"Yes." She stuck her nose in the air. "Yes, it does." She dared him to laugh at her.

Instead, he kissed her hard.

EPILOGUE

It was a farewell party for Julia's gran and Alice. Four months had passed since their time in Peru, and now the women were going back—to hunt for treasure. Only this time, they had the backing of the Peruvian Archaeological Society and a team of armed guards they'd hired from Benson Security. A team of newly recruited guards. Joe hoped they knew what they were getting into.

Joe looked over at his fiancée, who was standing in the corner of the grand room in her parents' house. Julia would never be the centre of attention, and that was fine with Joe. There were more than enough limelight hogs in her family as it was, and he liked that his woman only ever let her hair down with a select few people. She felt like a secret. His secret.

"Joe, darling." Libby Collins, Julia's mother and famed actress, bustled up to him. "I spoke to your mother last night and we agree that it would be fabulous to hold the wedding in Italy. Isn't that a great idea?"

"Almost as good as the one where you thought we should

have it in Cannes, or Lapland, or..." Nope, he couldn't remember. "Where was that place you shot your last movie?"

"Bora Bora. And you aren't taking me seriously." She pouted, but Joe was onto her. Libby Collins, like the rest of her family, was all about the drama. After each visit with Julia's family, Joe dug up his Catholic roots and lit a candle in thanks that Julia was nothing like them. He couldn't even begin to imagine the stress of living with someone who was performing all the time.

"You've tuned me out again." She smacked him on the chest, and Joe smiled.

"We're going to get married in the spot Julia picks. It's up to her."

"She wants to get married in Invertary. Can you imagine anything more boring?"

Joe thought back to the last wedding he'd attended in the Scottish Highlands, and laughed. Julia heard him through the crowd and caught his eyes. She made a slight gesture, which he read as her asking if he needed rescuing. He gently shook his head.

"It's a small town in Scotland. How will it cope with a crowd of celebrities descending on it?" Libby said.

"The same way it coped last time it happened." He cocked an eyebrow. "Julia and I aren't famous. We don't want to be famous. We want a quiet wedding with our friends and family, and then we want to settle down and pop out some kids."

"What a way to describe it." But her face melted at the thought of being a grandmother. "But Italy would be wonderful. We could borrow George Clooney's estate. He wouldn't mind; he's hardly ever there these days."

"Hey, it isn't me you have to convince. If Julia decides she wants to get married at Clooney's place, then it's fine with me." He gave Libby a sweet smile.

She narrowed her eyes. "You know full well that you're the weak link in your relationship. I'll never get her to agree to something she doesn't want. She's stubborn as a mule."

Yes, she was, and Joe loved it because Julia's stubbornness wasn't confrontational. She always listened politely and then either did what she wanted or manoeuvred people to do what she wanted them to do. It was highly entertaining to watch.

"I really appreciate it when you call me the weakest link. Makes me feel part of the family already."

Libby shook her head. "I'm going to call your mother again tonight and tell her you're being difficult."

"You get right on that." He kissed her cheek and made his way through the packed room towards Julia.

In a room the size of a ballroom, crowded with everyone from family members to A-list stars, Julia still shone the brightest. Tonight she was wearing a soft pink jumpsuit with silver heels and silver earrings. It was understated and classy. Just like she was. Even better, Joe knew what lay underneath. It seemed Julia had developed a recent fascination with lingerie. Sexy lace lingerie. And he had never been more grateful for her latest interest.

"Babe." He wrapped his arm around her waist and sighed when she cuddled into his side.

"Belinda was just telling me that we should get married in Kenya," she said to him. Her eyes were sparkling with mischief.

"You can get the Maasai tribes to dance at your wedding," Julia's older sister gushed. "Can you think of anything more amazing?"

"Nope, sounds good to me," Joe said, and Julia elbowed him in the ribs.

"I'll send you the links I have for the hotels I think are the best," Belinda said.

"You do that." Joe tried hard not to laugh as something behind him caught Belinda's attention.

"Got to go. We've put together a little band, and we're performing something for Gran. See you later."

She hurried off towards her *little band*, which consisted of two members of a chart-topping group, a daytime TV host and one of the biggest action movie stars in the world. They started to play as soon as she hit the stage at the end of the room.

"I don't think I'll ever get used to all the big names that hang around your family," Joe said.

"My family *are* big names," Julia pointed out.

But he was used to her family. They were famous, but they were also deeply insane and very hard not to like.

Julia's brother sidled up to them. "Heads up—Dad's coming this way. He wants to talk to you about getting married in the church that held his and Mum's wedding." The idiot started to laugh. "If I ever get married, I'm eloping to Vegas."

Joe looked hopefully at Julia, who shook her head. She was adamant that she wanted to get married in the place where they'd first met, and she knew he'd give her the world if he could.

"Last I heard," Julia said, "he also wants to talk to you about your *wild living*. He thinks it's time you settled down and grew up."

The twenty-two-year-old balked. "Time for me to go." And the coward headed for the door.

"If his fans ever knew their favourite superhero was a wimp, he'd never make a movie again," Joe said.

"He doesn't need to be courageous in real life. It's *acting*," Julia teased him. "He's pretending. For money."

He looked down at her. Damn, but he wished he wasn't in a room full of people. He'd much rather be alone in the bedroom of the apartment they'd bought close to the office.

"How come you don't act anymore?"

Julia's mother had made him sit through the DVDs of Julia's childhood TV show. She'd been electric on camera. Her presence lit up the screen, and she stole every scene she was in. Although he could have been a little biased in his assessment. He hadn't yet made it to the recordings of her singing, but he knew her mother had them all set aside for his next visit, much to Julia's dismay.

"Well, for one, I don't lie well."

"This is true." And something he loved about her.

"Two, I tend to have panic attacks when people are focused on me. Not all the time, but it can happen."

"Only people you don't know well." She hadn't hidden behind one plant since she'd come back from Peru. Although she had been known to duck under the desk when Callum was in a rage, which seemed like all the time these days.

She leaned in and whispered, "Three, I thought it was boring."

Joe threw back his head and laughed. He imagined such a confession was close to sacrilege in her family.

"What's funny?" Elle said as she came over to them, Ryan and Rachel at her side. Her hair was currently daffodil yellow, and made him think of Big Bird every time he saw her. He hoped this colour phase didn't last.

"Nothing," Julia said as she looked past them. "Where's Callum?"

Elle's face dropped. "He wouldn't come. I think he's still trying to get used to his new prosthetics."

Rachel snorted. "He's in a huff. He's been in one for months. His fragile male ego was damaged along with his legs, and he doesn't think he's macho enough anymore. He needs therapy. Or a smack on the head." Her eyes went wide.

"Oh, good, Cumberbatch is here. I have a bone to pick with him."

She charged off after one of Britain's best-loved actors, looking completely at ease in the room, dressed as she was in designer clothes and her trademark red-soled shoes.

"I hope we don't have to hide another body," Ryan said as he watched her go. As usual, he'd already visited the buffet, and was armed with a plate piled high with finger food.

"Any luck with the DNA database searches?" Joe asked Elle, who shook her fluffy yellow head.

"Nope. I've hacked all the countries I think are likely, but there's no match anywhere. Maybe I would have had better luck with fingerprints." She eyed Joe. "If you see David again, steal a print, will you?"

"Absolutely." He'd get right on it. After all, how hard could it be to get a print off a man known as a ghost who could kill Joe with his little finger?

Elle bounced up and down with joy at his agreement to help, and Ryan smothered a laugh.

"There you are." Julia's gran rushed up to them.

She was dressed in a formfitting silver dress that hugged her curves and made her seem twenty years younger. She was followed by Alice, who was dressed as a parrot and looked her age.

"Darling." Patricia hugged Julia tight.

"You all set for your trip?" she said when her gran released her.

"We have everything, don't we?" Patricia said to Alice.

"Except a finger." Alice held up her right hand. "I don't think it's fair that I can't get a prosthetic finger."

"You can't?" Ryan asked.

Julia smiled at him. "Apparently the little finger isn't considered essential, and although she could get a prosthetic to strap on to her hand, it wouldn't be bionic."

"What's the point it if isn't bionic?" Alice huffed.

"Yeah," Ryan said. "I don't see the point either. So, this trip? You really think you'll find treasure?"

"Even if we don't," Patricia said, "it doesn't matter. It would be amazing if we at least found evidence that the site had been used to store treasure. That way our theory about the textiles having a language within their imagery would be proven." She grinned widely, and it was easy to tell she was more interested in her textiles find than the treasure.

"I want the treasure," Alice said. "Although the Peruvian government probably won't let us keep any of it. You'd think after everything I went through, everything we *all* went through, they'd let us keep a teeny-tiny bit of the treasure. After all, we did hand them Esteban's head. Is it too much to ask for some gratitude?"

"Yeah, but we also handed them an airport full of dead bodies and the wreck of a burning plane," Ryan pointed out.

"At least we were able to get the plane crew back to their families and Ed to Lima," Julia said softly. "That's good."

He knew she still had nightmares about the crew being caught in the fire. He'd told her time and again that they were already dead before the plane exploded—he'd seen it himself—but Julia's subconscious wouldn't listen.

"That is good." He kissed her temple and breathed in her soft scent.

"What's also good," Ryan said around a mouthful of food, "is that Rachel's dad didn't charge us for the plane. Insurance covered it." His eyes went wide. "Fifty-five million. Million!"

"Don't think we'll be allowed to borrow the new plane, though," Elle said. "Pity. I liked flying private."

The *little band* Julia's sister had put together finished their mini set of travel-themed songs, which made people laugh and applaud.

Patricia smiled fondly in the direction of her eldest

granddaughter. "She is such an attention hound." She turned that smile onto Julia. "You ready to give me my present?"

Julia straightened her shoulders and rolled her eyes. Joe could practically feel the determination emanating from her.

"You know I'd only do this for you, Gran."

"As it should be." Patricia's haughty look was the mirror image of the one Julia used on Joe.

"Do what?" he said. "Do you need help?" He didn't like the grim set of her mouth. Whatever she was about to do was something she had to work herself up to.

"Not this time." She went onto tiptoes and pressed a sweet kiss to his lips. "This is for you too," she whispered against his ear. "Enjoy it. It will never happen again." She leaned back, looking anxious. "And Joe, please don't take your eyes off me."

"Never," he promised.

Then she turned and walked through the crowd to the makeshift stage.

"What's she doing?" Elle said in shock. "She isn't going up on the stage, is she? She's Julia. She can't do that."

"Her head will probably blow off from the stress," Ryan said, making Joe growl at him.

"And now," Belinda called over the sound system, "a special treat for all of you. Julia Collins is going to sing for us."

Joe sucked in a breath as gasps erupted around him.

The crowd clapped politely, and Joe caught Julia's eyes as the music began to play. She held his gaze as though he were her lifeline. And then Julia sang. The words burned into him, each one a declaration of her feelings for him. She was singing of her love for him, in front of everyone. Joe listened to the lyrics of "The First Time Ever I Saw Your Face" as Julia made it come alive. It was the most beautiful sound he'd ever heard, and the crowd were mesmerised, completely in awe of her ability. The stories about her award-winning voice as a child hadn't been exaggerated. He could only imagine it had gotten better with age.

He held her eyes and felt like there was no one in the room except them. He could feel the lyrics, the melody, like a caress. He could feel her love for him, and it was a boundless thing that humbled him.

"Isn't she wonderful?" Patricia whispered to him.

He didn't take his eyes off the woman who owned him. "She was wonderful before she even began to sing."

Patricia hooked her arm through his. "You'll do, Joe. You'll do."

READ THE FIRST CHAPTER OF RAGE

Four months earlier, London

Callum McKay sat on the floor with his back to the wall and looked at the wreckage he'd wrought. His TV was shattered, spreading glass across the room. His books were in shreds. There was a KA-BAR knife sticking out of what was left of his leather sofa. And every piece of wooden furniture in the room had been smashed.

Feeling no regret, Callum clasped the neck of a bottle of Glenfiddich. He brought the whisky to his lips and drained what was left. One swallow emptied it, and he tossed it into the mess in front of him, watching with some satisfaction as the bottle smashed.

He was done.

Totally.

Absolutely.

Fucking done.

He wanted to burn the place down. Let the flames take it all. And him along with it. But he'd need to find his damn legs if he wanted to get up and finish the job. His blurred gaze caught sight of the prosthetics he'd thrown across the room after he'd collapsed against the wall.

A dry laugh erupted from him. He'd have to drag himself over broken glass to get to his legs—if he wanted to get up. Which he didn't. Because he was done.

Totally fucking done.

He was done pretending he was useful. Done pretending he was normal. Done acting as though his life was the same as it'd been before his legs were blown off in Afghanistan. Before he'd become half a man. Before he'd become a liability to his team.

His head landed back against the wall, with a thump he barely registered, and his eyes focused on the ceiling. The pristine white ceiling. It was perfect. And that was wrong. He didn't want anything around him that was perfect. Unblemished. Unspoiled. Whole. He should have trashed the ceiling along with the rest of the room.

A loud thumping disturbed his thoughts, and it took a minute to register it was coming from the door and not from inside his head. Callum ignored it, as he'd been ignoring every well-meaning visit from his team for days. No. Not *his* team. Not anymore. Because he was done.

The banging got louder, and Callum frowned in the direction of his front door. They'd get fed up and leave. They always did. No one wanted to risk facing his wrath. That thought caused another mirthless laugh. He was a bloody cliché. A grumpy-arsed Scot who terrified women and children. He reached for his whisky before remembering he'd finished the bottle.

"Open the door." The shouted order snagged Callum's dulled attention. He almost jumped to comply—before he remembered that he'd need his legs to do it, and that Lake Benson was no longer his SAS commander, or his business partner. Because Callum was done—he just hadn't told anyone yet.

"Callum," Lake snapped. "Open the door."

"Go to hell," Callum roared.

He heard muttered voices and scraping. Bloody stubborn Englishman was picking the lock. Callum didn't care enough to try to stop him. Anyway, what could he do? Nothing. That was what. Because he was fucking useless.

The heavy door swung open and the room was suddenly flooded with light. Callum squinted against the glare. He could just make out the solid shape of Lake filling the doorway.

"It's time for this to end," Lake said.

"Get the hell out of here and leave me be," Callum said.

"Too many people have been leaving you be." Lake strode into the room, glass crunching underfoot. He crouched beside Callum, his forearms resting on his knees. "You're a mess."

That struck Callum as particularly funny, and he started giggling like a schoolgirl.

"And drunk," Lake said in disgust.

Callum's attention was snagged by the sound of movement in the debris that used to be his home. The women. Elle and Julia. Members of his team who smothered him with their pity.

"I've got his legs." Elle waved something in the air, but all Callum could see was her shocking blue hair.

"Don't touch those! Get out of my house!" Callum reached for something to throw at her.

A strong hand stayed him.

"Give the legs to me," Lake said.

They were ignoring him. As if he wasn't a person anymore. For a minute, he forgot where he was exactly. In his head, he was back in hospital being poked and prodded by the team fitting his prosthetics. A team that was more interested in the tech than the person who'd wear it. He'd felt invisible. A project. A pathetic problem to be fixed.

"Get out, get out, get out, get out!" His rage made him dizzy, and he tilted, slipping down the wall.

Strong hands pulled him upright again.

"Leave us," Lake ordered, and the room cleared.

Of course they listened to Lake. He was whole. He wasn't an invalid. He wasn't half a man. Callum stared down at what remained of his legs, hating the sight of them. Hating that there was nothing but stumps where his knees used to be. Hating that he couldn't see his feet, but could damn well feel them. That constant searing pain that never went away. That constant reminder of who he used to be.

"You get out too," Callum spat.

"You might be able to intimidate the civilians with your bad attitude, but all it does is piss me off. Now put these legs on so I can help you get out of this mess." Lake cocked an eyebrow. "Unless you want me to carry you."

"Fuck off."

Lake stared at him in reply.

The stubborn bastard would sit there until he got his way. With a snarl, Callum snatched a prosthetic from his *former* friend and tried to line the cup up with his stump. It wasn't possible. Everything kept moving. His stump kept slipping out. His hands wouldn't work properly. And his rage grew again. He lifted the leg, ready to throw it across the room. Lake snatched it from his grasp.

"You're too drunk to do it." He looked behind him and yelled, "Joe. Get in here."

"No!" Callum shoved Lake. He rocked back but didn't topple.

Callum wished he'd remembered to bring a weapon home. He could have shot the bastard.

"And we're all grateful you aren't armed," Lake said as he stood, making Callum realise he'd been thinking out loud.

"I should shoot you, you interfering bastard. You dragged me into this mess. This *team*. You should have known I'd be no use to them. I'm a fucking liability. I almost got them killed in Peru."

"Almost doesn't count." Joe stood beside Lake. "You're talking garbage. Which figures, because that's what you smell like."

"Fuck off," Callum said again, and the American paid about as much attention to him as Lake had.

"It's going to take the two of us to get him into bed," Lake said to Joe. "He might need to be restrained. He's a violent dickhead when he's drunk."

"Get out!" Callum roared. "I don't want you here. I don't want your help. Or your pity. Leave me alone."

The two men ignored him as, between them, they scooped Callum up. They carried him in a sitting position, their arms under his thighs and around his shoulders—as if he were a child or an old invalid.

Hell no.

Callum swung his fist and managed to connect with Lake's jaw.

"You hit me again and I'm going to hit back. You got it?"

Like Callum gave a crap. "Bring it on, English."

An arm clamped across his forearms, holding them in place.

"Hurry," Joe said. "He's strong."

Callum shouted obscenities until he felt the veins in his neck bulge and his head grew light. Suddenly, the cool cotton sheets of his bed were at his back.

"Get his legs," Lake said. "Put them on the chest. I'll put the wheelchair beside his bed. He's less likely to throw the wheelchair at us. If he wants his legs, he can roll over and get them."

Callum grabbed his alarm clock and lobbed it at Lake's head. His aim was off and the clock hit the wall and shattered.

Cold eyes caught his. "I *will* knock you out." Lake's voice was icy calm.

"Bring it on." Callum made a fist and waved it. "I can take you. You arrogant English bastard."

Joe shook his head and left the room. Callum could hear voices coming from the other room. All of his damn team were there. All of them. He'd locked himself away from them. And they were there anyway.

"I don't want them in here," he told Lake.

"What the hell *do* you want?" Lake folded his arms and glared down at Callum.

The question knocked the wind out of him. He sagged back into his bed and stared at the ceiling. But he didn't see it. He saw his past. The part of his life that was never coming back. The part where he knew who he was and what he could do. The part where he'd felt invincible.

"I want out," he said. "I'm done being part of Benson Security. I want to go home."

To Scotland. To die.

Because.

He.

Was.

Done.

Get Rage now to keep on reading!

ABOUT THE AUTHOR

I'm a Scot, living in New Zealand and married to a Dutch man. I write contemporary romance with a humorous bent – this is mainly due to the fact I have an odd sense of humour and can't keep it out of anything I do! If I wasn't a writer, I'd like to be Buffy the Vampire Slayer, or Indiana Jones. Unfortunately, both these roles have already been filled. Which may be a good thing as I have no fighting skills, wouldn't know a precious relic if it hit me in the face and have an aversion to blood. When I'm not living in my head, I'm a mother to two kids, several pet sheep, one dog, four cats, three alpacas, two miniature horses, eight guinea pigs and an escape artist chicken.

www.ingramcontent.com/pod-product-compliance
Lightning Source LLC
Chambersburg PA
CBHW020925110726

47900CB00001B/298